D1368494

Published 2003 by The M.O.T.H.E.R. Publishing Co., Inc.

Inquiries should be addressed to:
The M.O.T.H.E.R. Publishing Co., Inc.
PO Box 477
Rock Springs, WY 82902-0477
www.motherpublishing.com

First paperback edition 2003

Summary: A young girl inherits a wizard's power and finds herself thrust into a world of magic where dragons and wizards scheme to rule the world.

ISBN # 0-9718431-2-0

Library of Congress Control Number: 2003111296

1. Dragons – Fiction. 2. Wizards – Fiction. 3. Magic – Fiction I. Title

Printed in the United States of America

BRINN
AND THE
DRAGONS OF
PALLAN CLIFFS

PROPHECY OF THE DRAGONS
BOOK 2

DIANA METZ

M.O.T.H.E.R. Publishing Co., Inc.
PO Box 477
Rock Springs, WY 82902
www.motherpublishing.com

Tolago nodded without saying a word. The last jutting crag looked too familiar. He continued to sniff the air. "What does a king smell like, anyway?"

Felgrig headed for the southern mountain valley. "Probably the same as every other human, like dirt, only with a bit of gold mixed in. Must be inconvenient to have to walk everywhere. You don't suppose he's going to want us to *fly* him to that castle, do you?"

Tolago shivered. That would be taking this human-dragon cooperation just a bit too far. Guard duty was one thing, but he drew the line at being a pack mule. Tolago decided to change the subject before he got himself worked up. "I was flying over a village a couple of days ago, and I could have sworn I felt a shift."

Felgrig was preoccupied with trying to locate the royal party they were supposed to be guarding. "Shift? What do you mean, 'a shift'? Did a cloud move into your flight path or something? I think I smell a king just on the other side of that forest."

Tolago smacked Felgrig's tail with his wing. "You know: a shift in the *field*."

Felgrig glared at his friend, "Hey, what did you do that for?" He gave his offended tail a twitch. "How am I supposed to know what you're talking about? What kind of field do you mean? Corn, wheat, daisy? Look over by that lake; I'm sure I saw a king-type banner."

Tolago stopped in mid-air. "Aren't you listening to me!? THE MAGIC FIELD!" he shouted. "A SHIFT IN THE MAGIC FIELD!!"

*****

"We've been out here all morning, Tolago[*]. I think you're lost." The large yellow dragon searched the ground far below.

"I *am* not. I remember flying over that mountain, we go over that way." Tolago squinted down at the snowy peaks, they all looked the same. The broken pine tree looked familiar, but there hadn't been an eagle there earlier.

"If I had known it would take this long, I would have skipped breakfast and gotten an earlier start." Felgrig knew he shouldn't have had that third bear. "We've flown past that mountain goat twice, you know."

Tolago hoped Felgrig hadn't noticed. "Don't be silly, all mountain goats look the same. Anyway, they move around a lot." He sniffed the breeze. A faint scent of human floated on the wind. "He did say they would be coming by a direct route, didn't they?"

Felgrig wasn't ready to turn back and admit defeat. It was a great honor to be selected by the Chosen One for any task (even if it meant guarding a human), but it would be a great embarrassment if they arrived late because Tolago had no sense of direction. "I say we take a left at the next peak. They are supposed to be

---

[*] If you have trouble pronouncing the names of the characters go to the Guide at the back of the book and see how I pronounce them.

1

Many Thanks

To Kayne and Candi, for bringing my dream to life
To Darren, who lives the magic everyday
To My Guild Sisters: watch out for snowballs
To My Family, who make this a lot of fun

Felgrig paid little attention to his friend's tantrum. "Ok, so a dragon or wizard died and passed on his power. What's so special about that?" He began to spiral down toward the waiting royal party.

Tolago followed behind Felgrig. "I don't know, I just thought I'd mention it."

*****

Chapter 1

Brinn plunged her hands deep into the warm belly of the dragon she had just slain, searching for her father's ruby ring. She had to find the ring before the ogress returned and locked her up to be sold to the evil wizard. Even now she could hear the heavy footsteps coming down the stairs. She must not allow the ogress to get hold of her father's ring. If the monster learned how to wield the ring's power, the land would suffer untold torments. She picked up a knife and crouched behind the beast. She would have to dispose of the ogress first, then recover what was rightfully hers. It was *her* legacy. Her evil stepbrother had no right to remove it from her father's lifeless hand. And now he went and got himself eaten.

The sound of the ogress' bloated feet came ever nearer. The attack came from behind, surprising Brinn. She was grabbed by her tattered collar and pulled mercilessly to face the hideous beast.

"What in the world are you doing down there?!"

Brinn looked into to the face of Aunt Nethra. "Put the knife down!" Nethra shook Brinn and pulled her to face the worktable. "Look at the mess you've made of this dough!"

Brinn blinked several times to clear her thoughts. "I'm sorry, I wasn't paying attention."

"This is no place for your silly fantasies. Now get this bread on the hearth and take up the breakfast trays." The "ogress" Aunt stomped back up the stairs.

Brinn gave the dough an apologetic pat, kneaded it back into a smooth mound and covered it. Cut slices of bacon were set to fry; hot apples were spooned into dishes to cool. Brinn stirred the porridge, wishing it wouldn't take so long to cook. The dough had forgiven Brinn's insulting behavior, and she gently shaped it into loaves. She gazed out the kitchen window while waiting for the kettle to boil. Her imagination began to wander again. A gigantic bird flew into the garden. A man slid from the huge bird's neck (an awfully long neck for a bird). He stood for a moment seeming to speak to the bird before disappearing into the morning mist. The bird pushed with its massive legs (odd shaped legs for a bird), and thrust itself into the air (the wings were the wrong shape). Brinn shook her head; she needed to keep her mind on her work.

The whistling kettle brought Brinn's thoughts back to the kitchen. She dusted off her hands and placed teapots on trays, scooping fragrant leaves into their potbellies. Removing the pot from the fire, Brinn was pleased to see the porridge had hurried along and

out into the warmed bowls. Slices of bread
meal. Heated cloths were placed over the
Brinn carried the armload upstairs.

Once the breakfast trays had been delivered, the
bread set to bake, and the kitchen readied for the noon
meal, Brinn had a few minutes of her own before the
tavern had to be swept out. She went to the courtyard
and watched the traffic coming into town. Carriages
and wagons, massive stallions and shaggy mares, finely
dressed nobles, soldiers in chain mail, ragged beggars,
worn down farmers. There seemed no end to the
variety traveling on the road. Brinn wished she could
join their company. She would sit astride a powerful
black stallion, dressed in battle leathers. A jeweled
short-sword hung at her side, a bow and quiver full of
arrows across her back. If she rode through the night
she could join up with the king's army at Precanlin and
ride on to Velisia to help send Baron Taldar back to the
hole he had crawled out of.

A stable boy brought out a gray mare. Seeing Brinn,
he called across the courtyard, "Nethra's looking for
you!"

Brinn sighed, her only battle would be against the
pots and pans. The tavern sweeping would be delayed,
and her father would scold her for daydreaming again.
Some days she never caught up with her chores. She
slipped into the tavern and grabbed a broom. If she
looked as if she was in the middle of sweeping, Nethra
might let her finish before giving her more work.

Brinn was pleasantly surprised to find the floor of

weeping. Her father must have
It wasn't like him to help her
must have had a good night.
to find Nethra, a gentleman
t her attention.

in the tavern's door looked
ushed his hood back and stepped
xcuse me, do you work here?"
n't help but smile at the man's polite
lso approved of his clothes; from head to
black, no adornment. At first she thought
man, his long hair was white as new fallen
his face was definitely that of a young man.
be a nobleman, but not flashy about it. She
"Yes, sir. This is my father's inn."
you tell me if an elderly gentleman rooming
as supposed to meet him a few days ago, and
ng he's still here." The man's voice was
low in tone.
couldn't take her eyes from the stranger's
the cautious look she had seen in soldiers
w ted the tavern. There was a faded scar
above one eye, partially hidden by his wild white hair.
When she looked at his lips, she saw a smile on them.
She blushed and looked away. She recalled his
question, "There *was* an elderly gentleman rooming
here, but I'm afraid to say that he passed away two
days ago." Her memories of the friendly old man
brought tears to her eyes.

The stranger stepped close to Brinn and took her

shoulders. When she glanced up at him she saw an anxious look in his eyes. "When exactly did he die? Was there anyone with him? Are his belongings still here?" Brinn pulled away at the intensity of the man's questions. He let go of her suddenly, he stepped back, and stared for a moment. "Forgive me."

Brinn smiled weakly. "He told me his name was Thal. He died just as the sun rose, two days ago."

The stranger chuckled, "Just his style." He sat down at a nearby table motioning for her to sit also. "Was there anyone with him when he died?"

"None that I know of, sir," she answered slowly. "He didn't answer when I brought breakfast. When I went in he was still and cold."

The gentleman started to ask more questions when Nethra entered the tavern. "Brinn! I sent for you twenty minutes ago! What are you doing in—" She stopped in mid-sentence, stared blankly, then turned and left the room.

"Now, you were saying?" the gentleman asked casually.

Bewildered by her aunt's behavior, Brinn decided it would be best if her father dealt with this gentleman's questions. She certainly didn't want to anger Nethra. She stood. "I will fetch my father; he will be able to help you." She ran off before the gentleman could stop her. After locating her father, Brinn went to the kitchen and began work on the morning's dishes.

Nethra found enough chores to keep Brinn occupied until supper, and the evening was spent under her father's stern eye, serving and cleaning up after customers. It was only after the last dish was cleared from the tables that Brinn was allowed time to herself.

Not wanting to miss any of the cool evening breeze, Brinn changed quickly out of her work dress and slipped down the back stairs, avoiding the kitchen. She strolled down the dusty street, nibbling on a meat-filled roll she had slipped into her apron. She stopped to talk to the blacksmith, and visited with the daughter of the baker. A few pennies bought some ribbon at the dressmaker's just as they were closing for the night. On her way back, Brinn was startled when someone stepped out from the shadows.

"Hello Brinn, out for your evening walk, I see." Though the light was dim, the smell of fish identified Ruthic, the offensive son of the local fishmonger.

"You're very observant. I'd like to continue it, now." Brinn tried to step around Ruthic. He grabbed her arm and pulled her close.

"There's no rush, the floors can wait to be scrubbed." He laughed cruelly, as if his insult was amusing. "You have time to give me a kiss." He leaned his unwashed face toward Brinn's.

Brinn easily avoided the offensive lips. "You smell as if *you* could use a good scrubbing." She twisted in Ruthic's grasp.

Ruthic held her tight against his chest. "Think you're too good for me?" He grabbed Brinn's hair and held her twisting head still.

Fear and anger filled Brinn. She pushed against his chest. Her mind screamed out. She found herself suddenly free. Ruthic was slumped against a wall, unconscious. Brinn looked around for her savior, but he was nowhere to be found. "Thank you!" she shouted, hoping that whoever it was had heard her. She ran back to the safety of her father's inn.

Brinn didn't want to answer any questions about her disheveled appearance, so she took the back stairs to her room. With the door shut behind her, Brinn felt safe. She fumbled for the flint, but her shaking hands couldn't make a spark to light her candle. Her anger rose again, "Oh just light!" she said in frustration. She jumped back when the whole candle burst into flame, and quickly burned out. Brinn opened her door, letting the lights from the landing flood into her room. She stared at the smoldering wick in a puddle of congealing wax. "Wow," she laughed nervously, and shut the door. Deciding not to attempt another candle, Brinn dressed for bed by the light of the moon.

Nightmarish figures of huge fish filled Brinn's dreams; hidden heroes rescued her from being drowned by the scaly, rancid creatures. She woke several times to find herself twisted in her sheets. Another figure drifted in and out of her dreams, the black-dressed gentleman who had inquired about the old man. He always seemed to be hiding in the shadows, watching. An icy breeze woke Brinn and she shivered violently. She lay in the darkness, trying to think of anything but

Ruthic and his smelly hands on her shoulders. She considered the explosive candle for a moment. There must have been a flaw in the wick, or a bubble in the wax. She would have to clean up the mess before Nethra found it. Another chilling breeze made Brinn clutch the blankets tighter around her chin. Had she left the window open? Brinn reached down to where she had dropped her dressing gown, wanting to add an extra layer to her blankets. She did not touch the warmth of the flannel, however, nor the rough wood floor.

Brinn's fingers touched something cold and smooth. She immediately pulled them back under the covers, being careful not to touch her own warm skin. There must be a layer of ice on the floor, she thought. With this logical explanation, Brinn leaned over and reached for her slippers. The slippers were not there. Brinn reached further out. Her hand made contact with an icy wall, but it couldn't be *her* wall. Her bed wasn't near the wall; she shouldn't be able to touch it from the bed. A sudden, frightening thought occurred to Brinn and she hesitantly reached out on the other side of her bed. She sighed with relief when she did not touch a wall. Something must have been pushed up against the bed. The relief faded when she dropped her arm and her fingers met the cold hardness of the floor.

"This is ridiculous," she said to herself, "There nothing to be..." She fell silent. Her words had a strange ring to them, as if they were echoing back to her. Her mind raced for some answer, but she could find none.

Once more Brinn reached out. The sheets slid and she found herself falling off the bed, landing on the hard, icy floor. Her elbow banged painfully on the side of the bed. Splinters of pain ran up her arm and she smothered a cry. When her vision cleared, Brinn saw the bright moon shining through her window and found herself not on the frozen floor, but on wood warmed by the downstairs fires. As her breathing returned to normal, Brinn scolded herself for getting carried away in a dream.

She climbed back into bed and tried to stay awake as long as possible. When Aggie, Nethra's youngest daughter, knocked on her door just before sunrise, Brinn was grateful to be leaving the terrible dreams behind.

The halls were cool and comforting, Brinn was glad to be starting her normal routine. She heard the sounds of Aggie starting the fires in the tavern, and knew that the fire in the kitchen would be lit and a kettle of water set. She detoured to the pump and henhouse. The dim kitchen was beginning to warm from the fire. Brinn set down her load of eggs and water on one of the long scrubbed wooden tables and lit the lamp.

The bread was on its first rise, when stirrings from the rooms above began to filter down. Brinn poured a second cup of tea and began to cut the slabs of bacon when she heard the kitchen door open. "Tea's still hot, Aggie," she said without looking up.

"Thanks, I could use a cup." Brinn dropped the knife; it was not Aggie who had answered her. A shaggy-haired man was leaning over the teapot. He was dressed casually, and it took a moment for Brinn to recognize the gentleman from the morning before.

"Beg your pardon, sir; I didn't know it was you. I could have had a maid bring that up for you. Breakfast isn't normally served until seven. If you're hungry I can warm up some of yesterday's bread. I have eggs and bacon that I can make for you if you'll be needing something more." She didn't know why, but she felt nervous.

The gentleman leaned down to the fire and warmed his hands. "Please don't go to any trouble. I didn't come down here to have an early meal. I wanted the chance to talk to you without being disturbed."

Brinn turned quickly back to the bacon. This was not what she wanted to hear this early. "I'm sorry, but I have a lot of work to do this morning. I don't have time to talk." She wished she hadn't been so abrupt. "Please, if you need any more information about your friend..."

"No, thank you, your father was quite helpful. I was hoping for a more personal conversation."

"I'm sorry, but I'm not supposed to speak to the guests." She knew how silly this sounded. "Besides, you don't even know me." She didn't know why this man completely unnerved her.

He came closer. "You're right, let me introduce myself. My name is Talon. I come from high up the mountains. I have a number of very unpleasant friends, and I like my bacon thin."

Brinn noticed then that she was cutting the bacon

much too thick, and laughed at herself. She smiled at Talon, he didn't look dangerous, especially with ruffled hair and miss-buttoned shirt, he had the appearance of a young boy. Here in the kitchen, with a knife in her hand, there was no reason to be afraid. "My name is Brinn."

Talon smiled. "I'm sure you're father wouldn't mind your talking to me. He likes his guests happy, and as long as I keep my hands to myself and don't interrupt your work, I don't think he'll complain." He took a hot loaf of bread from the hearth and tore into it.

Brinn had to admit that Talon's assessment was correct. Her father was not as strict as Nethra, and did not ban her from talking to the customers, as long as it did not disturb them.

"I was a friend of Thal's, a very close friend. I talked to your father yesterday; he said you spent a lot of time with him."

Brinn continued cutting. "He was pleasant to me. I liked listening to his stories."

"Did he have any other visitors?" Brinn shook her head. "You said yesterday that he was alone when he died. Had he had any visitors the night before?"

Brinn turned away from the table and occupied herself at the fire. "No. But I think he was expecting someone. When I brought breakfast to him that morning something didn't feel right in his room." Brinn remembered the air in the room had the same feeling of an oncoming storm. "I knew then he was dying, he had that look in his eyes."

"Yesterday you said that he was dead when you took in his breakfast tray."

Brinn blushed at having her lie caught. "I didn't want anyone to think I had...I didn't...it wouldn't have looked right for me to be there, alone." She brought the dough to the table and began to work it into loaves. "There was no one there for him, I felt like I needed to stay with him until the end."

Talon reached out his hand and laid it on hers. "It must have been hard for you. Did he say anything before he died?"

Brinn shook her head. "If you mean something like who was to inherit his belongings, or where his treasure was hidden, or anything like that, no. The last hours he was delirious."

"Delirious? What do you mean?" Talon rose and came around the table; he took Brinn's shoulders and turned her to face him. "What did he say?"

Brinn pulled away. "Nothing, just gibberish. I couldn't understand anything he said."

Talon dropped his hands. He turned away, muttering to himself. When he didn't say anymore, Brinn finished the bread and set it by the fire. "I'm sorry I couldn't be of any help."

Talon helped Brinn lift the iron skillet to its rack above the fire. "Some of the gibberish Thal spoke, did it sound like: grintal slone vanglia mori shanool?"

Brinn stood slowly, her eyes wide. "Yes, that is what it sounded like. Is it a foreign language? I didn't recognize it."

15

Talon laughed and shook his head. "I don't expect you have. It's a very old language. When you are done here, could you show me Thal's room? I'd like to talk more about his last few hours." He didn't wait for her answer and passed Nethra as he walked out of the kitchen.

Nethra scowled at Brinn, but since the breakfast preparations were finished, she could find no reproach. "Get the trays upstairs before we get complaints."

Chapter 2

After the noon meal had been cleared Brinn went looking for Talon. She was startled when Ruthic cornered her in the tavern.

"I've been looking for you." His words sounded lewd.

"I've been working, as I always do." Brinn searched the tavern for any escape.

"I decided to forgive your behavior last night. But if I find out who the coward was that punched me and ran away, I'll kill him." Ruthic twisted his fingers in Brinn's hair. He pulled them swiftly away, as if they'd been burned. "I'll wait for you at the smithy after you finish the floors."

Ruthic left before Brinn could tell him she would rather eat raw eels than ever meet him *anywhere*. A few guests were staring at her, so she was unable to utter a few choice words. She went outside to continue her search.

Brinn found Talon sitting in the small back garden. He seemed to be deep in thought. She watched him, unnoticed. He was quite handsome. His eyes were bright and full of mischief; his face was tanned and leathery, either from age or weather. Brinn shook her head, bringing herself back to reality, this was no fairy tale, Talon was not the knight in shining armor come to rescue her from evil villains.

Talon felt Brinn watching him, and stood. "Thank you for taking your free time to help me."

Brinn felt her face warm, embarrassed that she had been caught. "Thal's room hasn't been used since he died." She turned to walk back inside. "I'll take you up." She didn't have to turn around to know that he followed her up the narrow stairs. She opened the door and stepped aside, she didn't want to enter the room.

Talon entered and looked around. "Your father said his things had been left untouched." He walked around and picked up a few belongings. "I am grateful that business has been slow enough to allow this room to be left alone." He brushed his hands on the bed; it had been straightened after the body was removed. "I am only sorry that he was buried so quickly."

Brinn watched with curiosity as Talon inspected Thal's belongings. He searched clothing, shuffled through papers, pulled out drawers. The search seemed desperate.

"Why didn't he leave me a message?" The anger in his words startled Brinn. "What am I supposed to do with this girl?"

Brinn stepped into the room. She tried to calm Talon, not understanding his outburst. "He was ill, he couldn't feed himself, much less write a letter."

Talon looked deep into Brinn's eyes. "Ill, yes, but not delirious as you suggested this morning. Fernley knew what he was doing right to the end."

"Fernley?"

"That was Thal's real name." Talon turned away and sat on the bed. He motioned for her to sit. "I'm sorry I lost my temper. We need to talk."

Brinn pulled out the bedside chair. "I don't know what more I can tell you. Thal—Fernley didn't leave any instructions or messages. He seemed content to have me sit with him, to keep him company."

Talon nodded. "Did Fernley happen to tell you he was a wizard?"

Brinn stared at Talon. Her first reaction was surprise, and then she laughed. "Wizard? There's no such thing. I'm not a little child who believes in fairytales." Well that wasn't exactly true. Brinn felt an uncontrollable need to defend herself. "Just because this is a small isolated village don't think that we are uneducated superstitious bumpkins."

With a snap of his fingers, Talon shut the door, another flick of his hand set the fire ablaze and scattered papers stacked themselves. "No, not uneducated, superstitious bumpkins, just isolated. There are many things in this world you have not been exposed to." A cup of tea appeared on the table next to Brinn. "I think you could use that." When she hesitated, looking at the cup as if it were something horrendous, Talon laughed softly. "It is only a tea cup. I brought it from the kitchen. Please drink." He watched as she cautiously picked up the cup and put it to her lips. "Fernley was a powerful wizard, though he didn't make a big show about it. His specialty was digging up histories, prophecies and that sort of thing. I knew he was not well, and was to meet with him. Now that he has died, others will come looking for his successor. We don't have much time."

The tea was exactly what Brinn needed. Not being without imagination, she didn't find it difficult to accept what Talon told her. Hadn't she spent many dreary days dreaming of wizards, princesses, dragons and knights? She should be thrilled that her dreams were becoming real, even if it meant an adjustment of her comfortable world.

Talon waited for Brinn to think everything through. "I know this is a bit of a shock, but there's more. When a wizard dies, their power doesn't die with him, but is given to a successor. This is normally an apprentice, or perhaps another wizard. On rare occasions the receiver of the power is an innocent bystander." Talon saw that Brinn didn't understand what he was getting at. "The incantation, the gibberish, Fernley spoke just before he died transferred his power to his successor." Brinn looked puzzled. "Has anything unusual happened in the past two days? Objects appearing just where you wanted them, tasks being completed faster than usual, coincidences that made life easier?"

Brinn thought of a dozen instances such as Talon described. The memory of Ruthic knocked unconscious came into her mind. Suddenly the horror of what Talon was suggesting hit her. She jumped to her feet. "Oh no, I don't want any part of this! You just take whatever it is away!"

"I'm sorry, but I can't. I know what you're thinking; I've been where you are. But you have to accept the gift that was given, you have no choice." Talon wanted to comfort the girl but knew sternness was better for her now.

Brinn paced around the room. A number of times she started to speak, but stopped, not able to put her thoughts into words. She sat down and stared into the fire. "No choice," she muttered.

Talon watched the battle of emotions on the young face. He tried to think of anything he could tell her that would ease her distress. "You won't be alone. You will be taught how to use your new power. You don't have to live like a hermit. It isn't like the fairytales, craggy old men living in caves. Many wizards live in towns, or castles, helping Normals in many ways."

Brinn looked intensely at Talon. "How much power do I have? What can this...magic do?"

Talon took his time answering. What did she need to know at this stage? He remembered his own beginning. Was she much different from what he had been? Talon chose honesty. "Your power equals that of Fernley's at his death. You will need to learn how to use that power, then you will be as strong as any of us."

"And just what can I do with this power?" Greed, ambition, compassion, excitement, all tumbled together in her thoughts.

"Just about anything you could want to do."

Brinn grinned. "Quite a temptation isn't it."

Talon hesitated at the tone in her voice. There was so much at stake. "And what would you do with such a temptation?"

Brinn looked at Talon and had to laugh at the serious, almost fearful, expression on his face. "Nothing as awful as you must be thinking. I have no inclination toward the evil that might tempt others."

Talon breathed a sigh of relief. "I thought for a moment my first impression of you had been seriously inaccurate. You are right about the inclination toward evil. There are too many novices that become drunk with their new power, or are led to evil by others."

Brinn took a sip of her lukewarm tea. "There must have been a flaw in their personalities to begin with, I think." She was silent for some time. Then stood, resolute. "I won't be able to stay here, will I?"

Talon stood. "No. You may come back after your training, but you are vulnerable now."

"Can we leave right away?" Brinn was eager to begin her new life.

"There are preparations I have to make. Will the end of the week be soon enough for you?"

Brinn smiled with satisfaction. "Yes."

Talon walked to the door. "It would be wisest not to tell anyone else of what we have discussed."

Brinn nodded, "My father would be too practical to understand." She followed Talon out of the room and went down to the kitchen. There was a new spring to her step.

Chapter 3

Nethra sent Brinn to the butcher, so speaking to Talon that evening was impossible.

The events of the afternoon occupied Talon's thoughts entirely as he sat picking over his dinner plate. He paid little attention to the influx of patrons in the tavern. That could have been fatal. A repulsive wave of hate distracted his thoughts. He turned with amazing speed, stopping the knife in mid-flight and sending it into the rafters. "You're losing your touch, Keldric."

The dark-cloaked figure at the door of the pub grunted and stilled the innkeeper with a wave of his hand. "Just checking to see if life with those beasts has slowed your reflexes." He moved smoothly into the crowded room, oblivious of the stares aimed at him. "I was unavoidably detained, has the old goat died yet?"

Talon sat next to his mortal enemy. "Is that what brought you out of your hole? I didn't know you and Fernley were so close." The sarcasm was wasted on Keldric. "Your information is a bit old, Fernley is no longer here." Talon felt Keldric's mind searching his. He let the distasteful touch find what it was looking for, but no more.

"Dead? Then you came to take his spirit. I would have thought that your mind was crowded enough with the old wizard and that *monster*."

"Are we counting? It seems that you have collected quite a few wizards' spirits lately. And most of them were unwilling donors." Talon's tone had become tense.

"I had little choice after you robbed me of my own power." Keldric's eyes burned with hatred. "You don't know how I suffered. I am justified using any methods needed to regain my rightful position. If you are wise you won't get in my way."

Talon only lifted an eyebrow at the threat. Talon had learned not to underestimate this enemy, but he would not be intimidated either. "If it will make you go away...I did not inherit Fernley's spirit."

Keldric seemed to accept this information. "You must have worked fast to find a successor, then." Keldric sent his thoughts to search the inn. "Where have you put him?"

Talon was grateful that Brinn had gone on an errand that afternoon. "What makes you think I had anything to do with finding Fernley's successor? Fernley knew for quite some time he was dying. I assume he arranged the whole thing."

Keldric looked suspiciously at Talon. "No, he put it off too long." Keldric was no longer concerned about hiding the fact that he knew more than he should. "Fernley could never bear to share his knowledge with anyone. He didn't take an apprentice. And he contacted you a few days ago. If the fool didn't have someone here to receive his spirit, then what happened to it?" Keldric looked intensely at Talon.

Talon smiled with an odd satisfaction. "Haven't your spies found that out for you?"

"They seemed to have disappeared. Something to do with you being here, I imagine." Keldric stood and pulled his cloak around him. "If you are still here, the novice must be close by. I think I'll take a room for a few days." He turned to leave.

"Hair's still black, I see," Talon said pointedly, running a hand through his own wizard-white hair.

Keldric self-consciously put his hand to the dark locks then shot a look of pure hatred at his enemy and swept out of the pub.

Talon waited a few moments then followed. He had to find Brinn before Keldric did. When his searching failed, Talon knew it would be less conspicuous to wait for Brinn in her bedchamber.

It was well past dusk before Brinn's tired feet took her upstairs. She knew before she closed her door that someone was in her room. For some reason though, she didn't feel afraid.

"I'm here." Talon's whisper warned her. Brinn lit a candle and saw Talon sitting next to the tiny window. "Have you seen a man, tall, wearing a black cloak?"

"Yes, he was in the livery stable when I returned from town. I saw him staring at me while I talked to the stableboy. He would have followed me inside, but the stablemaster, had some business with him. I don't think I like him."

"Listen to your feelings. The man is Keldric, an evil wizard who would destroy you if given the chance."

"That's a little harsh." Keldric pushed the door open and stepped into the room. "I'm aggressive in my tactics, I'll admit, but one must assert oneself if they want to get ahead." Keldric bowed theatrically to Brinn. "Have I the honor of addressing the esteemed daughter of Master Kippling?"

Brinn was confused, but curtsied. The man before her did not appear to be the monster Talon had described.

"You must forgive Talon; he has lived among dragons for so long he has forgotten his manners. I am Keldric Finnelias, at your service." Keldric pulled a chair close to the fire and offered it to Brinn.

An odd feeling of dread tugged at the back of her mind. She decided not to make any hasty judgments about this man. She sat in the offered chair. "I am Brinn."

Talon blocked Keldric from sitting across from Brinn. "This is a private conversation."

Keldric pointed a manicured finger and a chair appeared next to the fire. "Surely you don't expect me to stand by and let you poison this young girl's mind without some defense. It's terribly chilly in here," he waved his hand and two brightly burning logs appeared on the fire. "Much better. Dear Brinn, I'm sure young Talon, here, was informing you of my despicable reputation. Though I'm sure he left out the part about how he stripped me of my magic, or how he's spent the past fifty years in the company of ferocious dragons. He's a bit out of touch with humans. He is not the best of choices to teach a novice in the ways of *human* magic."

"And *you* are?" Talon scoffed.

"Unlike you, I have had the opportunity to train several novices in the art of magic." Keldric turned his attention to Brinn. "Let us put aside the differences between Talon and myself, what's important is you and your training. Talon has probably told you how amazing your life is about to become." The surprised look in Brinn's eyes was all Keldric needed. "Having lived among humans, I know what a young girl like you wants. Under my tutelage you will have everything you could ever want: a plush mansion with servants seeing to your every desire, a feast of delectable foods, all the latest fashions, anything your heart desires."

Talon had a strong desire to slap the smug look off Keldric's face. It was Brinn's laugh that wiped the superior grin from the wizard's lips.

"Your offer doesn't tempt me. I'm not a foolish young girl you can entice with jewels and pretty dresses. But I'll forgive your assumption because you have just met me."

Keldric tried to recover from his blunder, "I sincerely beg your pardon. I was only thinking of you. Your training would, of course, suit your individual needs."

Brinn stood. "I'm sorry. I know we are not well acquainted, but I feel that I am better suited to study with someone like Talon." She went to the door. "If you will both excuse me, supper preparations await." Brinn curtsied and left the two staring after her.

Talon slapped Keldric's satin covered shoulder. "I've got to congratulate you. That had to be the smoothest routine I've seen in decades."

Keldric pulled away and stomped out the door.

An hour later Brinn went in search of Talon, being careful not to find Keldric instead. She found him, again in the back garden. He was talking to someone, but the garden was empty. She quietly sat down on a bench opposite his.

Talon stopped speaking for a moment when he saw Brinn, then smiled and held up a finger to let her know he would be finished in a moment. "Tell Gontel I will take care of the matter personally. No, that's too important to be delayed. Can you help keep an eye on things here? Thanks old friend." A sudden breeze blew and Talon pulled his cloak closed. "I'm sorry, that must have seemed peculiar."

Brinn shrugged. "I'm sure today will be the beginning of many peculiar events in my life."

Talon looked concerned. "And do you feel up to the challenge?"

Brinn smiled broadly. "With all my heart. What girl doesn't dream of adventure, of being taken away from their mundane lives by a mysterious man?"

Talon looked away. "I'm afraid I won't be able to whisk you away quite yet. I have to return home tonight to take care of an urgent matter. You might have to be here a bit longer."

Brinn was disappointed. "Can't you take me with you?"

"I'm sorry, but I can't. I promise to return before the week is out." Brinn accepted this in silence. "I have to leave you with Keldric still around, but I have no choice."

"I can handle him."

"Don't be too sure. He's a powerful wizard. I don't think he'll try any magic here, but to be safe, you shouldn't be alone with him."

"Don't worry about me; he's the *last* person I want to spend time with." Brinn rose and turned toward the house, her spirits very much lower. "I won't detain you." She went quietly back to the inn.

Talon watched solemnly until Brinn disappeared inside, then he disappeared.

Chapter 4

The morning chores kept Brinn occupied. She was glad she had little time to brood over the delay of her departure. The idea of washing one more dish, scrubbing one more table, hanging out one more sheet was becoming intolerable. It had been ten days since Talon left. If only she knew how to use the power inside her, Brinn thought she could find ways to make the days speed by. She was so lost in thought that Brinn did not notice Keldric sitting on the garden bench when she took a moment to step outside in the clear air.

"This is a lovely garden," Keldric said casually.

Brinn was startled, the wizard had not approached her since Talon departed and she thought he might have left as well. She searched for an excuse to return to the inn.

"Please don't go." Keldric motioned to the bench opposite his. Brinn chose to remain where she was. "I would very much like the chance to apologize for my behavior when we last met. It was wrong of me to make such an assumption of anyone. I, myself, care little for the trappings of fashionable life. Power is what I seek. I gather together the most powerful wizards. With our combined strength we will destroy our enemies and take back our rightful place as leaders of the world."

The wild look in Keldric's eyes frightened Brinn. "I'm sorry to disappoint you, but I'm not a powerful wizard, and I don't really want to be one."

Keldric tried another approach. "But you want to get out of here, am I right?" Brinn had to acknowledge the truth. "Then let me at least take you away. Talon has deserted you. He came to take Fernley's power for himself. When he found out the old wizard out-smarted him, Talon ran off to his precious dragons."

Keldric's words mirrored the suspicions Brinn already had. She knew better than to trust Keldric, but what would she do if Talon did not return? Where could she go? Would her family consider her a freak? Or would they take advantage of her?

Seeing Brinn's turmoil, Keldric smiled. "Come with me. If you don't want me to teach you, I'll find a wizard who will." He held out his hand. "Trust me."

As tempting as Keldric was, something deep in Brinn's mind urged caution. "I'm sorry, but I think I will wait for Talon's return."

Keldric was careful not to let his anger show. He would not accept defeat so easily. "If that is your choice, I will have to wait." He got to his feet and left Brinn alone in the garden.

Brinn returned to her room. She got little sleep that night. A part of her wanted to take Keldric up on his offer. He offered her a way out from under the domination of her aunt, away from Ruthic's offensive innuendos, an alternative to the misery she would be destined to live if she remained where she was. The temptation of power was also strong. Once she learned the extent of the powers Fernley had given her, Brinn would be able to repay the years of labor and humiliation she had endured since her mother had died.

When she finally fell asleep, Brinn dreamt of living in a large castle with maids and servants waiting on her. Nethra would have twelve meals a-day to prepare, hundreds of chamber pots to empty, and acres of floors to sweep. But Brinn's vengeful dream was haunted by an eerie feeling that she was being watched. Just out of sight was something large, with glowing eyes and savage claws. And Keldric was always in the background, a self-satisfied grin on his face. Brinn did not know which was more dangerous, Keldric, or the creature with glowing eyes.

Brinn woke from her dream, hearing beautiful, bell-like laughter. She slipped from her bed and followed the enthralling sound down the stairs and outside. She saw two red eyes looking out at her from the treeline across the road. They burned into her mind, searching. Brinn was frozen with fear; she did not see the man approaching from behind. In the moonlight she saw the flash of a knife as it neared her throat. Still, the eyes held her motionless. She felt the cut of the blade against her skin but not the warmth of blood. From the trees burst a stream of flames. Brinn felt burning heat brushing her cheek, and tried to pull away, but the eyes bored into her, holding her still. A terrible scream tore the quiet of the night, the deadly blade dropped from Brinn's throat. The force that held her was released and Brinn ran back into to the inn. She turned for just a moment, the cloaked figure was slapping flames from his arms. Keldric's face was a mask of fury. The glowing eyes moved out of the trees to reveal a gigantic reptilian head and shoulders. The dragon never took its eyes from Brinn's as it came fully out of the trees.

"Remember which one was the monster." The voice was quiet and kind. The dragon crouched and sprang into the air.

Brinn ran up to her room and locked the door. She slid to the floor and burst into tears. It was some time before she could stand and return to her bed. Once there she fell quickly into dreamless sleep.

The next morning Brinn tried to recall the horrific events. She was beginning to think it was just a terrible nightmare. Her reddened cheek could have gotten chapped from the sheets; the scratch on her neck could have been made by something sharp in her nightgown's collar. She immersed herself into the morning's rituals and pushed the night's memories into the dark corners of her mind.

By late afternoon there was still no sign of Talon. Brinn found excuses to be outside most of the day to watch for his return, but became resigned to the belief that he was not coming. She could not stay away from the inn any longer and went to clear the tables.

From the corridor, Brinn heard her father mention her name. She turned to enter the room, but stopped at the sound of Keldric's voice.

"You are very wise. A young man will soon come and take your daughter away, this way you can make a profit. You will be able to afford *three* serving maids and still come out ahead." Keldric's smooth manipulating tone made Brinn shiver.

"And you assure me that you will take care of her?" The lack of real concern in her father's voice broke Brinn's heart.

"My mother has grown lonely since my sister married." Keldric sounded like a loving son. "She craves someone to talk to. Your daughter's life would be greatly improved. She will move in circles that will allow her to contract a most advantageous marriage."

Brinn heard the counting of a large number of coins. Her father had no more to say. Two hands were slapped together, sealing the arrangement. Resentment and fear were outweighed by anger. Brinn ran to her room and began to pack.

By the time she slipped down the back stairs, Brinn decided to have nothing more to do with her family or wizards. Talon had deserted her, her father had sold her into servitude, and Keldric's plans for her were dubious. Brinn took a seldom-used path out of town.

She didn't know if Keldric would be able to use magic to find her, and decided the best thing she could do was to empty her mind. She paid little attention to the path before her and stumbled over roots and caught her skirt on brambles.

The sun was beginning to set, but Brinn kept moving. She knew it would soon be too dark to continue, but she needed to get as far away as possible. In the dim light her footing was more uncertain and Brinn found herself on her knees. She looked back at the root that had brought her down. She was sure she had stepped over it. But here she was, sitting on the damp ground with sore knees. Brinn began to get back to her feet when she noticed the thorny root move. Thoughts of poisonous snakes and fanged reptiles slithered through her mind. The bushes began to shake, twigs broke, and Brinn's nerves snapped. She drew out a small kitchen knife and ran down the path. Crashing foliage followed close behind.

When the first huge claw stepped out of the bushes Brinn screamed and stumbled back, falling soundly on her bottom. She followed the claw to the foot and up the long leg. Brinn squeezed her eyes shut for a second; she must have hit her head when she fell. She opened her eyes and looked up into the deep blue eyes. The fangs were smaller than in her usual fantasies. The head of the green beast lowered and the great maw opened to eat her in one bite.

"No, the head's all wrong." Brinn reached up and grabbed one pointed ear. "These are supposed to be longer, and frilled." She tapped the smooth scalp. "And where are the horns. Dragons are supposed to have horns." Brinn patted the narrow cheek. "How do you expect to chomp me in half with small fangs like these?" she asked irritably. She shook her head. "This is just not up to your usual standards, Brinn."

The fierce beast pulled his head back. "Do you mind!" He shook out his offended ear. "What do you think you are doing?"

Brinn got to her feet and shouldered her pack. "Listen I don't have time for daydreaming. Will you just chew me up and get this over with."

The dragon laughed, or at least Brinn assumed it was a laugh, her fantasy dragons never laughed. "You are mistaken. This is no daydream," the beast said. "I am *not* a creature of your imagination."

Brinn shook her head disbelievingly but noticed her knee was bleeding, and it hurt. She looked back up at the monster, then turned to run. Brinn only got a few yards before she was grabbed by a large, fanged mouth and was lifted into the air. She slashed with the knife and made contact with whatever had hold of her, but it was to no avail. The beast shook Brinn roughly. She muttered a prayer and moved the knife to her own throat. Better to die quickly by her own hands than slowly in the bowels of a beast.

"No, I don't think so." A claw took the knife from Brinn's hands. "No need for such dramatics. Just calm down and I'll release you."

37

Brinn was stunned by the quiet voice. She took a few calming breaths and looked clearly at the beast she thought was about to eat her. Brinn found that she was not, in fact, in the jaws of a huge monster, but in one of its claws. The other was still holding her knife. She turned her head, looking for the source of the voice. Looking up, she saw the horrific fangs and screamed. This definitely was no dream.

"Stop that!" Brinn was gently shaken. "I'm not going to eat you." The claw holding the young girl lowered to the ground. "If you promise not to run away in hysterics I'll release you."

Brinn nodded wordlessly. She was gently set down. "But you're a dragon, aren't you?" she asked breathlessly. "You're supposed to want to eat me. No, wait." She remembered the glowing eyes and belching flames of her nightmare. "If you aren't going to eat me, why did you grab me?" Brinn was starting to get control of herself.

The dragon shifted its weight and made itself as comfortable as it could along the small path. "Well you were coming at me with a knife, and though I doubt it would have done me any harm, I thought you might trip and hurt yourself." The dragon looked down at the girl, squinted and looked closer. "You are a wizard."

Brinn brushed the dirt from her dress and adjusted her shoes. "So I'm told. Someone told me I was, but I don't know for sure. If you aren't going to eat me I'd like to be on my way." Brinn looked for a way around the dragon.

The dragon looked Brinn over and smiled broadly. "You're the girl who inherited Fernley's magic. Talon told me about you."

Brinn turned back to the smiling dragon. "You know Talon? Where is he?"

"He was called back to the colony. I thought he would be back by now. He asked me to keep an eye on that beast, Keldric. Shall I hazard a guess that he's getting out of hand again?"

Brinn didn't know what to make of this curious creature. It seemed friendly enough, but she wasn't completely sure. She didn't get a chance to make up her mind. A rush of air around her shifted Brinn's attention.

The dragon reached out and pulled Brinn close. "Trust me," was all it said before a flash of light appeared before them.

"Step away from her, vile monster!" Keldric stood regally on the path.

The dragon shifted slightly, as if to move toward the wizard. Keldric stepped back cautiously. "Go back to your hole, Keldric. You will not win here."

Keldric shifted from his imperious posture to one of caring concern. "Brinn, you are in grave danger. I know this beast; he'll gain your confidence, and then devour you."

The dragon laughed. "You're one to talk, wizard. We've been keeping track of your exploits. You are more dangerous than *we* ever were."

Keldric ignored the dragon's remarks and reached out to Brinn. "Step slowly away from the monster, I'll protect you."

Brinn was reminded of the words the dragon from her nightmare spoke. Brinn straightened defiantly. "*Protect* me? Is that what you were doing at the inn? Were you protecting me by buying me from my father? I don't like you, and I certainly won't come with you, now, or ever."

"That was plain enough," the dragon said smugly. "You will leave the girl alone."

"I will not take orders from the likes of *you*." Keldric pointed a finger at Brinn. "Come here!"

Brinn began to move away from the dragon's side; she looked down at her feet in frustration. "You're a wizard, too," the dragon whispered. Brinn clenched her hands into fists and took a deep breath. She didn't know what she could do, but she wasn't going to let Keldric win. She flung her arms out and shouted as loud as she could: "NO!" Whether the scream distracted Keldric, or Brinn had actually accomplished it with her own magic; her feet stopped in mid-stride.

The dragon put himself between Brinn and Keldric. "You see, she doesn't want to go with you. Your power is not strong enough to handle *both* of us. I suggest you leave...now."

Keldric's face was twisted in anger. Brinn felt a rush of cold air whip around the furious wizard. His cloak swirled, his hair stood on end. Eyes narrowed and lips moved in slow uttering.

The dragon turned quickly to face Brinn. "Get on!"

Brinn didn't argue. She scrambled up the extended foreleg and straddled the enormous neck. She was thrown forward and the hind legs thrust them into the air.

The downdraft of the mighty wings joined the air encircling Keldric. His hand rose into the air, hands outstretched. One word of the long spell broke through the tumult: DOWN.

Brinn felt a mighty force knock her sideways off the dragon's neck. She fell, screaming as she plummeted toward the treetops. She was jerked from death and dragged skyward. When Brinn dared to open her eyes she was greeted by the sight of two rows of sharp, white teeth. She panicked and began to twist away from their dreadful grasp.

"Hold still!"

The words were shouted directly into her mind. Brinn closed her eyes and tried to relax, putting together what must have happened. It seemed forever before Brinn felt the thud of landing. She was laid gently on the ground. Her clothes were wet with saliva and bruises darkened on her arms and legs, fingers and toes that had been exposed to the harsh wind were icy cold. When she dared to look up at the enormous beast, Brinn saw a concerned look in the dragon's eyes. She slowly sat up. "Thank you," she said weakly. Brinn realized for the first time that her belongings had been left behind. She laughed, "I don't have any dry clothes to change into." She bit her lip, holding back the hysteria.

The dragon chuckled, relieved the girl had not gone into shock. A pile of wood appeared a few feet away and after a gentle puff, briskly burned. "When you're dry I'll take you to Talon. Right now I think I'll take a nap." Curling around the fire, the beast dozed.

Brinn tried not to look at the sleeping dragon. She wanted to forget the past hour, the past weeks. Here was a solid reminder that her life had taken an unexpected turn. Very unexpected. Her fantasies were rapidly moving toward reality.

"Is there a problem with that?"

Brinn turned angrily. "Stay out of my head! It's very impolite and annoying." The dragon's eyes were still closed, but a grin spread across the huge jaw.

Great blue eyes opened and looked into hers. "You are a very interesting human. You stand up against a powerful wizard, ride atop a dragon, and nearly fall to your death. And yet here you are complaining about how your life is going to change. Now *that's* annoying."

Brinn shook out her drying dress. "I wasn't complaining. I was just thinking that I can't go back to the way it was."

"Would you want to?"

Brinn smiled wickedly. "Never."

"Good girl." The dragon rose slowly to its feet, stretching. "If you're ready to go, I'll take you to Talon now."

Brinn again climbed onto the back of the dragon. This time they lifted gently into the air. Brinn thrilled at the rush of wind and the passing of the world below. She held on tightly as they rose higher toward the mountains and shrieked as they dove between the peaks. It was definitely a disappointment when the dragon slowed at a cave entrance. She ducked her head as they passed into the cave.

Talon met them at a junction in the tunnel. Brinn slid carefully down, giving the dragon's leg a squeeze.

Talon laid his hand on the massive shoulder. "Thank you Graldiss, I hope you didn't have too much trouble."

The dragon smiled and winked at Brinn. "No trouble at all." He disappeared down a tunnel.

Chapter 5

Talon walked silently down the long passageway, taking branching tunnels until Brinn was lost in the maze. Warm air drifted through the passages, smelling slightly of leather and soot. The floor beneath Brinn's feet was gravelly and made a crunching sound as she walked. Most of the tunnels were large enough for dragons to walk easily through, but a few were narrow and the ceilings so low Talon had to stoop. The walls of the passages seemed to glow just bright enough to see the next turn. When she paused to look behind her, the glow disappeared.

Brinn was just about to ask Talon to stop and let her rest when she bumped into him.

"Here we are," Talon pulled back a sheet of leather. He waved his hand and a dozen torches lit.

Brinn was surprised by the hominess of the cavern. Brightly colored rugs covered the floor and intricately woven tapestries hung from the walls. The huge fireplace was flanked by a dragon-sized cushion and a much smaller overstuffed chair. A long worktable with a stool stood against one side next to the cooking area. A curtain partially hid the bed and wardrobe. Standing shelves were filled with books and odd-looking objects. The cavern looked comfortable.

Talon laid a book he had been carrying on a small table near the entrance. A kettle moved from the cooking table to the fire, which seemed to glow to life on its own. "Please make yourself at home." He motioned to the curtained area. "You can call that your own while you're here." He went to a workbench and stirred a glass of green liquid.

Brinn drew back the curtain. The bed was large and fluffy, nicer than anything she had seen in her life. She bounced a few times on the springy mattress and rubbed her hand on the velvety cover. A table with a small candle stood beside the bed. A dark red robe lay over a simple chair, matching slippers lay next to it. Brinn rose and lifted the robe, a simple white dress lay under it. They looked to be her size. She took off her dirty dress and stockings, slipped on her new dress and pulled the robe over her head. The hood was more decorative than useful in the warm cavern. Brinn tied the soft rope belt and slid her feet into the fur-lined slippers. She felt luxurious.

Brinn pulled the curtain aside and went to the fire. Talon looked busy, so Brinn pulled the boiling kettle off its stand and looked for cups and tea. She found bread, butter and plates on one of the shelves. Talon set a small metal pot filled with smoking green liquid on the table.

"Thank you very much for the clothes." Brinn noticed Talon was wearing a similar robe. "Do all wizards wear robes like these?"

Talon chuckled and brought a small steaming pot and a bowl of sugar from his workbench. "Some wear cloaks, like Keldric. They can be very dramatic. But I found this style of robe is perfect for these caves. Loose fitting, not too warm, keeps out the drafts." Talon took a slice of buttered bread. "Are you ready to begin?"

Brinn put her cup down and sat up excitedly. "Are you going to teach me some magic now?"

"No, we'll get to that later. I'm going to release Fernley."

Brinn looked confused. "Release him? Where is he?"

Talon tapped Brinn's forehead. "That gibberish he recited just before his death allowed his thoughts and power to enter into your mind. It's sitting in there like a forgotten memory. I will finish the spell to release that power. You'll feel odd for a few days, maybe a few weeks. You'll remember things that never happened to you. You may even have conversations with Fernley's residual thoughts."

Brinn understood little but just accepted it. "Will I be able to do magic right away?"

"Not really. The power to manipulate your surroundings, which people call magic, will be given to you, but you will have to learn how to use it." Talon pushed the cooled pot in front of Brinn. "Drink this."

Brinn looked into the pot and grimaced with distaste. Nothing about the contents was appealing. It was a curdlely, green slime that smelled like rotten potatoes. When it blurped Brinn pushed it away. "You can't be serious."

"I'm going to be bumping around in your mind, Brinn. That isn't going to be pleasant for you. When I find the pocket of Fernley's memories and release them, it will be very unnerving. It would be better if you were completely unconscious during this."

Brinn looked at the goo again and shivered. "Did you have to do this?"

"Not all of it. The Ceremony of Transference was performed within twenty-four hours of Olwin's and Magrid's death. You didn't have that option. Fernley's only alternative was to place his essence inside your mind without the benefit of the ceremony." Talon poured a spoonful of sugar into the pot and stirred. "Drink up."

Brinn lifted the offensive substance to her mouth and closed her eyes tight. Luckily the glop was slick enough to slide down her throat quickly, because she didn't think she could stand the taste of it longer than the few seconds it slid over her tongue. Her head felt suddenly as thick and goopy as the potion she had swallowed. She didn't know that Talon caught her head just before it hit the table.

Talon carried Brinn to the overstuffed chair. He put his hands on either side of her head, closed his eyes, and slowly slid his thoughts into her mind. Talon coalesced his thoughts into a semblance of a physical self. He kept his attention on the search, ignoring the thoughts and emotions that crowded in on him. The landscape he traveled through was varied. Forests and swamps, fields and craggy mountains, all these were the forms Brinn's memories took. Weeds, and drifting leaves were mixed in, patches of flowers and occasional boulders; each one was an emotion Brinn had experienced at some time in her life. He brushed a flower with his hand and felt the joy of playing with a kitten. A drifting leaf brought the contentment of lying in her father's arms. Knowing how tempting it could be to remain here and experience Brinn's emotions, Talon moved quickly on. He passed a large flat stone set in the ground, feeling a chill as he stepped around it. Talon caught his leg on a thorn, and saw a flash of one of Brinn's memories of being pushed off a rock by a childhood friend. A wave of anger and hatred flowed over him. He quickly shut his mind, and took more care where he 'stepped'.

It seemed to take hours to traverse Brinn's mind, but eventually Talon found what he was looking for. It had the mental appearance of a large, glowing, yellow bubble. Talon gently felt the sides of the bubble. Satisfied that this was Fernley, Talon held out a small gold pin and carefully pierced the skin of the orb. "Crren nillya ssik roon jall fa. Come forth and reveal your true self."

With a soft chime of a bell the bubble burst. "Oh yes! At last. Thank you, Talon. Didn't like being bound up like that." The essence was definitely Fernley's. The yellow glow spread a bit, but did not disperse. "That's *not* how I wanted to spend eternity. A mental picture of the old wizard began to take shape. "Thank you, again. How did you find me?"

"You were lucky in your choice of recipients. I found her still at the inn where you died."

"The maid, yes. How is she taking all this?"

"Better than could have been expected."

"Yes, there are stories of unprepared recipients that have gone mad. I had to take the chance."

"They won't accept her, you know."

"Never been a female wizard before, I know. I saw that Keldric showed up. I tried to help. Praise the Ancients for that dragon of yours." Fernley looked around. "Interesting place. Never been in a mind before."

"You're avoiding the problem."

"What do you want me to say, kill the girl to preserve the status quo? I think it could be time for a change. If it turns out that a female can't handle the power, then you will have to deal with it as you see fit. But there's something special about this girl. It feels *right*, somehow. Watch over this one, Talon."

Talon nodded.

"I wonder how long it will take before I'm absorbed by the girl's mind."

"A few weeks, I imagine."

Fernley's spirit smiled. "Well, it will be an interesting experience to say the least. I think it's time you left."

Talon agreed. "Roon blonn linn krra. Your spirits are one." He shook his old friend's hand. "Billian taa." He retreated from Brinn's mind.

When Brinn woke, she was disoriented and weak. She found herself in a wonderfully soft bed. It took her a few minutes to remember where she was and what had happened. After several tries, Brinn sat up, she felt as weak as a newborn. She took her time swinging her feet from under the covers and standing up. When she pulled back the curtain Brinn saw the dragon that had brought her to the caverns, Graldiss, Talon called him, sitting on the cushion by the fire. Talon was lying on a simple cot.

Graldiss turned his head and looked at Brinn. "You'll be hungry, there's meat and cheese in the cold-box."

Brinn was concerned about Talon. "Is he all right?"

"He's just tired. Wandering around in someone else's mind can be exhausting. He just needs to sleep it off."

Brinn nibbled on some bread and cheese. She looked at Talon. In sleep he looked hardly older than herself. "He's awfully young for a wizard, isn't he?"

Graldiss looked at his dozing friend. "I suppose he *did* start young. But age is relative. Next to you, I believe he's the most recent addition to the clan."

Brinn brought a plate of meat and bread to the fire. She sat down on the rug.

Graldiss was amazed that the young girl would be so relaxed around him. She was either very brave or very stupid. He reached out a claw and speared a piece of meat from Brinn's plate. Her only reaction was to hold the plate out and offer him another slice. Of course she now had the memories of a wizard running around in her head, and dragons wouldn't be unknown to her, but he remembered how calm she seemed in the woods. She had guts, yes, and a cool head on her shoulders. He liked this human.

Brinn popped the last bit of bread into her mouth. She stretched her feet out and wiggled her toes in front of the flames. "How long has Talon been a wizard? I mean, he seems quite natural about it all."

Graldiss lay his chin on his forearms. "He inherited his power almost fifty years ago. But in reality," the dragon continued, "Talon was touched by magic much earlier. He's the only human ever to be born with magic. Unlike dragons, humans are only able to tap into magic through apprenticeship and inheritance, as you did."

Brinn was stunned, but it answered a question that had been in the back of her mind: "So that's why his hair is so white."

The dragon chuckled. "Actually, when a wizard receives his power the outward sign of his new status is the whitening of their hair."

"But Keldric's hair is dark," Brinn said, bewildered.

Graldiss grinned hugely. "That was my doing. He was being a nuisance so I arranged a permanent reminder that he wasn't invulnerable."

Brinn laughed, she really liked this beast. "Fifty years is a long time. Why does he look so young?"

A slab of cheese and a loaf of bread appeared on the plate next to Brinn and a log was added to the fire. "It has to do with personal identity. As humans age they come to a point where they imprint their appearance on their mind. They will age, gain weight, stoop over, but in their mind they still think they look like they did when they were eighteen, or twenty-five, or forty. Unconsciously, a wizard uses magic to retain that imprinted appearance. There have even been a few wizards that purposely...unaged themselves."

A story popped into Brinn's mind. "Yes, like Wilfret Brumbek. He liked being a child so much that he reverted back to himself as a seven year-old. He had a great time, but the complications drove him mad." Brinn looked puzzled. "How did I know that? I've never heard that story before."

"That would be a bit of Fernley. Your predecessor made a hobby of collecting stories. You are remembering them because the spirit of Fernley is within your mind."

Brinn was horrified. "I have his thoughts in my head? He's going to be there the rest of my life? I don't think I can deal with that."

Of course you can. A voice said from within Brinn's mind. *I chose you because I knew you could handle this.*

"He won't be there for long." Graldiss reassured her. "I've never actually experienced the process before, but from what I understand they don't stay around for long, too confusing for the recipient." The dragon got up and cleared away the dishes. "Now might be a good time to meet your predecessor."

Brinn was uncertain how to go about doing that. "Do I just talk to him? Say hello, nice to see you again?" It sounded so silly.

Graldiss laughed. "Why don't you lie down and take a nap? That's how Talon did it. I understand it's easier to communicate with your predecessor if you're asleep."

Brinn saw the logic in this and went to the curtained nook. She lay down on the soft mattress.

Brinn closed her eyes and let herself relax. She felt an odd swirling sensation. A dim light became visible in the darkness, growing slowly brighter. She couldn't tell if she was moving toward the light, or the light was moving toward her. Either way, she soon recognized the light was coming from a fireplace. As the light grew, Brinn could pick out details of her surroundings: tables, chairs, plates, and mugs. Just as the room came into full focus Brinn realized she was in a tavern; and not any tavern, her *father's* tavern.

A movement at a corner table caught Brinn's attention. Brinn's stomach knotted for a moment when she thought it might be Nethra. But when the figure stood and came toward her, Brinn saw that it was a man and she relaxed. In the fire light Brinn recognized the man who had come to the inn a week before; the man who had changed her life, only he looked younger.

"Interesting place you've chosen," Fernley said, taking a seat next to Brinn.

Brinn looked around. She knew every detail of this room from years of cleaning and scrubbing; she hated every inch. "Why are we here?"

Fernley looked around casually. "*You* chose the setting. If you'd rather, I'll find someplace more friendly."

"Yes, please."

After a dizzying blur Brinn found herself sitting in one of two overstuffed chairs next to a cozy fireplace. Fernley was seated next to her. She looked around, admiring the brightly colored rugs, ornate candle sconces, and shelves of musical instruments. Intricately woven tapestries hung on the walls along with carved and elaborately painted masks.

"Welcome to my home," Fernley said with pride. "Well, it's really *your* home now."

"It's beautiful."

The wizard leaned over and poked a stick into the fire. "This is just the conservatory; where I come, or I guess I should say 'came', to relax. I'll give you a full tour later."

Brinn was excited to find that she had a real home someplace. She held back the multitude of questions that flooded into her mind. "Is this a dream?"

"No. We are in that place between dream and awake. You are asleep, but in control of your thoughts just as if you were awake. Your mind perceives what you do here as real. This gives us a place to talk and study. I'm a jumble of memories waiting to take up residence in your mind. I don't have much time before my memories become yours. We'd better get on with your training." He leaned forward and took Brinn's hands. He looked into her eyes, but she felt him searching her mind. "Yes, just as I first suspected. You have a strong, quick mind. That will make this much easier." Fernley sat back; a pipe appeared in his hand. "Magic!" he said dramatically. "The stuff of fairytales and myths. You now know that it's all too real."

Brinn interrupted Fernley's oration. "I've been wondering. Talon seemed surprised at my inheriting your power. Do you know why?"

Fernley puffed on his pipe. "Well, you're a girl, and there's never been a female wizard. We always assumed that women and magic were incompatible. Of course there were stories of witches, but they were just village midwives who knew which herbs healed and which ones poisoned. Curses and love potions need no magic to make them real if your customers have enough faith. But there was something about you. I couldn't put my finger on it. You made me doubt the old belief. And of course here you are, proving us all wrong."

Brinn felt uncomfortable under Fernley's proud gaze. "I haven't done much."

Fernley's bushy eyebrows rose. "Really? Without any training you've speeded up any number of tasks around that inn, created flame, translocated a young fisherman, used telepathy to speak to a dragon, broke Keldric's spell, and now you're sitting here having a conversation with a dead man. These are more than simple parlor tricks." He stood and moved around the room. "What you've accomplished so far is nothing compared with what you will be able to do once you've reached your full potential. Now if you'll come over here I will show you where we'll begin." Fernley led Brinn to a paneled wall. "Touch the scuff marks on the lower right panel."

Brinn bent down and looked at the chair rail and put her hand on the scratched paint. A gentle movement of air was the only indication a secret door was opening. Brinn looked at the paneling, expecting to see a torch-lit tunnel, but there was none. She turned and looked questioningly at Fernley.

He smiled and disappeared through an oak wall-panel. Brinn touched the panel and was startled when her hand went through it. When her hand reappeared with no damage, Brinn shrugged, closed her eyes and walked through the wall. She felt a slight tingling sensation, like walking through a light rain. When she opened her eyes, Brinn found herself in a library. Shelves of books and scrolls lined three walls and a large desk was placed in front of a fire.

"This is where I work...worked. Everything you need is here. You'll add your own scrolls as time goes by."

Brinn ran her fingers over the scrolls, taking one down and unrolling it. The writing was strange, perhaps in a different language. As she stared at the incomprehensible scribbles they began to make sense. Within a few minutes, Brinn found she could read and understand them.

"See how nice it is to have my memories? You will be able to read and speak many different languages."

Brinn read the scroll's title: "'Fireballs and Lightning Strikes'." She looked at Fernley. "These are all spells?" She indicated the stacks of tightly rolled parchment.

"Yes, each scroll holds an individual spell; all of my own creations. The books over there are spells I gathered from around the world." He pointed to a wall-length shelf on the far side of the room.

Brinn read through the spell. There were a series of neatly worded verses accompanied by details of hand movements. "I'm confused. The magic I've done during the past few weeks didn't include any spells."

Fernley nodded. "You used pure magic. Pure magic is the process of drawing energy from within yourself and your surroundings and redirecting it. Spells allow you to take that energy, shape it, and give it form and detail. Forming and casting spells is an art. Pure magic is crude and simple by comparison. It's nice for spur of the moment events, but there's no finesse."

Brinn read the scroll. "Caution: this spell must only be used in the presence of cloud formations." She looked questioningly at Fernley.

"It has to do with charges. Inside every cloud there are...well, good and bad charges; when they bump into each other they make a lot of noise and sparks. In the really dark clouds these charges gang up on each other and have a terrible fight. Lightning is when the charges fall from the sky." Fernley hoped the girl would comprehend something so complicated.

Brinn hid her smile. She knew the wizard was oversimplifying his explanation in the extreme. "Then there's not enough energy in one place to create lightning without a cloud?"

When Fernley realized Brinn didn't need a lesson in thunderstorms he felt just a little silly. "No, at least not of any amount. Easier to borrow what you need from the source." He pulled down a small scroll. "Since there aren't any clouds handy, why don't we start with something simpler: Levitation." Fernley unrolled a scroll and laid it out on the desk, placing four beautiful glass paperweights on the corners. He set a spoon next to the parchment.

"Encircle the object to be lifted," Brinn read after the mystic writing clarified itself. She put her hands around the spoon.

"No, no. Not physically. Magic is the redistribution of energies. You borrow energy from the world around you to make things happen." Brinn looked baffled. Fernley struggled for the words to explain something that had been second nature to him for centuries. "Look, a fire gives off energy that you feel as heat, right? Well, that same energy flows in and around *everything*. Collect the energy, draw it into yourself and redirect it. That's Magic. Spells focus thought and energy to be more efficient. Now, create a...bubble of energy around it. Not too tight. Now gently draw in energy from objects around you. This room is specially designed with an abundance of energy. Use the plants in the corner and on the shelves, the fire, the mouse under the woodpile, even the stones under your feet. No, not from me. You don't need much, the spoon isn't large. Now, repeat these words: *Tibbin Gougash* and push slowly on all sides; a little more on the bottom to lift it."

Brinn spoke the words and the spoon quivered for a moment then flew to the ceiling. Brinn gasped and the spoon dropped to the floor.

"Try again."

Brinn closed her eyes, picturing a blue glow around the spoon. She felt the fern and fire eagerly lend her their energy. "Tibbin Gougash." She held her hand out, and lifted it as if lifting the spoon herself, making sure to keep pressure above as well as below. She peeked between her closed lids to find the spoon hovering next to her hand. A wide grin spread across her face.

"Very good. This may not be as difficult for you as I thought, but you might want to keep your eyes open."

They worked together for hours. Brinn was thrilled to find she could read and understand many different languages. She enjoyed working with spells and incantations; they seemed more exact than the magic she had used before. She felt in control. When it became more and more difficult to draw energy from around the room Fernley decided the lesson was over.

"We don't want to exhaust you." Fernley saw the look of disappointment on Brinn's face. "Don't worry; you will have plenty of time for practice. A long lifetime to practice. Until Talon takes you to your new home, you may want to explore some spells the dragons use."

Fernley led Brinn back to the conservatory and sat before the fire. While nibbling on dream-created cookies and tea they spoke of many things. After many hours Fernley found himself fading slightly. "It's time for me to go."

"When will we meet again for more lessons?" Brinn asked.

"This is our only time together, in this form. I am only able to remain separate from your mind for a few hours. From now on I will only be part of your memories."

This was more than a little daunting. "Are you sure I'm ready?"

Fernley smiled. "You'll do fine; besides I'm not deserting you, just backing off and letting you do things your own way. You don't want me banging around in your mind, anyway. Talon will see to it you are well prepared for your new life." Fernley's image began to fade. "It's time for you to go back now. Close your eyes and breathe deeply."

Brinn did not want to leave, but could not fight the urge to close her eyes. She felt herself drift toward sleep.

An icy chill woke Brinn. She opened her eyes and found herself in total darkness. There was no sound from the sleeping dragon or wizard, and her own breathing seemed too loud. She slowly got out of bed. Her feet stung from the icy surface of the floor; it was hard and smooth, not dusty, as she had remembered it. She recalled the dream she had a few weeks before.

"I'm still sleeping," she reassured herself, "and this is just a dream." The air around her was dry and had a smell of rock. Talon's cave had a smoky, herbal smell about it. She reached down to touch the bed, but it was no longer there, neither were the curtains or the bedside table. "OK," she thought, "I'm not in the cave." Believing she was only dreaming, Brinn decided to explore.

She held her hands out in front of her and slowly walked forward. After a few steps, Brinn's hands made contact with an icy wall. She warmed them with her breath and touched the smooth surface again. It didn't feel natural. Brinn reached up but found no indication of a low ceiling. With the wall as a guide, Brinn walked on. The passageway did not curve at all, and after walking for a while, Brinn began to feel that she was going no where. She decided to sit down and wait for whatever was going to happen. It didn't take long.

The sound started as a low whistle, and then became melodious. The music moved through Brinn, taking up the beat of her heart and rhythm of her breathing. Brinn thought she could pick out words, or at least the impression of words.

"Hello? Is someone there?" Her words disappeared down the passageway. She stood up when the music stopped.

From faraway a voice called to Brinn. It was soft, a whisper carried on the cold air.

"Where are you?" Brinn called out. She held her breath and listened with all of her being.

Faintly, pleadingly, the answer came: "Help me..."

Brinn took a step down the passageway and found herself falling...falling.

Chapter 6

"How long has she been out?"

"Since last night. Almost as long as you were."

"I've never waded through anyone's mind; it's not easy. She'll be hungry."

"I've taken care of the food; Silgaa is bringing some fruit and bread."

Brinn knew the two voices belonged to Talon and Graldiss, but she couldn't tell which one was which, they both sounded alike. She listened to them for a while before she realized they were speaking some foreign language and she was able to *understand* them! Brinn silently thanked Fernley. She wondered what other surprises awaited her.

"She's awake."

Talon pulled back the curtain. "Welcome back. Drink this." Brinn looked suspiciously at the cup Talon held out to her. "It's just tea."

Brinn sat up slowly and took the cup. "Thank you." She sipped the warm liquid, feeling the weariness of her body drain away. "That was an interesting experience. I hope I never have to do it again."

"One spirit is all you get," Graldiss said stoking the fire, "unless you're the Krrig Daa."

Talon glared at his friend. "One is more than enough for anyone."

Further discussion on the topic was prevented by the arrival of a dragon carrying two baskets. Brinn could smell the fresh baked bread from across the cave, and her stomach began to rumble.

The dragon, Silgaa, put the baskets down on the table and stared for a long moment at Brinn. His eyes grew wide and he pulled Graldiss aside. "She's glowing," he whispered urgently.

Graldiss nodded. "I know."

"Wizards don't glow like this."

"I know." Graldiss tried not to stare.

"Doesn't *he* notice?" Silgaa glanced from Talon to Brinn.

Graldiss looked at Talon who pulled bread and cheese from the large basket. "I don't think so." He led the other dragon out of the cave.

Talon didn't seem to notice this odd discussion. "This should help you." He handed Brinn a full plate. "It's amazing how much energy it takes for a purely mental exercise."

Brinn was full of questions, but when she saw the food in front of her she decided they could wait. She stuffed the food into her mouth in a very unladylike fashion.

Graldiss returned to the fire and chuckled at the ravenous girl. "Maybe I should have had a whole cow brought in."

Brinn swallowed. "Maybe later," she said, ripping off another hunk of bread.

When the last grape was eaten and the crumbs brushed from her robe Brinn sighed with contentment. "Thank you."

"How do you feel?" Talon asked.

Brinn thought for a moment. So much had happened since she had arrived. She didn't even know what day it was. How long had she been unconscious, talking to Fernley? Her dream of the dark tunnel had shaken her a bit more than she would have liked to admit. She found she could not just dismiss it as a simple nightmare; there was something...*real* about it. And what had that dragon meant...'she's glowing'?

Talon cleared his throat. "I just wondered if you had recovered your strength."

Brinn laughed. "I'm fine, thank you."

"Good. And how was your experience with Fernley?" Talon looked more closely at the young girl.

This time Brinn put little thought into her answer. "It was like having a light turned on."

Talon nodded, he knew just how she felt. "Do you feel up to testing your new knowledge?"

Brinn's eyes lit up. "Yes!"

Talon stood and held out his hand. Brinn took it without hesitation. In an instant the two were transported to the valley floor. Brinn squinted against the brightness of the morning light.

"Magic can be as instantaneous as that. Little thought, no preparation." Talon sat casually under a tree. "But such use of magic has its hazards. If a goat had been nibbling here it would have been squished. The first lesson you must learn is there are consequences to every act of magic. While some are small, most are not. Never use magic haphazardly. Moving one rock, picking one flower, shifting one cloud, can change the world."

"Oh brother! You sound like old Viggot." Graldiss landed a few feet away from Brinn and Talon. "What a stodgy old coot. He never let us have any fun."

Talon scowled at his friend. "Better to be informed of the risks from the beginning rather than regret your mistakes later."

"That's not the Talon I know." Graldiss turned to Brinn. "This sage advice comes from the boy who shrank me down to the size of a cat! Without concern for the consequences, he chatted with ducks to find a lost cloud, talked mice into starting a riot, removed Keldric's powers, diverted a landslide, and convinced King Simiat's crops to grow despite a three year drought."

Talon was not put off. "Those were all well thought out...well at least some of them."

Brinn couldn't imagine Graldiss the size of a cat. "You don't have to worry about my understanding the risks of magic," she reassured Talon. "Fernley covered that last night. I think I can safely say that I won't be moving mountains any time soon."

Talon was satisfied. "Then let's begin.

Brinn watched as Talon closed his eyes and took a deep breath. She felt an odd pulling sensation and tentatively pushed. Talon was taken by surprise and fell over. Graldiss rolled on the grass, laughing. Brinn apologized.

"Serves you right," Graldiss said, wiping tears from his face, "taking energy from someone without asking."

Talon sat up, smiling. "I guess we can consider that a lesson. Always know where your energy comes from. Don't just take it randomly from around you. It is impolite to take energy from others without permission. And keep your eyes open." His face took on a look of concentration. Talon spread his arms wide. A moment later his arms dropped to his side and he let out a heavy sigh.

Brinn felt a wave of energy spread around her and out onto the grassy knoll. She held her breath, waiting for some magnificent magical event to occur. Nothing happened.

Talon stood abruptly and looked toward the mountain.

"Well, that was a bit anticlimactic," Graldiss said, watching Talon.

"What happened?" Brinn asked.

The dragon shrugged his massive shoulders.

"*That* happened." Talon pointed to the growing spot on the horizon. As they watched, a large orange dragon joined them on under the trees.

"Forgive me, Krrig Daa, but I have an urgent message from Prince Selane." The newcomer handed Talon a rolled parchment. "He asked me to convey you with all possible speed to the castle."

Talon read the parchment, muttering to himself. With a wave of his hand his clothes changed from a loose robe to heavy leather riding gear. "I'm sorry," he said to Brinn. "It seems the prince is having a bit of trouble handling the dragons sent to help him. He wants to replace his palace guards with them." He rolled his eyes. "Graldiss, would you mind taking care of Brinn? I'll be back as soon as I can knock some sense into Selane." Talon grumbled as he vaulted onto the orange dragon's back and was soon disappearing over the treetops.

Brinn stood staring after the wizard. She had hoped for an informative afternoon and she felt let down. She looked to Graldiss.

The dragon was nibbling on a toe. When he saw the young girl looking at him Graldiss gave his foot a last lick and nervously looked around. "What?"

"What happens now? Do we just wait here?"

The dragon shrugged and rolled onto his back. "I don't expect Talon will be back anytime soon. Selane isn't bright, but he's obstinate. I'm sure some advisor, looking to move up the ranks, suggested that having dragons as palace guards would be impressive for visiting barons."

Brinn put her hands on her hips. "So what do I do?"

Graldiss looked at the irritated girl. "Why can't you just enjoy the day? The sun is warm and the grass is green. A good roll never hurts." He rolled once to demonstrate.

Brinn sat on the grass and watched the comical view of a huge dragon wiggling on his back. The grass *did* feel soft and the sun *was* warm compared to the coolness of the caves. She lay down and stretched out. In the quiet of the morning, Brinn thought about everything that had happened to her in the past few days. She was thrilled at her new life. She was living with dragons, she was a wizard, and Nethra was no where in sight. She didn't know what lay ahead for her, but it couldn't be worse than life at the inn, could it? A loud, beastly growl roused Brinn from her thoughts. She looked over at Graldiss as either the source of the growl or her rescuer from another beast.

The dragon looked a little embarrassed and rubbed his stomach. "Must be getting close to lunch time." Graldiss rolled to his feet and shook out his spines. "Are you hungry?" he asked.

Brinn smiled at Graldiss and nodded. She got to her feet and brushed the grass from her hair and robe. She half expected to have a meal magically appear before her, but instead Graldiss shook out his wings and knelt down on his front legs. Brinn stared at him.

"Climb on."

Brinn hiked up her robe and climbed up the muscular leg. When she had settled, Graldiss spread his wings and with two mighty beats, they rose into the air. Brinn's expectations of the great dragon hunting for his food were again wrong, and rather than flying to some unsuspecting herd of deer, they returned to the mountain.

Graldiss flew high over the peaks rather than toward the cave entrances lower down the mountainside. Brinn noticed the mountain peaks did not culminate in one ultimate pinnacle, but rather, formed a circle around an open pit. As they drew closer, Brinn realized the pit was actually a tremendous cavern exposed when its domed ceiling caved in. As they neared the edge of the peaks Brinn could see down into the heart of the mountain. Ten to twenty dragons were delivering their catch of the day while others were arranging piles of fruit that magically appeared. Huge loaves of bread were being brought in on trays and gigantic barrels of drink were stacked into piles. Three dragons were tending a massive fire, roasting meat and warming cider. A few humans moving about in various tasks looked tiny in comparison to the dragons.

Graldiss landed off to the side. Brinn carefully climbed down, but stayed close to the dragon. Graldiss smiled playfully. "Don't worry, you aren't on the menu."

A large yellow dragon drifted gently to the ground next to them. "Graldiss, you know humans are served only on the night of the second full moon after the first day of winter."

Graldiss glared, but Brinn had seen the yellow dragon's grin and pretended to be horrified. "Please spare me, I'm much too bony."

"Best use you for broth then." Some near-by dragons chuckled. "I am Riffa," the yellow dragon bowed slightly. "Haven't seen one of your kind before, most unique."

Brinn looked puzzled.

"A female of your species...wizard. They usually limit themselves to males...a pity. If you ask me they could use a woman's viewpoint." Riffa bowed again. She looked curiously at Brinn then gave Graldiss a sidelong glance and turned to join the meal.

"You'll have to forgive Riffa; she has very strong opinions about the way humans treat their females." Graldiss led Brinn toward a great table. "But on the other hand, she has some pretty strong reservations about too many male dragons sitting on the High Council."

As they joined the other dragons, Brinn had the oddest feeling that she was being looked at with more than idle curiosity. They found an empty spot at the table. A boulder-seat appeared next to Brinn so that she could reach the food. A large platter of roasted meat was placed in front of them as well as two of the large bread loaves and a bowl of fruit. Human-sized eating utensils and mug found their way to Brinn. It was evident the dragons were used to humans joining the feast. She was glad not to be the only human at the table; a few men were seated further down the table.

"You seem distracted," Graldiss said, tossing six apples into his mouth.

"It's just being around all these dragons." A few nearby dragons turned at the comment. "Well," Brinn shrugged, "you aren't at all as I expected." She felt nervous with all the large eyes looking at her. "Our children's tales always depicted dragons as ferocious man-eaters. You aren't like that at all."

A smallish green dragon sitting opposite Brinn joined their conversation. "And as hatchlings we were told of cold-blooded knights killing defenseless dragons, thieves stealing hard earned treasure, and using our body parts in potions and ornaments."

Brinn had to admit she had heard those stories as well, but had never thought about how the dragons felt.

"There was some truth to both sides of the story," Graldiss said. "But that's over now, thanks to Talon." Dragons within earshot banged their cups at the mention of Talon's name.

Now there was something Brinn did not understand. "What makes Talon so special? How did a wizard come to live with dragons and take such an active role in your lives?"

Graldiss swallowed a mouthful and started to speak, but a larger dragon a short way down the table answered: "A prophecy was handed down through the ages that spoke of a savior who would mend the rift between dragon and man; to end the wars and return us to our true place in the world. Our greatest queen gave her spirit to the one sent to save us."

The dragon's words sounded familiar and Brinn checked Fernley's memories. She saw the Rite of Transference Talon had gone through almost fifty years ago. After the wizard Olwin had transferred his spirit and power to Talon the meadow around the ceremonial stone slab had filled with dragons. To the shock and amazement of the wizards gathered to witness the rite, a dragon's corpse had appeared on the slab and a second transference took place. Magrid, the late queen of the dragons Brinn now shared a meal with, also gave her power and spirit to Talon. No wonder these dragons thought of him as something special.

"Since then, Talon has been an ambassador for our race," Graldiss added. "He has stopped the killings on both sides and is bringing our races together."

Not all the dragons at the table were in awe of Talon. "We are no closer to returning to our rightful place. Humans use us as slaves and lackeys." There were grunts of agreement from a few dragons, and cautious silence from the humans.

The large dragon who had spoken before threw a chunk of bread at the grumbler. "Not a single dragon has been hunted down in forty years, Manett. And it took centuries for humans to turn against us, I think we owe the Krrig Daa a few more years to put things back to the way they were."

73

Manett got to her feet and turned so quickly that her tail knocked off a side of venison and two bowls of fruit. A few other dragons left the table and followed her out of the cave.

"Don't pay too much attention to Manett. Before Talon arrived, she was set to become Queen Ittra's head councilor."

A young dragon joined the table. He was content with devouring his food until he looked up and saw Brinn. His moose haunch dropped onto the floor and his elbow knocked over his neighbor's cup of cider. Everyone at the table looked at the young dragon, and then looked at what he was staring at. It seemed that for the first time the dragons noticed Brinn was shining a bit more than the average wizard. Their gaze turned to Graldiss, who shrugged and went back to eating as if it were nothing special.

Brinn tried not to feel self-conscious and quietly finished her pear. The remainder of the meal was eaten in silence. Though Brinn had at first enjoyed eating with the dragons, she decided it was really no place for a human. She was relieved when Graldiss led her back to Talon's cave.

Brinn tried to keep track of the turns and landmarks, but was soon lost. She stopped keeping track of how many lefts followed the next right and enjoyed peeking into the side caves. Some were very spartan with only a firepit and a pile of bedding; others were clearly utilitarian with huge wash basins and cooking fires like none Brinn had ever seen before;

many of the side caves were cozily decorated with tapestries and rugs. One particular cave made Brinn stop in amazement. Through the lacey curtains she could see piles of pink cushions, embroidered tablecloths, multiple glowing balls of light, and two ornately canopied beds (one dragon-size, one human-size). The scent of roses wafted through the slightly parted curtains. Brinn took a step toward the inviting cave.

"They aren't home," Graldiss said, waiting for Brinn a few yards up the tunnel. "They always go flying this time of the day."

"They?" Brinn asked. She rejoined Graldiss and they continued walking.

"Enikka and Oriana. They are one of Talon's...experiments. He arranged a treaty between Ittra and a neighboring kingdom. The king's first-born spends a year living up here with one of us. The next year the dragon lives at the castle. They are quite a pair. They have tea parties and slumber parties, picnics and dances. Quite a few young female dragons have started wearing color on their claws and dangly ornaments on their ears. Silly if you ask me. If you are here for a while I'm sure the Princess will invite you to one of their parties."

Brinn could not picture a dragon with earrings and nail polish. She didn't think she would fit in with a group like that, but her life had taken quite a turn already, so maybe a tea party with a princess living with a dragon would not be so remarkable.

Talon returned early in the evening. He was tired and glad of the warm fire. "He's a fool," he grunted when Brinn asked how the meeting had gone. "Some day I would like to see intelligence be a requirement to rule a country. Selane wanted those poor dragons to dress in pointed caps and leather collars!" Talon threw a fireball into the flames. "Spiked bands around their ankles!" Another fiery ball sprayed embers on the hearth rug. "Selane claims to have thought it up himself, but he lacks the—"

"I know what you need," Graldiss interrupted before more sparks destroyed the rug. A flute appeared in the air near Talon's head. "What do you say we have a little music?"

Talon grinned and took the flute. "Tired of my ranting so soon?" He played random notes. "Well what did the two of you do this afternoon while I saved the dignity of Dragonkind?"

Brinn brought a pillow to the fire and leaned against Graldiss. "Oh, we talked about you, of course."

"I took her to lunch," Graldiss added.

Talon moaned. "You didn't take her to the *pit* did you?" He leaned down and spoke softly to Brinn. "Dragons are horrible slobs."

Brinn patted the dragon's foot. "I don't know, they can be dainty eaters when they want to impress a lady."

Talon choked and almost fell out of his chair. Graldiss gave Brinn a shove. "You should be more respectful of your superiors." He grinned hugely.

"It sounds like you had more fun than I did." Talon played a few quick notes.

"Maybe tomorrow will be better," Brinn said hopefully.

Talon lowered his hands and let the flute drop to his lap. "Tomorrow will definitely be interesting. I'll be taking you to see Queen Ittra."

This news came as a shock. "The Queen?" She looked nervously at Graldiss. He nodded reassuringly.

"When I came in," Talon explained, "she cornered me and asked why I hadn't brought you to see her yet."

"I've no idea how to act around the Queen of the Dragons."

Graldiss chuckled. "Not *all* dragons."

"Ittra's only the queen of this colony," Talon explained.

"You mean there are *more* of you?" Brinn stared, trying to picture a world filled with dragons. "How did you keep hidden?" She laughed at the mental picture of dragons hiding under bushes and behind trees. Talon and Graldiss laughed along.

Talon began playing a tune; he was joined by the low humming of Graldiss. The glow of the fire was comforting and Brinn began to doze. Talon suggested that she call it a night. "You'll want to be rested for your visit tomorrow."

Brinn said good night and crawled into bed. Soft flute music drifted across the cave. Brinn's eyes grew heavy.

A fragrant wind bringing the scent of wildflowers roused Brinn. The glow of the fire was gone as was Talon's flute music. Brinn suspected she was dreaming again. She sat up and hesitantly pulled back the bed curtain. Instead of the pitch-black cave, she was out in the open. The meadow before her was still and pristine, very story-like. There were no indications anything had been there for quite some time. Brinn stepped into the scene. She felt a strong urge to find something in this beautiful meadow, something important. The urgency was so strong that it took Brinn's breath away, but she didn't rush out into the grass. Something didn't feel right; there was something wrong with the perfection before her. Brinn was used to these dreams feeling too real, but there was an oppressive weight of magic this time. The urgency became panic. She had to find what she was sent for before...before it was too late. Too late for what? Her thoughts were muddled. Someone didn't want her to find...what?

Brinn stepped into the meadow, gasping at the weight suddenly thrust upon her. She took a deep breath and calmed herself. The fear weighing down on her lifted and Brinn walked out onto the meadow. Something was familiar about this place, the color of the flowers, the movement of the waist-high grass. As Brinn walked she felt that she was being...led in the right direction. Her foot stubbed into something hard, bringing Brinn down to her knees on a flat stone slab. Brinn moved her hands across the somehow familiar smooth surface; even in the sunlight the stone was icy cold. A shiver ran through her body.

Brinn pulled back the tall grass and took a look at the stone. It was translucent black, cracks could be seen throughout its depth, but the surface was so smooth and glossy that it looked wet. The stone seemed to be a perfect circle, almost four feet across. Its edges were unnaturally rounded and at least two inches thick. The grass touching the slab was brown and dry. Had touching the stone killed it? She shivered and backed away.

Heavy oppressive panic filled Brinn. She wanted out, out of the meadow and out of this dream. She turned and began to run. Would the dream let her leave the meadow? A dizzying wave hit Brinn and she found that she was again standing in front of the stone. She heard a faint voice calling her name and her eyes fell to the glassy surface. In a daze, Brinn knelt down and grasped the rounded edge, this time the stone was warm. She made a tentative attempt to push the slab, then put her whole weight into it. The stone did not move. Brinn carefully pulled in energy from the grass and flowers around her. She rubbed her hands together and laid them on the stone. When her palms touched the black rock, Brinn was violently thrown back. After a moment her head cleared and she rubbed her sore hands on her nightgown.

When Brinn's knees stopped shaking she stood and approached the stone again. She reconsidered using magic. Tentatively touching the smooth surface, Brinn searched the edge for someplace to hold on to. She found two slight grooves on one side and wiggled her fingers to get a better grip. She tensed her arms to lift. The rock moved easily. Caught unprepared, Brinn fell across the opening, catching herself on the rim. A burst of air blew against Brinn, she heard a triumphant laugh and felt herself fall into the dark, icy pit.

Chapter 7

The shockwaves of Brinn's dream echoed throughout the mountain. Dragons in the far caverns thought it was a mild earthquake. Closer in there was no doubt something highly magical had happened. In Talon's cave it looked as if a disaster had struck: not a single item was upright. Talon had been thrown out of bed and Graldiss was covered with debris that had fallen from the ceiling. Talon immediately got to his feet and looked around, stunned. He looked to Graldiss for some kind of explanation, and saw his friend staring at the sleeping nook where Brinn should have been asleep. Talon followed the dragon's gaze. Brinn was standing, her eyes stared blankly into the room she lit with her glow. The vacant look scared Talon. "What's wrong with her?" he asked Graldiss, but something was terrifying his friend. He went over and slapped the dragon's nose. "Snap out of, Gral. I need your help."

The dragon's mouth slowly closed, and he turned his vision away from the still body of the girl. "There's nothing I can do."

"Why are you so frightened?" Talon was baffled by his friend's behavior.

"Can't you *see* it?"

"The light? Of course. Rather extraordinary." Talon took a few steps toward Brinn.

"She's been glowing for the past three days."

Talon turned to look at Graldiss. "What do you mean? Like *I* glow?" Talon had always been suspicious about the dragons' assertion that he emanated an aura. "But this is the first time I've see this sort of thing. This can't be the same thing, surely."

"Of course not," Graldiss said, irritated.

"Well then, what is it?"

"It's a dragon," Graldiss whispered, glancing for only a second at Brinn.

"A dragon?" Talon couldn't understand what his friend was telling him. "Do you mean to say a dragon's spirit transferred into her?" That would account for the disturbance in the mountain.

"No...not like that. It's taken possession of her mind."

Now Talon was really lost. He took a moment to search Queen Magrid's memories for some reference to dragon possession. There was only a vague reference to a Rite of Transference gone wrong where the recipient dragon was overpowered by the spirit of the dying dragon. Talon had heard of this type of thing happening with aggressive wizards as well. "Well, one of us has to do something about it." Talon paid no attention to the dragon's mumbled words of warning.

Talon pulled in energy from everything he could, even from Graldiss. With an urgency that was dangerous for himself and Brinn, Talon pushed his conscious mind into an energy stream and flew across the cave to the still body. In Talon's amorphous state the light emanating from Brinn took on a physical form and it wasn't friendly. It battered at him and pulled at his energy. The only thing that kept Talon in one piece was that the dragon responsible for the vicious light was still adapting to the human source of energy. A few quick flashes later Talon was inside Brinn's mind.

While Talon collected himself into a safe mental image he felt he was being watched. Talon was shocked at the change in Brinn's mind. The natural landscape of her memories was now shrouded in a heavy white mist. The sky that had been clear was now dark with thunderclouds. Talon felt chilled. An icy wind blew at him but he stood his ground. Something large flew out of the darkness at him; Talon knew it could not harm him here.

"Get out! This is *my* world!"

Talon stood tall, straining against the darkness to see the dragon. "This is not your world; this mind belongs to the girl."

A harsh wind blew past the wizard. "She locked me away, but now I am free. This time I will lock *her* away. It is my right!"

"No, it is not. I won't let you."

A vaporous form took shape in front of Talon. Misty wings spread wide, glassy claws dug deep, black scales glistened. "Who are you to stop me?"

The glowing eyes looked into Talon's, not through him. It was blind. "I am the Krrig Daa! You will obey me!" Talon made his voice larger and deeper.

"There is no Krrig Daa. He would have come to rescue me. I do not believe you." A ghostly claw swiped in Talon's direction.

Talon closed his eyes at the sight of the dragon's arm passing through him. Waves of emotion from the beast tore at his soul. He had to grit his teeth to keep from crying out with pain and fear, loathing and...shock.

"You are human!" A tremendous sheet of flame shot toward Talon.

Icy flames engulfed the wizard. He calmly stepped from the inferno. With a simple wave of his hand the fire died. "I *am* the Krrig Daa." Talon said firmly. "You will leave this child and return from where you came."

"NOOOO!" the dragon began to wail.

The unrelenting screams shook Talon to the core; it was too much for him and he fled Brinn's mind. Once returned to his own body, Talon collapsed. Ittra caught him.

It hadn't taken long for the source of the magical disturbance to be pinpointed. When the dragons started filtering into Talon's cave they were confused to find their Chosen One being carried to a chair by their queen. They stared at the female wizard who was glowing intensely. Graldiss was hiding behind his bed.

Talon opened his eyes when his head stopped spinning and was relieved to find Ittra standing over him.

"You silly man," Ittra said, carefully giving Talon some of her own energy. "Subtlety was never your strong suit. Did you think to find out *why* the dragon was there?"

Talon smiled weakly and shrugged.

The imposing queen went to Brinn's side. The barrier of light did not pose an obstacle for the dragon, who easily entered the young mind.

Ittra did not like what she saw. Never had she seen a mind so filled with hatred. She saw the dark dragon drifting amongst the clouds, singing a sorrowful melody. With gentle sweeping movements, Ittra's wings swept away the heavy mist. With a blow of sweet breath, the dark thunderclouds dispersed. A paw delicately brushed the wildflowers at her feet, bringing forth a fragrance of Brinn's childhood memories.

The dark dragon landed angrily, crushing the flowers beneath large claws. "Go away!" It charged straight at the Queen. But instead of passing through Ittra as it had Talon, the ghostly beast slammed into the Queen as if both were solid beings. The dark dragon sat, dazed, in the flowers. "You are not the human." It looked up blankly. "Who are you?"

Ittra passed her paw in front of the unseeing eyes; they blinked rapidly then widened as they focused on the magnificent creature before them. "I am Ittra," the Queen said quietly.

Through sobs and sniffs, Ittra heard the broken story of how Neesha had been captured by an evil wizard and held prisoner in a pit of glass. After what seemed centuries, someone had lifted the spell that held her, but before she could savor the taste of freedom, she was again plunged into darkness. "Please don't send me back," Neesha pleaded, and then growled: "I *won't* go back!" She tore herself from Ittra's comforting hold and flew into the last remaining cloud.

"You can not stay here," Ittra said firmly.

Neesha slowly returned. "You wouldn't put me back there, would you?"

Ittra put a calming paw on Neesha's shoulder. "Never. I will show you the way out." The queen led Neesha to a crystal waterfall. She raised her arms and the water parted, revealing a dark cavern. A single beam of light pierced the darkness. "Fly free."

Neesha gratefully touched her head to Ittra's. She flew toward the cave. Ittra heard a faint shout of laughter.

Talon had recovered enough to stand and was leaning on Graldiss' shoulder. Before their eyes the glowing light around Brinn coalesced into a sphere above her head. It rose slowly toward the ceiling then disappeared through it. Talon was surprised when Ittra's voice spoke to him. "Tell the others to return to their caves. I'm taking the girl with me. Try to get some sleep and come see us in the morning."

Talon told the gathered dragons that nothing more was going to happen and sent them away. Moments after the last dragon left with a disappointed last look, Ittra and Brinn disappeared. "Do you think you can get back to sleep?" Talon asked Graldiss.

Graldiss turned to Talon with a look of disbelief. "You can't be serious. After that?"

"Yeah, I know. What do you say we get something to eat?" The fire was lit and a plate of fruit appeared on the table. "We should clean up this mess anyway."

Chapter 8

Brinn thought she must be dying. Her body was numb. She couldn't move, not even to wiggle her fingers. Her eyelids refused the command to open. No sound was heard. She had no memory of what happened after...the dream, the awful dream. It seemed so real now. Was it possible that it really happened? From somewhere distant came the wonderful smell of baking bread...and humming. A heavy sigh escaped her, at least two of her senses were working.

"Careful, little one, you had quite a rough experience."

Brinn felt a warm glow at the sound of the gentle voice from across the room. She found that she could slowly open her eyes. The light of the fire was too bright and she closed them again. The humming continued and Brinn felt warmer with each note. Soon she was able to turn her head and shift her feet. A piece of warm bread was slipped between Brinn's teeth and she slowly chewed it. Her stomach growled noisily and a soft chuckle was followed by more pieces of bread entering her mouth. It wasn't long before Brinn started feeling alive again.

"I've brewed some mint tea, if you can sit up to drink."

Brinn opened her eyes, hoping to catch a glimpse of her guardian angel, but saw only the glow of the fire. With slow, determined movements, Brinn sat up and pushed away the furs. A cup of fragrant, steaming tea had been placed on the floor next to the low bed along with another slice of buttered bread. She gratefully consumed them. She concentrated on each bite, focused on the intricate glazing of the cup, and the jewel-like quality of the sandy floor, anything to keep her mind from the memory of the dream.

"You will have to come to grips with those memories sometime."

Brinn was not too surprised that her thoughts were clearly read; little would surprise her anymore.

"And I think there are other memories we need to address." The speaker stepped into the light.

Brinn stared in awe at the small dragon. Its scales had the appearance of highly polished silver and reflected the firelight like sunshine on a lake. The spines were small and rounded, almost ornamental; the tail was long and delicate. The claws were definitely *not* ornamental; they looked sharp enough to slice through the toughest hide. Unlike the longish muzzle of Graldiss and the other dragons Brinn had seen, this dragon had a short, roundish nose. Brinn was most amazed by the dragon's face; it did not have the hard, beastish appearance she had grown used to seeing. The eyes, Brinn couldn't name the color they were, looked at her with tenderness.

Brinn drank the last of the tea and placed the cup on the ground. "Thank you. I'm feeling much better." There was no answer from the dragon who seemed preoccupied by the fire. Brinn pulled a light fur around her shoulders and looked around. The cave was decorated with hanging tapestries, but other than a low table and a single, human-sized chair, there were no furnishings. Brinn thought the furs she sat on must be the dragon's bed. She breathed in slightly and noticed a scent of rose petals. Brinn realized for the first time that she assumed dragons smelled like other reptiles, she hadn't thought to sniff Graldiss to disprove that notion.

The dragon laughed at Brinn's thought. "Technically we're not reptiles. We may have scales, but we have never been dirt grovellers. If you are smart you'll never use the "L" word around a dragon." Two gigantic loaves were removed from the fireplace. "Would you like another slice?" Brinn shook her head. The dragon cut off a steaming chunk and sat down next to the bed.

Brinn looked up into the dragon's face. She was startled by the gentleness there. But there was a strength about this dragon that set it apart from the others. "You're different," she said trying to put her finger on what was different.

The dragon smiled. "I come from separate bloodline than the other dragons, a very old bloodline."

Brinn thought for a moment. "You're the Queen, aren't you?"

"Yes, my name is Ittra."

Brinn looked away from the queen's face. Her mind raced to remember if she had done anything that might have been offensive. "I beg your pardon; I hope I have not behaved badly."

The Queen laughed. "Don't be silly. I'm not the tyrannical type." Ittra took a bite of bread, butter dripped down her chin. "You gave us quite a scare last night." Brinn looked baffled. "You released enough magic with that dream of yours to shake the very core of this mountain."

Brinn pulled the fur blanket closer at the mention of her dream. "It was different from the other nights." Brinn saw the Queen's inquisitive look. "The night before I met Talon, I dreamt of someplace dark and icy cold." She shivered at the memory. "The second dream I was in a pitch black cave...the floor and walls were smooth, like glass or smooth stone."

"And last night's dream?"

Brinn shut her eyes and shook her head. She didn't want to remember.

"You used magic to do something," Ittra prompted.

Brinn thought for a moment. "No...I tried, but it didn't work. I just picked it up...the stone slab." Brinn shuttered and put her hands over her face, she couldn't go on.

Ittra changed the subject. "Can you tell me the first time you saw a dragon?"

Brinn thought for a minute. "I bumped into Graldiss in the woods, and I'm pretty sure I dreamt about him the night before that." She remembered something she saw the morning she first met Talon. "The bird...I thought it was just a big bird, but it must have been a dragon that brought Talon to the inn that morning." Brinn also remembered the daydream she had had that same morning, but decided not to tell Ittra about that.

"Any other time? Maybe when you were younger?" The piercing blue eyes looked into Brinn's.

Brinn shook her head, but searched her memories. "I remember an orange dragon, on a large stone table, and a field filled with—"

"No, that's your wizard's memory of Magrid, my mother. What about when you were a child? What memories do you have of dragons from that time?"

Brinn shrugged her shoulders. "I don't know. I read fairytales of princesses and knights fighting vicious...sorry."

"You might have been five or four?"

Brinn shook her head, she remembered little about when she was a young girl.

"Maybe three?" Ittra reached out a paw and a claw lightly touched Brinn's head.

Though the dragon's claw barely touched Brinn, she screamed out in terror. "No! No! No!"

The Queen put her arm around the sobbing girl. "It's only a memory, it can't hurt you. There was a dragon, wasn't there?"

Brinn nodded, sniffing. She huddled against Ittra's chest.

Ittra stroked the long black hair. "You know, it's strange," she said casually, "your hair didn't turn white like the male wizards. I wonder why?"

Brinn pulled back and looked up at Ittra. "White?" She unconsciously touched her hair.

"Yes, hadn't you noticed? It comes with the power that's given them by their predecessor. But yours is still black."

Brinn pulled her hair around and looked at it. "It used to be brown," she said absently.

"Do you want to tell me about your dream?" Ittra asked casually

Brinn shook her head wildly. "I don't want to think about it. It was a dream. It didn't really happen. Mother didn't change, she was killed by wolves." She stopped. What did her mother have to do with her dream?

"Wolves?" Ittra asked, probing.

"Yes. Father said they found her clothes torn to shreds."

"But the wolves didn't eat *you*, obviously." Ittra said.

Brinn said nothing.

Ittra waited for the girl to continue.

Brinn was confused. What was real and what was a dream? She looked to Ittra. "Can you help me?"

"What do you want me to do?" Ittra wanted Brinn to say the words.

"Help me to remember," Brinn sounded like a small child.

Ittra nodded, slipped into Brinn's mind and found the field of wheat. She created a breeze with her wings. When she felt the memories stirring, Ittra pulled out.

Brinn began to remember. "I was three, almost four," she told Ittra quietly. "Mother had taken me into town. We stopped for lunch by a field of grain. The wind was blowing and the grass looked alive. We ran through the long stalks, hiding from each other. I tripped on a rock. It wasn't very big...black...shiny. I turned away, but it called my name. The stone was cold. I covered my hands with my apron and picked it up. A strong breeze blew...blew through me. I fell. When I got up I saw Mother. The wind was whipping around her, howling. Her beautiful yellow hair was wild. Her arms were twisting. Her head whipped back and forth. Her mouth was open, but she didn't scream." Brinn squeezed her eyes shut. "I didn't want to see. I put my hands over my face. The wind went quiet. I put my hands down. Mother wasn't there anymore. *It* was there."

"A dragon." Ittra added.

"Yes. A large black dragon. I looked into its face. For a moment its eyes looked into mine, pleading. Then they went cold...cruel. It leapt into the air. Horrible laughter trailed behind it." Tears flowed down Brinn's cheeks.

"They said she was killed by wolves," Ittra said with finality.

"Father came looking for us. I was asleep in the wagon. I think I was still hoping she would come back. He went wild when he found the clothes. There was no blood of course, but what else was he to think? I always felt he wished it had been me the wolves ate."

"Did you ever see her again?"

"The dragon? Yes, once. I was...five. It was at night. The moon was full, shining into my window. I heard a voice, Mother's voice, calling me. I looked out my window. Across the road, just outside the woods, I saw her, it, in the moonlight. Our eyes met. I felt some strange pull. She turned and flew away." Brinn looked down. "She never said good bye."

Ittra stroked Brinn's hair. "It wasn't her fault. She didn't want to leave you. Neesha didn't give her the chance. She must have loved you very much to be able to make the dragon return that night."

"Neesha? Was that its name?" Brinn felt anger toward the beast that had stolen her mother. "How did you know?" Brinn asked accusingly.

"When Neesha's spirit was released from her prison it tried to inhabit you first. I think your mind was too simple for it to take hold, so it found your mother. But a small piece of that spirit stayed behind...got caught in your mind. When you buried the memory of that day you put that small piece of Neesha back into the hole, imprisoning it."

"My dreams." Brinn began to understand.

"When you came into contact with other dragons the forgotten memories began to work their way back into your subconscious. Last night you lifted the stone again." Ittra showed Brinn everything that had taken place in her mind the night before.

"How did you get her to leave?" Brinn asked.

"Old magic, older than...well *really* old magic. Normally a spirit residing within a mind, like Fernley's within you, can only be released at death. I...cheated. I can't explain how I did it, but I can tell you that Neesha is gone, free to roam the world. Maybe she will find the rest of herself some day."

Brinn was just glad it was gone. She thought of her mother. "Last night, why didn't I end up like Mother?"

"Neesha wanted to take over your mind, there wasn't enough power left to change the body." Ittra felt it was time to change the subject. "You are quite unique, you know."

"So I've been told." Brinn was glad to have something else to talk about. "Why is that?"

"I don't really know." Ittra went to the fire and poured more tea. "Maybe men didn't want to share the power. Odd thing about your race, the women haven't demanded to be treated as equals, much less taken on roles of power."

Brinn joined Ittra by the fire. "True. I can't argue that. Is it so different with dragons?"

"Oh yes." Ittra thought for a moment. "Centuries ago mothers were allowed to hatch their own eggs and raise their hatchlings as they saw fit. That controlling attitude naturally transferred to the running of the colony. No one seemed to object. The males like to spend their time hunting and telling stories around the fire. This was one less thing they had to worry about."

Brinn thought this sounded peculiar; two sides of the coin. "Then how does Talon fit into the scheme of things? *He's* a male."

Ittra smiled. "When the Prophecy mentioned a male as the Chosen One some saw it as a sign that a king would arise. Many males have always taken the Prophecy as a sign that they were destined to be the real power. When Talon was revealed to be the Krrig Daa everything turned upside-down."

"Everyone blames me," Talon appeared at the cave entrance, "I didn't have any say in the matter." He went to the Queen and bowed low, touching his hands to her front paws. "Thank you for taking care of Brinn."

Ittra leaned down and kissed Talon's head. "Well, someone had to," she said with a smile.

Talon rose and went to Brinn. "How are you feeling?"

Brinn smiled weakly. "I've had better days. My head still feels foggy."

Talon moved behind Brinn and put his hands on her head. Two fingers pressed gently on her neck and two on her forehead.

Brinn sensed a tingling as energy was drained through her scalp. She felt light headed, then found that she could think clearly again. Brinn sighed deeply. "Thank you."

Talon poured himself a cup of tea and sat down on the floor. "You had a lot of traffic in your mind, that can leave residual energy." He turned to Ittra. "She was quite powerful. Who was she?"

"Her name is Neesha." The Queen said respectfully. "She had a lot of time to build up energy."

"When I was young," Brinn explained to Talon, "the larger part of Neesha's essence transformed my mother's body. Someone locked her away in a pit. A dark pit." She shivered at the memory of her dreams. "And I opened it.

Ittra nodded. "The monster was Targis Orlag." Ittra spat.

Talon shivered at the name. Orlag had been the most evil wizard in history.

She patted Brinn's knee. "We are lucky Brinn was strong enough to keep from losing herself."

Talon sighed. "I guess I shouldn't be surprised that Neesha was angry," he said. "Where did she go?"

Ittra scowled at Talon and glanced at Brinn.

Talon realized he was more concerned about Neesha's spirit than Brinn's. He took Brinn's cup and refilled it. "This must all be a bit frightening for you."

"Yes it is. I have to admit these last few days have strained my hold on reality. I don't know that I would be surprised at anything now."

Ittra grinned. "Oh, I wouldn't start getting cynical just yet. There is a world of wonder out there." She sighed and stood. "They're gathering." Ittra said absently.

Talon nodded. "It started just after you took Brinn away. Amazing how fast rumors fly."

Ittra came back to the fire. "What are they saying?"

"Do you think *I* listen to rumors?" Talon looked innocently at the Queen, who glared back at him. "They think Brinn's a reincarnated dragon, they think she killed Neesha to get her power, they think she is the true Krrig Daa, they think she's faking it to get attention."

"What is reincarnation?" Brinn asked.

"In a nutshell, they think you were Neesha before you were born, and her spirit transferred into your body at the moment of your birth."

Brinn didn't like any of the rumors. "Hasn't anyone told them the truth?"

Talon shook his head. "Sure, but the truth means little to a mob."

"It'll take a while for this to quiet down," Ittra said with little enthusiasm.

Brinn felt obligated to say: "Maybe I'd better leave."

After a silent moment, Ittra said honestly: "I think you're right."

Talon was shocked.

"Well how would you handle this...event?" Ittra asked with interest.

"I'm becoming an old hand at managing catastrophes." Brinn thought he was joking, but there was no smile on the tired face.

"You have too much on your plate already. Training Brinn was one thing, but having to deal with zealots and angry mobs is quite another."

Brinn was confused. "Mobs?"

Talon motioned toward the curtained cave entrance. "There are twenty dragons jammed in that tunnel, and they all want a chance to touch you. And there are twenty behind them wanting to throw you over the nearest cliff."

"Don't be so dramatic," Ittra scolded Talon. She turned to Brinn. "You have to understand, we tend to think in absolutes; something *is* or *isn't*. We have an innate distrust of humans, even though Talon has brought our two races closer together."

"If you were to stay, we wouldn't be left alone long enough for me to teach you what you need to know about your new abilities. Those crowds won't go away anytime soon." He turned to Ittra. "Do you have any ideas?"

"Your cottage?"

Talon shook his head. "Two younglings are studying there. One of the other colonies? How about Betto's?"

"No, she's got some radicals telling the colony they should each have a *choice* in who their leader is. Something called *elections*. Ridiculous! Most of the other colonies have been slow to accept humans, and a wizard would definitely be unwelcome."

Brinn didn't like having her future discussed as if she were a stray kitten. "You don't have to worry about me," she said testily, "I *have* a home to go to, remember?"

Talon shook his head. "I've spoken to Fernley's man and the time is not right for you to move in. He's in Precanlin, and won't be back for a month. I wanted to train you before you went out on your own."

"What about Graldiss?" Brinn asked. "We get along. He could teach me until I —"

Talon shook his head. "Something about last night spooked him. He left without a word after Ittra took you away."

Ittra saw the discussion was distressing Brinn; she was on the verge of tears. There was no doubt Talon wanted the girl to be close-by for a while, but it would be best for everyone if she were out of the caves. There seemed to be only one solution. "The widows."

Talon smiled. Brinn just looked confused. "Do you think they'd agree?" Talon asked.

"Two old ladies? They would love the chance to have a visitor to pamper."

"And tell their stories and complaints to." Talon looked at Brinn. "Do you think you could stand two old biddies for a while? I'll warn you, you'll probably be spoiled."

Brinn grinned at the thought. "How long would I stay with them?" She was intrigued by the idea.

"A few weeks, I imagine," Ittra said offhandedly.

"At least a month," Talon said forcefully.

Brinn found that she liked the idea of stability. It was exciting to fly away with a dragon and live with a wizard in a mountain cave, but it would be nice to be in a normal house again. "How soon before I leave?" She tried not to sound too anxious.

Talon and Ittra looked at each other. Brinn had the impression they were speaking mentally. "Tomorrow." Ittra hoped she was not hurting the girl's feelings by making it sound as if they were trying to get rid of her. "Afternoon."

"I'm glad I don't have much to pack," Brinn said with a light tone.

Talon and Ittra relaxed a bit. With a sigh Talon stood. "I think it's time I took you back to my cave."

Ittra kissed Brinn's forehead. "Sleep well."

Brinn threw her arms around the small neck. "Thank you...for everything." She looked at Talon and motioned to the door.

Talon glanced at the Queen and transported himself and Brinn back to his cave.

Brinn didn't know if she liked the sensation of instant travel. There was a feeling of being pushed and pulled at the same time. A tingling of energy being drawn and released. It wasn't like flying on a dragon, the joy of moving faster than she had ever traveled before. There was no feeling of movement at all, just a gone-from-there - come-out-here sensation. Her apprehension was not eased by appearing a foot above the ground.

The look on Brinn's face seemed to require some explanation from Talon: "It's safer not to 'arrive' at ground level, you never know where that might be, or what might be there." They floated gently to the dirt floor. Talon held Brinn for a moment more, until she was steady enough to stand on her own. "It takes a few minutes to adjust," he explained.

When Talon released her, Brinn went to the bed and sat down. She desperately wanted to sleep, but was worried about her dreams. Talon seemed uncomfortable, looking around the cave for something.

Talon didn't know what more he could do for the girl. Why wasn't Graldiss there to help him out? For the first time in a long time, Talon regretted not having spent more time with his own race. Here was a girl that needed comforting and he didn't have a clue how to do it.

"What are they like?"

Talon shook off his uncertainty and looked blankly at Brinn.

"The widows, what are they like?"

Talon sat next to Brinn and told her the story of the elderly knight and the old dragon who fought a duel to the death and how their widows, brought together by their common loss, crossed social boundaries to become friends.

"They sound wonderful. I can't wait to meet them." Brinn said drowsily.

Talon pulled the blanket over Brinn's shoulders and quietly wished her goodnight.

Chapter 9

The smell of roasting bacon and mint tea was a wonderful way to be awakened. Brinn's stomach rumbled and she peeked out of from under the blankets. She could hear the muffled conversation of Talon and Graldiss. She sat up and quietly got out of bed. The wizard and the dragon were crouched around the fire, dipping their toast into steaming mugs. Graldiss turned the bacon roasting on sticks over the flames. When he caught sight of Brinn he dropped a thick slice into the flames. The fire sputtered and flared. Talon was about to scold his friend when he saw Brinn.

"Good morning."

Brinn smiled and sat down between dragon and wizard. She smiled a sleepy smile and yawned. "Smells wonderful." She reached for a piece of toast. "Any jam?"

Talon pushed a pot of sticky red jam toward Brinn. "Slept well, I hope."

"Best in days." She licked her jam-covered fingers. She smiled at Graldiss, and was worried when he did not smile in return. "Do we have to rush off this morning, or do I have time to say goodbye to Queen Ittra?

"Loris isn't expecting us until this afternoon." Talon said and turned a piece of bread floating over the flames. "There are some dragons that would like to meet with you before we go."

Graldiss silently stood up and left the cave.

Brinn stared after him, then at Talon, who was looking into the fire. "Did I do something wrong?"

Talon sighed. "He's pretty upset. He was shaken by the events last night. When he heard about Neesha being trapped he was furious. It seems he was trapped once when he was very young and has never really gotten over the trauma."

"But why is he angry with me? I was the one who let Neesha out."

"That's not what Graldiss holds against you," Talon said quietly.

Brinn looked unbelievingly at the cave entrance the dragon had exited through. "But I didn't have any control over that. I was a young child; I didn't know I was locking away the remnants of Neesha's spirit."

"That's just the way dragons are. Gral will get over his anger; I'll see to that. It will just take some time." Talon stood. "I put a new robe next to your bed, why don't you go put it on and we can get this parade of the curious over with."

Brinn didn't want to see any more dragons if they were going to hate her for something she had no control over. But she didn't see how she could get out of it. She rose and went to her sleeping area; stomping her feet on the dirt floor did not have the effect she wanted.

The new robe Talon had given Brinn surprised her. The fabric looked like spun gold, intricate patterns were embroidered in a rainbow of colored threads; the collar was high and the hem cut to trail behind her as she walked. She put the beautiful robe on slowly, relishing the feel of it on her skin. Her pleasure was cut short when she heard Talon bringing in the dragons.

"Wait for a few moments," Talon's voice sounded in Brinn's mind. "When you come out don't be intimidated."

Brinn waited until the outer cave was silent. She pushed her hair behind her ears, squared her shoulders and pulled aside the curtain. She was startled to see the cave filled with dragons and more were waiting in the passage. A cushioned stool had been brought in and the fire pit was gone. She held her head high and walked slowly to the center of the cave. She nodded imperiously to Talon and bowed slightly to the dragons before she sat on the stool.

Talon spoke to the assembled dragons in Dragonese, "This is Brinn, rightful heir to Fernley the Bard, from succession through Canik of Flintcairn, Benian the Wise, The Beast Utor, Short Hassial, Stannt the Ancient, and Ahdin who was given magic by Bisellia, Matriarch of the Fittiak Mountain Colony."

Brinn was surprised to hear the list of her predecessors. Talon's recital triggered an odd branching of her memories. She felt the presence of each wizard as their name was revealed. In a split second their lives were exposed to her and she felt small and young. Brinn desperately wanted to learn more about her...ancestors and now was impatient with the dragons gathered around her. "What do you want of me?" she asked shortly.

The dragon nearest Brinn was not put off by her tone. "I am Krittlik, descendant of Neesha the Brave." The reddish dragon leaned down and kissed the hem of Brinn's robe. Brinn saw the tears in the dragon's eyes; she reached out and touched his rough head. He said no more. As Krittlik left the other dragons parted to let him pass, reaching out to touch him.

Brinn's anger melted away and she turned to the next dragon before her. Over the next hours Brinn found herself honored, gawked at, worshiped, and threatened. She lost track of how many times she pulled out a strand of hair for a memento, or said a blessing, or touched a head. The dragons that despised her for keeping even the smallest piece of Neesha's spirit locked away were a refreshing break from the solemn adoration, the pleading petitioners that hoped she knew where their lost ancestors might be, and the curious.

The final visitor was Manett. Brinn was tired and not prepared for the dragon's attack. The gray dragon appeared suddenly in the cave; with no warning she slapped Brinn with the back of her paw. Brinn fell to the floor. Talon tried to put himself between Brinn and the dragon, but found himself immobilized. Before his eyes, the elderly dragon was thrown across the cave, slamming into the wall. Talon looked disbelievingly at Brinn, whose bleeding arm was thrust in front of her. Manett's wing moved swiftly and a sheet of flame shot out. Brinn uttered a single word and stood untouched by the fire. Before the glow around her dimmed, Brinn's knife appeared at Manett's throat. Manett shifted instantly to the opposite side of the cave, her tail cutting at Brinn's legs but only managing to shatter the stool. Brinn hung unharmed near the ceiling of the cave.

The two glared at each other, panting. Talon fought to free himself. It was only the appearance of Ittra that ended the fight. "That is enough," she said firmly. "Are you satisfied?"

Manett grunted and vanished.

Brinn drifted down from the ceiling and Talon found he could move again. He confronted Ittra. "What was that about?" he demanded. "Did you know that was going to happen?"

"Of course." Her tone was scolding. She turned to Brinn. "There were some that thought you might still possess Neesha's spirit. Since one dragon never attacks another, you would have defended yourself but not counter-attacked had you held any of her spirit. This was the only test that would silence them." She smiled proudly. "Your skill is quite remarkable."

Talon stormed up to the Queen. "She could have been killed!"

Ittra laughed. "A wizard? Of her lineage? I'm sure I felt the influence of at least three of them at one point. Do you understand so little of the power you hold within you?"

Talon had never really considered the multiple powers that lay folded within *himself*. The line of wizards leading up to Olwin was imbedded in his subconscious. How could he have not realized it before?

"You are too self-centered. The thought that there might be others in your mind vying for control of your actions is abhorrent to you. Brinn doesn't seem to have a problem with it." Ittra grinned at the girl. "It was good for Manett to learn wizards aren't easy to defeat. There is one more who would like to speak with you before you leave. If you are not too tired."

Brinn nodded.

The Queen turned to Talon. "Let us leave them alone." Talon was confused, but left.

Brinn wiped the blood from her arm and straightened her robe. She was surprised when Graldiss walked into the cave.

The dragon looked for Talon, and was glad to find him gone. He went to Brinn and held out his forepaws. "Forgive me. I realize now that it wasn't your fault."

Brinn ran into the open arms and hugged as much of the dragon as she could. "I couldn't bear thinking you were angry with me."

"Queen Ittra made me see how silly I was being," Graldiss admitted. "She told me what happened when you opened the vault. It must have been awful. How could I have been so cruel?"

Brinn drew back and wiped her tears. "You couldn't have known." She sat down on the dirt floor, exhausted physically and emotionally. She was thankful when Graldiss changed the subject.

"We could feel your battle with Manett throughout the whole mountain. You impressed a lot of dragons."

Brinn smiled weakly. "I don't know that I had much to do with it. From what Ittra said, the other wizards in my head took over and handled the whole thing."

"They couldn't have done that without your willingness to hand over control. After the first blow you fought back. *You* chose to do that, whoever else did the fighting. That took courage."

"Thank you, but I didn't feel very courageous, just angry. Hour after hour they came through here as if I were a freak or a holy woman. What did they want from me?"

Graldiss remembered watching Talon go through the same thing when he first came to the mountain as the Krrig Daa. "Reassurance. Only one other human has had the spirit of a dragon within his mind. They want to know if *he* is the savior of our race, or *you*."

Brinn thought this must be a joke. "I'll leave that job to Talon, thank you. No offence, but I didn't care for the experience of having one of you in here." She tapped her head. "I have too much to handle just being a wizard."

Graldiss grinned. "And a very good one you'll make, too." He turned to leave. "I'm proud to have met you." As Graldiss walked through the cave entrance he turned. "Remember who the monsters are," he said with a smile, and disappeared.

Brinn wiped a final tear from her cheek. She thought about the dragon's words. She used to know who the monsters were: Nethra and Ruthic and Keldric, but Graldiss had thought *she* was a monster for submerging the spirit of the dragon that took her mother away, and she felt Manett would gladly have blasted her to dust. It seemed that monsters were in the eye of the beholder.

Brinn went to her bed and began to fold her clothes. She changed out of the elaborate robe and into the simple dress she wore when she started her journey. She wasn't left alone for very long, Talon returned with a tray of food and a brown cloak over his arm.

"You must be starving." The fire pit reappeared in the center of the cave, flames crackling cheerfully. "We'll be carried by dragon part of the way," Talon handed Brinn the cloak. "More for protection from dragon scales than the cold."

Brinn nibbled on the fruit as she put the last of her belongings in the pack Talon provided. When she finished she sat down by the fire. "I haven't had the chance to thank you for everything you've done for me."

She stared into the flames. "I don't know what I would have done without you."

Talon took her hand. "No thanks are necessary. It was worth it just to see that old buzzard slammed against the wall." He laughed. "Besides, I only got you away from that inn. Now you have your whole life ahead of you, and I won't be able to be around for you as much as I'd like." He pulled Brinn to her feet. "The Queen is waiting for us, and so are the widows."

Brinn thought Talon would take her to the Queen's cavern, but instead he led her to a large ledge where dragons were landing and taking off. Silgaa was waiting for them. Talon helped Brinn climb to a comfortable position between the dragon's shoulders, then slid behind her. "Hold on."

Brinn was about to remind Talon that she had, in fact, ridden a dragon before, but she was too busy scrambling for a handhold as Silgaa took off. She felt Talon laughing behind her and was pulled back to lean against him. She decided it would be safer to put aside her indignation and accept his secure hold while they were a thousand feet above the rocky peaks.

After they cleared the mountains Brinn felt Talon begin to pull in energy. Within a few minutes she felt the odd sensation of instant transportation and in a blink of the eye, they were over an open field. "Why travel by dragon at all?" Brinn shouted back to Talon. "We could just 'move' to wherever we want."

"Noise." Talon didn't shout, but allowed his words to be heard in Brinn's mind. "The mountain responds to magic. The power it takes to travel long distances would deafen anyone in the caves. Besides, it's more polite to arrive the usual way. You wouldn't want someone to just appear out of thin air, would you?"

"I didn't know there was an etiquette for magic," Brinn thought to Talon.

"I'm sure Kaalla will be able to help you out with those lessons."

Silgaa began to descend. Brinn could not believe her eyes when she saw what had to be the cottage where she would be staying. It looked like someone had built a cottage onto the side of a barn. Brinn spotted the Queen and a second dragon sitting in a garden. When Silgaa landed Talon helped Brinn down, steadying her for a moment. Brinn thanked the dragon for a comfortable journey. Silgaa bowed and rose into the air.

Talon led Brinn round to the back of the cottage. She was amazed at the variety and lushness of the flowers that encircled the cottage, and wondered if they were helped along with a little magic. As the two rounded the rear corner Brinn stopped. Before her was the most beautiful garden she had ever seen. Mounds of squash, yam and potato plants nestled next to rows of lettuce, turnips, beets and carrots. Bushes of berries, peppers and tomatoes were bordered with marigolds and poppies. Huge stands of corn and vines of beans and peas walled in one side of the orderly garden with fruit and nut trees a short distance away.

Brinn saw movement between the stalks of corn. An elderly woman stepped out from one end, her apron filled with plump ears, which tumbled to the ground at the sight of Talon and Brinn. The startled woman huffed and leaned down to pick up the load, but the corn disappeared. "I don't need any help, Kaalla," the woman grumbled. She turned on Talon. "Don't you have better manners than to sneak up on an old woman? Thoughtless child." She looked at Brinn and winked. "You were supposed to be here an hour ago," she scolded Talon. "Left all the work to me."

Talon put his arm around the bony shoulders. "Is this any way to greet your benefactor?"

The woman elbowed Talon's rib. "Benefactor? An impolite upstart, more like." A weathered hand slid under Brinn's arm. "I'm Loris, sweetie. You must be Brinn. Come and have some juice and cobbler." Talon followed after the pair.

They walked toward the two dragons talking under an apple tree. As they neared, Queen Ittra rose and bowed to the large elderly dragon who in turn lowered her head to the small feet. Ittra greeted the three humans. "Thank you for your hospitality," she said to Loris. "I can't wait to try your rhubarb jam on my toast this evening."

Loris curtsied gracefully. "Thank you for the venison, I'll prepare some mince pies for your next visit."

"Gridlinn would like you to stop by before your return," the Queen said to Talon.

Talon sighed and nodded. "She's having trouble with a group of younglings playing with Baron Veatel's herds."

"The poor sheep are too scared to eat," Loris added. "And their wool is falling off from fright." The old woman took Talon's arm and led him to the table.

Ittra turned and smiled down at Brinn. "I wish we had had more time to get to know one another. I'm sure we shall become best of friends."

Brinn blushed.

"I will visit from time to time," Ittra said. "I am sorry your stay with us was not very pleasant. I'm sure you will be comfortable here."

"Thank you. I would like to visit with you some more. Please don't worry about...well it's over now, no sense dwelling on it." Brinn squared her shoulders. "Time to move on."

"You are very courageous." Ittra smiled. "I will discourage my dragons from venturing here to worship at your feet. If you should need anything, don't hesitate to ask." The Queen bowed.

Holding back tears, Brinn leaned down and put her head on Ittra's foot, then stepped back and watched the beautiful dragon fly into the blue sky. She turned to join the others and saw Talon walking toward her. "You're leaving, too," she said simply.

Talon looked uncomfortable. "I have to...I...I hate long goodbyes, I never know what to say." He put his arms around her and hugged her tight. "I wish I'd had a sister like you." He turned quickly and vaulted onto

Silgaa's back. The two rose quickly and blinked out of sight.

It took a while for Brinn to get her emotions under control. She slowly joined the others. A large hankie appeared on the table in front of Brinn. She sniffed, blew loudly, then smiled weakly at Kaalla. Loris patted Brinn's arm. They sat in silence for a moment. Kaalla poured chilled juice from a large clay pitcher. Loris spooned out raspberry cobbler.

"Not a good beginning to the day," Kaalla said gloomily. "And here I thought it was going to turn out to be such a nice day, with the Queen visiting and all."

"They were both rather impolite, if you ask me," Loris huffed and took a bite of cobbler.

"No one did, dear." Kaalla turned to Brinn. "You must be finding yourself in quite an interesting situation."

Brinn was quietly eating the delicious cobbler. Her mouth was too full to answer. She used the large hankie to wipe red juice from her chin. "I feel a bit out of control of my life. Only a week ago I was slaving away at my father's inn. Now here I am, a wizard consorting with dragons and queens. What will happen next?"

Loris put another spoonful of cobbler into Brinn's bowl. "It's best not to ask questions like that. I heard you had a dragon in your head." Loris wiggled in her chair. "Gives me the willies just to think of it."

Kaalla swatted at Loris with her wing. "Don't be rude. It must have been a humbling experience. Such a noble dragon."

"Actually," Brinn said honestly, "I don't remember any of it at all. And I didn't think she was very noble when she took my mother away." Brinn knew she shouldn't be so cold, but she was really tired of the whole thing.

"Leave her alone, Kay. She's feeling a little low right now." Loris stood and took Brinn's hand. "Come along. We'll find a place for your things." She led Brinn into the cottage.

Brinn's mood was brightened by the inside of the cottage. Half of the interior was wide open, with a large cushion and a high table, numerous lamps hung from the ceiling, and the most incredible quilt lay across an enormous bed. The other side of the cottage was tiny in comparison, and sparsely furnished with a rocking chair, and a shelf of books and knick-knacks, a writing desk, and a cooking area with shelves of spices, and cooking pots. The center of the cottage was an odd mix of large and small. A large table with smallish chairs on one side, a gigantic fireplace with normal-sized cooking utensils, two small slippers next to four huge slippers.

"You're room is through this door." Loris led Brinn to the small side of the cottage and through one of three doors. "It's a bit light on frills, I'm afraid. Didn't have much time to bring anything in from town."

Brinn put her bag down next to the canopied bed. Despite Loris' words the room was beautiful. She had to choke back tears.

"Why don't you take a bit of a nap while I finish gathering vegetables for supper?" Loris softly closed the door as she left.

Brinn collapsed with relief onto the bed and was asleep instantly.

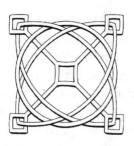

Chapter 10

Brinn was disoriented in the darkness. Only the sound of arguing women reminded her where she was and she sat up. She remembered seeing a candle on the small, window-side table. As gently as she could, Brinn sent out a thought of flame. A very small flicker of fire floated above her head. Brinn giggled and the tiny light seemed to giggle back. She sent the happy flame to the candle. It danced around the candle for a minute before settling onto the wick, giving off a warm glow. Brinn smiled, this magic stuff might be a lot of fun. As she brushed her hair, and changed into a fresh robe, she thought about the peculiar pair that had welcomed her into their home. There was no doubt they were the oddest couple she had ever seen. Checking her appearance in the mirror, she left her room.

Brinn's arrival went unnoticed, so she was able to study the two elderly females. Loris was busy at the table preparing the evening meal. Her shoulders were straight and proud. The short, wild hair had passed through gray and into white. The old woman seemed to be much older than Brinn had first assumed. Loris wore a white peasant blouse and a full red skirt colored with multiple patches; on her feet were a pair of bulky, mismatched socks, darned with yellow thread. Kaalla was sweeping imagined dust from the gleaming floor with a large, neatly trimmed broom. Brinn didn't know how elderly dragons were supposed to look. Kaalla's scales had lost their brilliant shine and her back spikes were rounded down to smooth curves. Her tail had a noticeable kink toward the tip and Brinn noticed she favored her left rear foot.

The two worked at their own tasks, seeming to pay little attention to the other until Kaalla spoke. "You should cut those a bit thinner, dear," she said helpfully.

"They are fine just as they are." Loris hacked at a thick spike of carrot.

"They will cook faster if they are thinner." Kaalla was not actually watching Loris to see how thin or thick the carrots were being cut, but from years of living together the dragon knew how the old woman cooked.

"Do you want to come over here and take over?" Loris did not pause in her cutting, she did not expect Kaalla to take her up on the offer.

Kaalla put the broom away in a corner and set the fireplace log aflame with a puff. A kettle appeared magically over the crackling flames. "Lemon tea or mint?"

"Can't you put a kettle on the fire like everyone else? You know I don't like magic done in here. Mint." Loris moved on to chopping turnips.

Kaalla squeezed into the cooking area and took the small tin of tea from the shelf. "If you hadn't insisted on a human-sized kitchen, I would be able to move around more easily." Looking clumsy with her large paws, the dragon scooped out a measure of mint leaves into the large teapot. "A bit of bacon in the soup tonight?"

White cubes were added to the soup pot. "I would tire myself lugging pots across such a large kitchen." Loris made no comment to the instant appearance of a side of salt pork and began slicing off thin strips. After she placed them in a hot skillet Loris noticed Brinn standing at the guestroom door. "Come, little one. A cup of mint tea will set you to rights. Kaalla, bring out some scones."

Brinn took a seat at the table. Kaalla poured out the tea. "Raisin or pumpkin?" A tin of sweet scones was held out to Brinn. "Take two or three, it will be a bit before supper is ready."

"All things at their proper time," Loris said sagely.

"And the proper time is when the carrots are tender," Kaalla whispered to Brinn.

Brinn sipped her hot tea and nibbled on a tender scone. She knew Kaalla would have many questions for her and she braced herself for the interrogation. She was halfway through with her third scone before Loris asked a question. "Did they feed you properly in that drafty mountain?"

Brinn hid her smile in her teacup. "Yes, ma'am, fresh fruit and roasted deer."

Loris scoffed. "Undercooked if I know dragons."

Kaalla dropped a scone into her mouth. "Did you get a chance to eat in the main cavern? Dissal, my mate, and I went every new moon. What a feast we would have. Great bowls of the freshest grains, whole tables of gently roasted meat." The dragon became lost in her memories. "Only the most succulent pigs and sheep were chosen, mighty bucks and tender fawns, there were platters of salmon, eagle and geese, tiny mice and chipmunks for appetizers. Once there was a centerpiece of apple trees. Oh, and on the Longest Night we would have a huge bonfire with sweet cakes and sticky treats, rabbits on sticks and tender, juicy—" Kaalla stopped, and looked away, embarrassed. "But that was decades ago," she mumbled. Loris and Brinn stared at the dragon. Kaalla turned to confront them, her head held high. "Things were different back then."

Loris patted her friend's leg. "Yes, they were."

"Actually," Brinn said smiling, "they're still serving people." It took a moment for the joke to sink in, but Brinn was glad to see the two laugh and break the tense moment. "Actually, I wasn't in the caves long enough to judge the quality of the food," Brinn told Loris. "But they sure don't know how to make a decent pudding. Not nearly enough sugar and they didn't whip the cream long enough."

Kaalla stared at Brinn. "You know how to make puddings?"

Brinn shrugged. "I preferred to work in the kitchen rather than wait tables at my father's inn."

Kaalla grinned broadly. "So...do you like to cook?" she asked hopefully.

Loris glared at the dragon. "Shame on you! Talon did not bring this little girl here to cook your supper!"

Kaalla pretended to be ashamed, but winked at Brinn.

Loris took a hotpad and reached for the soup pot.

Brinn stepped toward the fire. "Please, let me get that," she said helpfully.

Loris shooed Brinn away. "The day I can't lift this old pot is the day I fold up my apron and stop cooking."

"Can today be that day?" Kaalla asked from her spot in front of the fire. "Your cooking is getting hard to digest."

"This from a beast who would eat a sheep, wool and all, if my stew is delayed an hour." Loris absently handed the pot to Brinn. "If my cooking offends your stomach you can just go eat in the barn."

"Don't tempt me, hag." Kaalla made no move to carry out the threat. "Why don't you let the girl cook, I'm sure she was taught all the proper methods of preparing foods." The dragon winked again at Brinn.

"Why don't you get off that pillow, do your job and leave mine alone." The old woman didn't blink when the plates appeared on the table. Loris dished up the stew and they ate in silence. After the first bite, Brinn understood Kaalla's enthusiasm over her ability to cook.

When the dishes were cleared from the table and the teakettle freshened, Loris and Kaalla settled into their respective chairs. Kaalla motioned for Brinn to sit in the plush chair next to her cushion. Loris opened a well-worn book and Kaalla brought out a very large pair of knitting needles. Brinn stared into the fire. It wasn't long before the gentle snores of both ladies filled the cottage. Brinn smiled, feeling quite at home with these two friends. She poured herself a cup of tea and washed the dishes before she went to her room.

Brinn was up before dawn. She put on her blue robe and went out to the main room. Loris was still sleeping by the fire, but Kaalla had moved to her bed during the night. With a smile, Brinn started breakfast. As she prepared biscuits, Brinn wondered just how much a dragon ate. Last night Kaalla had six helpings of Loris' soup, but the bowls were the same size as their own. Brinn decided to make a few *large* biscuits for the dragon.

It wasn't long before the wonderful smells coming from the kitchen woke Kaalla. "Mmm, is there anything that smells as good as bacon in the morning?" She inhaled deeply then turned. "Pardon me." The dragon disappeared. After a few minutes she returned. "Sorry, nature called."

Brinn hid her smile as she dished up eggs and bacon. "What about Loris?"

Kaalla buttered one of the large biscuits that was still only a nibble. "Don't worry about her, she'll sleep all morning." The dragon eagerly ate the fluffy eggs and flaky biscuits. When only the old lady's portion was left, the dragon sat back and sighed. "That was wonderful. I'll take care of the mess." Brinn felt a rush of magic as the dishes were instantly cleaned and stacked on their shelf. Bits and pieces of food disappeared in a blink of the eye. "There. Now why don't we go outside and start your training."

Brinn followed Kaalla to a huge apple tree and sat down next to the dragon. "I don't understand why Talon and Ittra feel that I need to be trained. I have all of Fernley's memories in my head, why can't I just use *them*?"

Kaalla smiled at Brinn's innocence. "Being *told* how magic works is not enough. Magic takes direction of thought and we all think differently. The Krrig Daa didn't bring you here because he thought you needed to be *taught* magic, but rather for guidance."

Brinn wanted to shout that she didn't need guidance. She wasn't a little child playing with a knife. But in reality, that's exactly what she was. Just knowing the knife was sharp didn't mean she wouldn't get cut. "Ok, where do we start?"

Kaalla smiled, the girl had grit. She held out her paw and an apple instantly dropped onto it. "Now you."

Brinn looked up at the tree and a spell came to mind. "Valincia tordina komak." Bits of apples showered down on Brinn.

Kaalla didn't hide her smile. "Interesting."

Brinn tried again. "Valincia tordino konak." A single apple fell from a nearby branch, but rather than land neatly into her outstretched hand, the red fruit shot toward her head. Brinn ducked and watched the apple disappear into the orchard. She looked sheepishly at Kaalla. "What went wrong?"

"First off, do you have any idea what you were saying?" Brinn shook her head. "No, I thought not. This Fernley of yours must have put a lot of stock in words." Kaalla popped the apple into her mouth. "I don't know why humans ever used words to direct their magic. Why complicate something so natural?" Brinn looked confused. "Using spells transfers your power to words. Get the words wrong and you cannot control the outcome. Wizards who use spells to direct their magic are being lazy. It takes effort of mind to focus power and release it."

Brinn thought about the times she had *made* things happen without thinking. It had seemed easier than trying to remember the right combination of words. "What did those words mean? They definitely weren't a spell for making an apple appear."

Kaalla had to laugh. "No, they weren't. The first time you called for the apple to burst before you, then you told it to 'shoot forth'. How can anyone know what they are talking about if they can't even get the languages right. Why don't you try again without the spell?"

Brinn concentrated, trying to picture the apple dropping into her hand and released a small bit of her own energy. Nothing happened. She tried again, specifying a particular apple from the lower branch. Brinn was rewarded with a thump on the head.

"You forgot to hold out your hand," Kaalla said seriously.

Brinn picked up the apple. "Do I have to be so exact?"

"When you get the hang of visualizing it will come more easily. I'll also show you a few shortcuts."

Brinn held out her hand and an apple dropped neatly onto her palm. By the time Loris called them in for lunch, Kaalla had Brinn relocating small things all over the garden.

Over the next few days Brinn advanced to collecting fallen tree limbs, and moving the garden table, even levitating herself high enough to reach the last of the autumn pears.

Loris never joined them for Brinn's lessons, Kaalla said magic made Loris nervous. "Unnatural," the dragon said in a perfect imitation of the old woman. "You'll find a lot of people who feel the same way." Kaalla became serious. "Dragons weren't always hated, you know. It wasn't until the wizards took magic out of the every-day and turned it into mystical claptrap that our lives became endangered. By inciting dragocide, wizards were hoping to eliminate the last vestiges of uncontrolled magic. There are whole populations that have forgotten magic ever existed or who are frightened by anyone, or thing, that displays such abnormal abilities."

Brinn understood perfectly. Until a month ago she would have put wizards and dragons in the same fictional category as faeries and trolls. She had grown out of believing in magic when she became old enough to carry a serving tray. And her memories from Fernley told her of the terrible war against the dragons, when wizards incited a great quest against the 'heartless, vicious beasts'. The memories also told the stories of the many villages that perished from dragon fire. "But didn't some humans have good reason to fear dragons?"

Kaalla looked away. "Yes, that's true. I could explain that we were in fear of our lives, that we were just striking back, protecting our young, but that isn't completely true. I would like to believe that in the beginning the burnings were a defensive measure, but it got out of control; hatred took over and too many dragons wanted to eliminate all humans. I'm not proud of that." She sighed and reached up for an apple. "But now the Krrig Daa is helping us change things. Though how well he has convinced the other wizards to cease the antagonism has yet to be seen. At least we are once again free to fly the skies."

"You two look too gloomy for such a beautiful day." Loris had walked up from the cottage; she was wearing a new dress. "Why don't we go into town?"

Brinn's mood brightened immediately. "I'll be right out!" She ran into the cottage. She changed into her best dress and dug out the few coins she had horded away from Nethra's greedy fingers. She sighed wistfully, these were the last vestiges of her old life.

Brinn clutched the coins tightly, as if squeezing that life out of them. She dropped the coins into her pocket and ran outside. When she returned to the apple tree, Loris was sitting on a saddle strapped to Kaalla's broad back. Brinn climbed up the dragon's bent leg and slid behind Loris. Handhold straps made keeping her balance much easier than her previous dragon rides.

The traffic around the fair-sized town appeared to be mostly dragon. A tower that must have once housed the town guard was now used to direct incoming dragons to one of four landing areas indicated by flags of differing colors. Flags displaying large black and white shapes seemed to be used to let dragons know when they could safely take off. Kaalla landed gently, two boys hurried to help Loris and Brinn dismount and removed the saddle. The three moved off the field just as a small yellow dragon began to land. The three women joined the rest of the foot traffic into town.

Kaalla was the first to separate, going off to have tea with an old friend. Loris made sure Brinn felt comfortable on her own before she went off to have a discussion with the butcher about the proper way to season pepper sausage. Brinn didn't mind being left alone at all. She preferred wandering around on her own.

Brinn marveled at the wide streets of the town. Her own village had very narrow streets with overhanging second floors. This town must have been built, or enlarged for ease of movement by the dragons. There were open balconies high up with goods displayed for dragons to purchase. Brinn visited many of the shops, purchasing several large balls of yarn in multiple shades of blue for Kaalla and a set of measuring spoons for Loris (in hopes the old woman would learn to season in moderation). She bought a raspberry bun at a bakery where gigantic bread loaves and cookies were displayed along side normal-sized cakes and rolls. She found a bookshop and spent an hour roaming through the stacks.

Happy with her purchases, Brinn made her way to the Town Square. Tables were arranged outside nearby restaurants and there were many people and dragons watching the entertainment offered in the busy square. The usual human performers were joined by dragons performing feats of magic. Brinn sipped an exotic, icy chocolate drink while she listened to a mixed species quartet. As she glanced around, Brinn noticed for the first time that many of the dragons were glancing over at her rather than looking away. She did not recognize any of them from the caves and she started to feel a bit uncomfortable. One dragon, small with shiny red scales and tufted ear, was courageous enough to approach Brinn.

"I beg your pardon, Lady Brinn, might I sit with you for a moment?"

Brinn smiled at being referred to as a Lady and nodded. "You have the advantage over me, Sir Dragon, for I do not know your name." Brinn spoke easily in Dragonese, thanks to Fernley, which did not seem to surprise the dragon.

The dragon sat on the bench. "I am Kartek. I am from a colony where our queen reigns with a firm paw.

"Greetings. I am curious to know how you knew who I was."

Kartek smiled. "By your aura we knew you to be a wizard and you are a female. You are quite easy to pick out of a crowd."

Brinn was surprised to find knowledge of her was widespread. She nodded then motioned to the singers. "They're quite good."

"Who knew humans had the heart for music?" He looked intensely at Brinn. "May I be so bold as to request a favor from you?"

Brinn had no idea what favor a dragon could ask of her; she looked over at Kartek's friends who were looking expectantly at her. "There is no harm in the asking, if there is no harm in the declining."

The dragon nodded seriously. "Indeed." He looked at his companions. "My friends and I would like you to speak to the Krrig Daa on our behalf." He didn't pause for her response but rushed on. "Many of us believe we should have an equal part in deciding what path our future should take. We would like a voice in the direction we are taking to fulfill the Prophecy. Should its outcome be in the hands of so few? Long has our species been kept from returning to our rightful place in the world. Our own queen, though noble and worthy of all honor, has begun to lead our colony away from...the True Path. If we could get an audience with the Krrig Daa I'm sure he will see the truth of our words and understand his proper role in the Prophecy." He stopped for a moment. Did the girl understand how earnest he was?

Brinn was beginning to understand what Kartek, and his friends, were involved in. She remembered hearing Ittra mention one of the other queens was having trouble with a rise in the idea of democracy. She surely didn't want to get caught in the power struggle. "I'm sorry, but I really have no sway with your Krrig Daa. In fact, it was thought best for me to be removed from the Crinnelian caves many days ago, and I haven't seen Talon since."

The small dragon drooped a bit. Then he remembered he was sitting next to a wizard. "You know...our cause would gain attention if you were to join us."

Brinn regretted encouraging this dragon. She saw the corner she was being backed into. She didn't want to make enemies on either side of this coming conflict. Pleading ignorance seemed the only way out. "I do not deserve the importance you have placed on my opinion. I am not important in the world of wizards. My lack of knowledge about dragons would also prove an obstacle to your cause."

Kartek thought about this and nodded. "I see the wisdom of your words. I thank you for your candor." He jumped down from the bench. "If there comes a time when you can consider joining us don't hesitate to contact me." He bowed and turned to join his companions.

Brinn watched the group of small dragons talk quickly for a moment. A green dragon looked around nervously while some decision was being made. The group separated and each dragon faded into the crowd. Brinn relaxed again and finished her drink.

Brinn found Loris haggling with a tinsmith over a water pitcher. The tinsmith threw up his hands and gave in. Loris was grinning as she led Brinn away. "Always makes me feel young to beat a swindler like that one." She put her arm around Brinn's. "Well, my dear, have your enjoyed your day?"

Chapter 11

Brinn stirred the lumps out of Loris' gravy. The elderly woman was gently snoring in her chair. Kaalla was happily knitting with her new yarn. Brinn had laughed the first time she saw the four-foot long wooden knitting needles, and she was amazed at the speed of the large hand (she couldn't think of them as paws). Kaalla and Brinn chatted while she finished preparing the evening meal. The dragon talked about her visit with two clutchmates and finding the perfect headdress for the Hatching Festival. Brinn promised to read her new book to Kaalla and remarked that she should have bought some seasonings for Loris to use in her cooking.

"Not here to be put to work." Loris roused at the mention of her name and scolded Brinn for not waking her when the meat needed turning. She mumbled with a mouthful of flaky biscuit. She gave the roast a poke and the gravy a stir. "Best eat before you burn the meat."

Kaalla winked at Brinn and put down her knitting. "I rather like my meat on the dark side."

"No one is asking you for your culinary preferences. Bring in the butter, please." Loris brought out the plates and cups.

Brinn magically lifted the roast from the fire and placed it onto the serving platter, ducking as a bowl of butter floated in through the window. Brinn laughed and shot the biscuits onto each plate. With a flourished wave Kaalla cut thick slices of juicy meat. Loris stood with her hands on her hips. "Alright, enough of that silliness. You two aren't so feeble you can't raise a knife for slicing or take a few steps to set bread on the table."

"Biscuits," Kaalla corrected, manually pouring glasses of cold tea. "Sugar, dear?"

Loris glared at the floating sugar bowl but took a heaping spoonful.

After supper Brinn helped clear away the dishes before she settled onto the rug by the fire to read to Kaalla. The fire had burned low when Brinn woke to find herself drifting through the air toward her bed. She rolled over in mid-air and curled into a comfortable ball. She let Kaalla pull the covers over her and fell back to sleep.

Loris woke before Brinn and had a pot of oatmeal bubbling on the fire. Kaalla was not in the cottage when Brinn sat down to breakfast. "She likes to hunt early in the morning," the old woman informed Brinn. "I'm sure she thinks it offends my sensibilities." She offered the jam to Brinn. "She's a dragon for goodness sake, how else is she supposed to eat? I'm not so silly to think she can survive on stew and corncakes." Loris poured herself a cup of dark tea and scooped in three heaping spoons of sugar. "She'll be expecting you by the apple tree as usual." She took a long gulp of tea. "What's a nice girl like you needing all that magiky stuff anyway? Find yourself a good man to take care of everything for you. That's the ticket." Loris thought for a moment then shrugged. "But then again, most men are looking for a good woman to take care of everything for *them*." She laughed. "I suppose being a wizard-thingy is as good a job as any."

"It's better than working at an inn." Brinn put her dishes in the pan of soapy cleaning water and headed for the door.

Kaalla wasn't sitting under the apple tree as Brinn expected, but drifting on the warm air currents high above. She spiraled down when she saw Brinn approaching. "Lovely morning," the dragon said, not a bit out of breath. "Couldn't resist a morning soar." She curled around the huge tree trunk. "What would you like to do today?"

Brinn stared for a moment. She hadn't expected that question. She thought for a while before remembering something that had intrigued her. "How about disappearing and reappearing?"

Kaalla smiled and nodded. "That should take us a while. Have you had a good breakfast? You'll need plenty of energy." An apple appeared in the dragons paw. "So far, you have practiced moving small objects around. Having them drift through the air can be very disconcerting for people around you and it can be very tiring. There is also the matter of obstacles." The apple drifted thought the air, bumping into Brinn and the tree before making its way to the garden table. "Relocation is a quick method for shifting things from here to there." A second apple appeared in Kaalla's paw before it blinked out of sight and reappeared next to the first on the table. Kaalla smiled at the glint of excitement in Brinn's eyes. "But there are dangers." A third apple appeared and disappeared. Brinn was surprised to see half an apple sticking out of the side of the wooden bowl. "You *must* know exactly where your object is going to land. Line of sight is the best rule to follow. Be sure you can see your object to begin with and can see where it will land. The dangers are obvious."

Loris looked up from her gardening and glared at Kaalla. "You *are* going to fix that, right?"

Kaalla waved her paw and the bowl seemed to spit out the intruding apple and re-grow itself around the hole left behind. "Think about what it's like to move around in the dark," she told Brinn. "If you don't know where the chairs are, you are going to stub your toe. The hard part is the instant change in perspective. Something is here, then it is there. You must erase the thought of the *here* and create the thought of *there*. There is no movement." Kaalla disappeared from around the tree and reappeared in the air above the garden.

Loris gave a startled cry and fell to the ground. She quickly got to her feet. "You evil beast! If you insist on playing these tricks in my garden then I am going *inside*." The old woman stomped inside, wiping dirt from her backside.

Kaalla laughed and flew back to the tree. "She could use a little shake up now and then; good for the heart. Now you give it a try. Start with something small."

Brinn took a deep breath. She found a small stone near her foot and picked it up. "Do I have to memorize what it looks like?"

"No, self preservation will keep most things stable; their own energy will keep their ears or roots in the right spot."

Brinn stared at the stone in her right hand and held out her left hand. She pictured the spot just above her palm then looked at the stone again. Brinn shut her eyes and pictured the stone just above her left hand. She instantly felt the weight of the stone vanish from one hand as the stone dropped into her other. She opened her eyes and grinned. She clutched the stone to her chest as if it were a precious gem.

"Good job. But practice not closing your eyes. By starting small you didn't have to draw in energy to relocate that stone. As you learn to move larger things you will find using your own energy is too draining, or not sufficient for the task. Rather than drawing power from a specific entity, try a general inhalation of ambient energy."

Brinn looked bewildered.

"Take it from all over instead of from one place."

Brinn nodded. She put the stone in her pocket and looked around for something else to relocate.

It wasn't long before Brinn was exhausted. She decided it would be easier to manually put back the garden furniture than to use magic.

"If you feel up to it," Kaalla said, proudly looking down on her pupil, "you can try transporting yourself around tomorrow."

Brinn wasn't sure she was ready for that.

Loris looked out the cottage door. "Are you two finished playing around?" She came out, carrying a basket and a glass of lemonade. "Thought you could use this," she said to Brinn handing her the glass. "Looks like it was raining firewood out here." She waved her hand at the scattered logs. "Will you take care of that, please," Loris said to Kaalla in an irritated tone. When Brinn finished her drink Loris handed a basket to her. "Would you fetch some corn for supper, please?"

Brinn took the basket and walked between the rows of turnips and carrots to the green wall of corn stalks. The cooks at her father's inn had never let Brinn pick vegetables from the garden, so she was not really sure how to tell which ears of corn were ripe enough. *Ask them*, Fernley's memories hinted. *Plants are like any other living thing, talk to them. Before ending its life, it is always polite to ask for permission to do so. If it does not wish to give its life for you, respect its wishes.*

This seemed a bit silly, but Brinn figured Fernley knew more about this than she did. She stood before a stalk of corn taller than herself. How do I be polite to a corn stalk? Brinn wondered. "Good morning," she said tentatively. "Your stalk is very...noble, your tassels...silky. With your permission, may I pick some ears of your corn?" Brinn was startled when the whole patch of corn stalks started shivering and waving about.

Loris stomped through the potatoes to see what was happening. "Be quiet!" she shouted and the stalks stilled. Loris turned to Brinn. "What did you do to them?"

Confused at being scolded, Brinn looked down and murmured: "I was just asking them politely if I could pick some of their corn."

The stalks began to shiver again, and this time Loris joined them. "It's just corn," she said, laughing, "not the Duke of Fellicia."

Brinn turned beet red, realizing how silly she had been. Kaalla came to her rescue. The dragon appeared next to the rows of corn and looked tenderly down at Brinn. "The corn's purpose in life is to be food. All plants know this, most animals as well. It's the loop of life: plants grow to feed insects, birds, squirrels, and man; and in turn each of these provides food for others. We don't weep when the butterfly is caught by the sparrow, or the sparrow is fed to the fox kits. And though we weep when our loved ones die, their bodies are returned to the earth to become food for insects and plants, and the loop is complete."

Though this all made sense to Brinn there was still some confusion. "But I've seen Loris talking as she picks vegetables, and she seems to know when they're ripe."

It was Loris' turn to blush. "She likes to hear her own voice," Kaalla said with a smile, "no one else is listening. Loris has been gardening for *centuries*; she could tell if a radish was ripe from thirty yards."

Brinn felt foolish again. She turned again to the corn stalks and grasped a fat ear. She pulled it off quickly, waiting for some cry of pain from the stalk, but there was none.

"See? It's not offended that you have taken the fruit of its labor. Oh, it's true plants can speak, if you are patient enough to listen, but they will probably be more concerned with the weather or a weed creeping too close than with what you want to cut off them."

"What about animals? Aren't their thoughts more complex, like ours."

"Yes, and most of them would rather not be a source of food. But if you stop and take the time to ask permission to take their life, I'm sure they'd run away and you would have a very dull diet of plants. Certainly all life is precious, that's why it's not always easy to kill animals, including dragons and humans. Never take a life out of malice or for sport," Kaalla added seriously.

"If you are finished with the object lesson, I would like to get that oh-so-intelligent corn shucked and into a pot of boiling water." Loris bent and cut off a head of lettuce.

Chapter 12

The next morning, Brinn waited for Kaalla under the apple tree. She noticed more leaves on the ground than usual and remembered she had drawn energy from the magnificent tree the day before. She laid her hands on the rough bark. "I hope I haven't hurt you," she apologized to the tree.

To her surprise, Brinn felt a wave of golden energy flood through her hands. "Don't be silly, little one," the deep voice of the tree spoke slowly, "the days grow short and the frost begins to creep onto my leaves."

Brinn leaned against the trunk. "I was afraid I had taken too much energy from you."

A deep laugh filled Brinn's mind. "My roots run very deep, it would not drain my power to move a few rocks." The tree seemed to take a deep breath.

Brinn thought again about the day before and the corn. "Do you mind when we take your apples? Kaalla says it's the way of things."

The tree did not laugh at Brinn's innocent question. "If you enjoy eating my apples, then I am happy to share them with you. And despite what the dragon says, plants like to be acknowledged when you take from us. A simple 'thank you' is always appropriate."

Brinn turned and put her arms around the wide trunk. "Thank you."

A quick wind signaled Kaalla's arrival. "Good morning. Visiting with the apple tree, I see. She's very wise." Kaalla knelt down near Brinn. "Climb up, I found a nice meadow to practice our lesson."

Brinn took hold of a back spike and climbed up the offered leg. "Why aren't we working here?"

Kaalla leapt into the air. "Well, besides harming Loris' delicate sensibilities, I thought it would be safer if there were fewer obstacles around."

Brinn experienced a quick sucking of energy before blinking away from the space above the garden and into the blinding light above a field of grass. Brinn jumped off Kaalla as soon she set down. She felt a thrill of excitement and couldn't wait to get down and try instant travel by herself. She stood in the tall grass; an eerie feeling of being here before began to creep in on her. Brinn unconsciously looked around for the large flat stone. She couldn't keep from screaming when Kaalla touched her shoulder.

Bewildered, the dragon watched helplessly as Brinn raced through the grass, terrified. She gently looked inside the girl's mind to try and understand her sudden fear. The memory of Neesha's release and her mother's transformation came to life for Kaalla. Tears streamed down her face. No wonder the girl didn't want to talk about what had happened to her. She sunk into the grass, trying to think how she could help.

Brinn ran as fast as she could from the beast. She didn't look back, afraid that she would see her mother's eyes looking out at her from the monstrous face. The grass whipped and cut at her hands. Brinn tripped and fell to her knees. She lay flat, hiding in the green stalks.

"Get up! She's coming after you!" A voice whispered.

Brinn scrambled to her feet. She caught the sight of the horrible creature crouching in the grass. "She'll see me," Brinn said to the disembodied voice.

"I'll keep you hidden, trust me."

Brinn headed for the treeline. She felt the dragon's breath on her neck. In a panicked moment Brinn hastily drew in energy, aimed for a gap in the trees and disappeared. Thick darkness engulfed her. Agonizing moments passed but she didn't reappear in the trees. She heard a scream of frustration. Wherever she was, Brinn had gotten away from the beast. She was safe in the darkness.

Brinn wondered if she were in her own bed and this was just a nightmare. Maybe everything had been part of the nightmare: Talon, the caves, the dragons, the widows, Ittra...

"Me? A nightmare? That's not very flattering."

Brinn twisted around, squinting to see in the blackness.

"You are being very silly." A bright point of light shone in the darkness, growing larger as the crystal voice spoke. "What made you think this was the meadow where you released Neesha?"

"The grass...the breeze..." Brinn began to doubt herself.

"I've seen that meadow and it was nothing like this meadow." A tender touch warmed Brinn's mind. "Someone put that thought into your head. The aura was familiar..."

The light became a blinding flash. Brinn couldn't see for a moment. The darkness was gone; she was floating in a warm glow, the peaceful orange, yellow and pink of sunset. Her thoughts cleared, and the fear of the meadow faded.

"Come back now."

Brinn felt a gentle tug and found herself lying in a grassy field. Two dragons were standing over her. Brinn's heart jumped at the sight of Ittra. She sat up and realized what had happened, looked apologetically at Kaalla. "I don't know what made me panic like that. I'm sorry, I thought you were—"

Ittra put her paw on Brinn's shoulder. "It wasn't your fault. Someone was influencing you. We're just glad we didn't lose you. Transporting like that was very dangerous."

"Influencing me? I don't understand." Brinn got shakily to her feet, looking around.

"I have my suspicions." Ittra hissed. "I don't know how he knew you would be here. He may have been watching you for some time. The memory of what happened to your mother is still very fresh in your mind. It didn't take much to trigger a flashback."

"Who was it?" Brinn asked. "The one triggering those memories?" Ittra didn't say. Brinn tried to remember the voice that told her to run. She had heard that voice before. Keldric! It had been Keldric's voice urging her to leap to the woods. It was his style. Was he waiting for her there, or did he count on her not being able to reappear? Brinn suddenly thought of something. She looked at Ittra. "How did you get here?"

The queen smiled at the elderly widow. "Dear Kaalla called for me. You scared us both when you disappeared. We are lucky you didn't get a clear picture of wherever you were transporting to."

"But how did I get back? I was floating around in darkness until I saw a white light." Brinn looked up at Ittra. "That was you, wasn't it?" Ittra nodded. "You brought me back."

Kaalla stared at her queen. Was that true? Was this possible? She had heard of dragons 'leaping' when they were scared and getting lost in the Void. It was said that no one could find their way out of the utter blackness. How had the young queen found Brinn and brought her back?

Ittra saw the look on Kaalla's face. The elderly dragon suspected Ittra of doing the impossible. But the young queen did not dare reveal the secret powers she and Talon alone held. The only being who knew of these ancient powers was Talon, who had inherited those same powers when he received Magrid's spirit.

147

Ittra did what she had to do to protect the secret, she lied. "I saw the darkness in your mind," she told Brinn. "I replaced it with a picture of the meadow. You did the rest."

Brinn knew this was not entirely true, but did not question Ittra. She saw the answer seemed to comfort Kaalla. "Am I still in danger? Will you be taking me back to the caves?"

Ittra smiled but shook her head. "No. You will have to learn to handle the dangers that come your way. I do feel it's time for you to move on, though."

"But I haven't leaned everything Kaalla has to teach me. Who will help me?" Brinn knew that she sounded like a young child.

Kaalla laid a paw on Brinn's shoulder. "You are stronger than you realize. All you need is some fine tuning."

Ittra agreed. "I'll have Talon make arrangements with Fernley's man."

Brinn, no longer excited with her new powers, thought things was moving too fast. "I would feel better if I could finish the lesson Kaalla and I came here for."

The queen nodded. "I don't think you are in any danger of another, shall we say, panic attack. Keldric is not that stupid." She moved back and spread her wings. "Don't hesitate to call if you need me." Ittra rose into the air and blinked out of sight.

Brinn sighed heavily and turned to Kaalla. "This wasn't at all what I expected today. Thank you for taking care of me. I guess I'm going to have to learn to take care of myself from now on." She sighed again. "Shall we begin our lesson and hope for no further interruptions?"

Kaalla gave Brinn an encouraging smile and began explaining the dangers of instant transportation.

Brinn found that her overactive imagination came in handy when she had to hold a picture of her destination in her mind. She spent the next hour blinking in and out. She was relieved to find she spent no more than a few seconds in the blackness between thought and arrival. When Kaalla felt Brinn was ready, they attempted the more closed-in environment of the woods. By the time the air turned cool Brinn felt comfortable with her new ability.

When it was time to return home Kaalla didn't give in to Brinn's pleadings to relocate back to the cottage. "It's not polite to pop in on someone. Besides, I promised Loris I'd pick up something for supper." Brinn mounted and they rose into the air.

Brinn was half afraid Kaalla was going to swoop down and snatch a buck or cow and cringed when the dragon began to descend toward a cottage with numerous livestock milling around in corrals. Rather than grabbing a bull on the go, Kaalla set down close to the large cottage and rang a bell that hung from a post. Brinn's mouth watered at the smell of smoking meat in the air. A tidily dressed woman came out to greet them; she didn't seem at all surprised to see a dragon in her yard.

"Good evening Kaalla." the woman looked up at Brinn. "Good evening Miss. What can I get for you today? I have a lovely lamb leg, and Gillin's just mixed up a batch of sweet sausage. Butter was churned this morning, and bacon slabs came out of the smoke yesterday."

Brinn smiled at the idea of a dragon going to a butcher.

"Loris would like a ham and two pots of butter. I'll take a bag of goat cheese, if it's fresh," Kaalla added.

The woman scribbled the order down. "The hams are still smoking. Will Loris mind one of last week's?"

"No, not at all. Most of it will end up in a pot of beans anyway." The dragon and the butcher's wife laughed, both knowing how Loris cooked. "The cheese was pressed day before yesterday. Would you like plain or herb?"

"Herb, please. Did you want anything, Brinn?" Kaalla craned her neck to look back at Brinn.

"No, thank you."

The woman nodded and went back inside the cottage. She returned shortly with a large leather bag. "I put in some cracklings for the young miss." The bag was slung over Kaalla's neck. "Now don't let Loris overcook this fine ham, and take the salt jar away from her. Never known a woman so devoid of a sense of taste as that old crone. Oh, I put in some sweet cakes she's partial to as well; Gillin ate his fill at lunch."

Brinn felt a surge of magic from Kaalla. In payment for the food the dragon moved a heap of cow manure from the barn to the garden, several field-rocks were shifted to the growing wall, and the corrals had a fresh layer of straw. With the transaction complete Kaalla leapt into the air.

The sun was below the trees when Kaalla set down near the garden. Loris was sitting at the garden table, peeling pears. Brinn took the large leather bag from Kaalla and carried it into the cottage. She flopped down on her bed, weary from the events of the day. She didn't want to think about having to leave in the next few days. She was just beginning to feel at home here. It wasn't fair. Sadly, she changed her dress and joined Kaalla and Loris.

The rest of the evening was uncomfortably quiet. No one wanted to talk about Brinn's impending departure. Loris stomped around the kitchen when she discovered Brinn *adjusting* the cornbread batter. Kaalla despaired of getting a sweater finished for Brinn, and settled on knitting a scarf instead. Brinn was torn between depression over leaving and excitement for her future. After supper Brinn continued reading to Kaalla and Loris reworked a section of her needlepoint while nibbling on one of the sweet cakes.

Chapter 13

During the next few days Brinn put aside her lessons and did as much work around the cottage as Loris would let her. It was fun to see the different ways she could use magic in the everyday chores of gardening and cleaning. Brinn spent many hours talking to the ancient apple tree, chatting with the rose bushes, and receiving weather reports from passing clouds.

One afternoon, while wandering over the grassy hills around the cottage, Brinn heard the sounds of agonized screams. She transported herself to the top of a hill. The sight below was too horrible to believe! In the meadow below humans were being scooped up by a horde of young dragons. Their screams as the dragons spiraled high into the sky made Brinn's skin crawl. Other dragons were dropping rocks or boulders on pleading villagers and flying off to get more ammunition. Brinn couldn't take her eyes from the horror. When a man was viciously clawed by a diving dragon Brinn didn't care about her safety, she could not stand by and let this go on.

With a mighty yell, Brinn transported to the meadow. With a wave of her hand a descending dragon was thrown against the far trees. She ran to the injured man who didn't seem to notice the gash on his arm but waved away the dragons.

"Hold still!" Brinn tried to stop the blood while keeping the dragons at bay.

A huge purple dragon landed nearby and stomped across the grass. He didn't pay any attention to Brinn but rather shouted at the dragon hovering overhead. "Jegga! Why aren't you down here taking care of your human?"

The floating dragon shrugged his wings. "She won't let me, Nessig."

The purple dragon glared down at Brinn. "Is there a problem?" He said in perfect Humanish.

Brinn stood protectively over the injured man. "Dragons attacking humans? Yes, I'd call that a problem! I am a very close friend of the Krrig Daa, and I don't think he would approve of your actions here today."

A crowd had begun to gather. Brinn thought it curious the other humans weren't afraid of the dragons that had attacked them. "You aren't one of the trainees, are you?" The purple dragon took a closer look at Brinn, its head tilted after a moment. "You're that girl-wizard. What are doing out here? I can't vouch for your safety around these raw recruits. They might drop something on you."

Brinn was becoming more and more confused by the minute. "I heard screaming...this man has been wounded...dragons are dropping rocks..." She tired to sound reproachful but it wasn't coming out that way.

Numerous smiles and chuckles came from the crowd. Nessig glared at them. "What are you grinning at? Get back to work, wyrms!" The crowd scattered. "I'm sorry if you were unduly worried, just a bit of target practice."

"Target practice? With humans as the targets?"

The dragon laughed. "Yes, a bit unorthodox but oddly enough it's been great for human/dragon relations. We have no shortage of volunteers from the nearby towns."

"But humans as targets?" Brinn repeated herself.

Nessig thought this girl must be a bit light in the head, then he realized she had no idea what was really going on. He laughed. "You think we're...oh, that's funny. No. You see, there is a growing call for dragon-transport. The younglings are practicing picking up and delivering packages." He pointed out a young woman catching a bundle dropped by a passing dragon. "We are also perfecting a method of picking up and transporting humans. Oh, we get our injuries from time to time, like young Grigs there, but we are designing a suit that will protect the passenger from our sharp claws." The dragon leaned down and quickly cauterized the cut on the boy's arm with a thin stream of flame and sent a wave of healing energy into the injured limb. Grigs got shakily to his feet and rejoined the others.

Brinn stood and stared for a while. It was clear now this was no massacre, but organized training. Groups of humans were using sheets of canvas to catch large bundles, while others used hand signals to help orient the dragons. Some individuals worked one-on-one with a dragon. On the other end of the meadow a catapult was used to throw bundles into the air toward flying dragons. Sometimes it took a few tries before the humans or dragons on the receiving end caught their package. Brinn doubted this method would be used to carry fragile objects. The most unreal sight was that of the dragon swooping down and grabbing onto a leather-clad human. The screams she had heard before were really shrieks of laughter from the excited humans as they were lifted into the air. It all seemed to make sense now. "But why would anyone need to be picked up in such a hasty manner? Can't the dragons just land and pick up their passenger?"

"Oh sure, that's how it would work in most cases. Sometimes humans need to get someplace in a hurry, and since they can't fly...well, it's a service we can render. But there isn't always time or space for a dragon to land. This practice is mainly for messenger and delivery services."

Brinn saw the logic of the dragon's word and the potential benefits of such a service. "I feel more than a bit silly."

The dragon smiled. "Actually, it's rather commendable that one of your kind would care enough about someone else to make the effort. Most wizards would rather not get involved unless it's advantageous to them."

Brinn didn't know enough about other wizards to know if Nessig was stating fact or assumption, and she didn't really care. This whole affair had drained her. "I think I'll leave you to your training. If you see Talon anytime soon, please send my regards."

Brinn turned and walked back up the hill. After a few short 'hops' she was back in Loris's garden. She thought it would be best not to share the story of the afternoon's adventure with the widows. She picked the last of the peas and went inside to help with supper.

It was a few days before the next disaster struck. Brinn was helping with the late autumn harvest. The last of the lettuce and tomatoes were picked and their remaining greenery tossed onto a growing pile of limp vegetation. In the clear, crisp sky, an ominous dark cloud appeared. The gardening continued. Brinn was not afraid of a little rain, and she wanted to finish clearing the mustard greens.

The first suspicion that this was no ordinary storm cloud came when it settled over the garden, no longer moving with the breeze. It began to rumble, like an angry bear. A blinding bolt shot out of the black mass. There was no randomness to the direction of the lightning, it struck Brinn's basket. The sharp scent of scorched air mingled with the smell of charred lettuce.

Loris lay flat on the ground, hands pressed over her ears. Kaalla stared at the cloud. Brinn stepped away from the smoldering basket. The cloud shifted slightly, following Brinn. She could feel it drawing in energy. After another threatening rumbling a second lightning bolt singed the ground directly behind Brinn.

There seemed to be no doubt as to the evil cloud's intention. Brinn felt Kaalla draw in energy. "No! Get her out of here!" Brinn pointed to the prostrate Loris.

"I won't leave you." Kaalla stood protectively by the terrified old woman.

"I don't want Loris hurt." Brinn shouted. "I can handle this. Get her inside."

Brinn turned and faced the black cloud. She began softly humming a tune from Fernley's memory. She swished her cloak around her legs, raising a gentle swirl of dust. Brinn never took her eyes off the cloud as she paced back and forth in front of it. She felt the hairs on her arms stand up, and braced herself, hands out as if they pushed on an invisible wall. She closed her eyes tightly and mumbled a protective spell for her ears.

A bolt of lightning tore from the billowing mass and struck directly at Brinn. Her invisible wall held. Thunder boomed so loudly that even her protected ears rang with its intensity. The cloud rumbled its frustration at the ineffectiveness of the attack, drawing in energy for another strike.

Brinn filled her lungs and slowly blew out through pursed lips. The gentle breeze she had gathered around her took the hint and moved in the same direction as the exhaled breath. Brinn took a step toward the cloud, inhaled and again slowly exhaled. She could feel the wind gathering behind her.

The cloud felt it too. With each step the girl took, the wind followed and the cloud was pushed back. An inch...two...three. It sucked energy mercilessly from the ground, leaving a strip of burned grass. It didn't have time for a single strike. A dozen small lightning bolts flew out uncontrolled toward the advancing girl.

Brinn easily handled the charged streamers, deflecting, dodging, and absorbing their energy. The rumble of thunder was much less intense, a moan of aggravation. She began to slowly spin, twirling around and around. Her cloak opened and lifted with each turn. Again the accompanying wind followed Brinn's example and began to twist.

At the sight of the growing cyclone, the cloud began to panic. Rumblings became whimpers. It dared not retreat; its master would not accept defeat. The cloud made one last gasp for energy and lunged at Brinn.

Brinn was unprepared for the enveloping darkness, the whipping coldness, the encompassing static that pricked her and pulled at her hair. She could hear the wail of the twisting wind she had created and knew she would be caught in its path along with the black cloud. Brinn stumbled over a row of rocks and through a patch of flowers. Only a few feet to her left was the apple tree. She tried to reach it. Each step took great effort, and Brinn felt her strength fading. She stretched out her arms.

The cloud rumbled with laughter. If the wind was going to drive it off, the girl would meet the same fate, and the master would be satisfied. The cloud felt the intrusion of a solid object, a tree, and easily engulfed it.

Brinn cried out as her arm raked across rough bark. She twisted quickly and threw her arms around the chilled trunk. Her cyclone was nearing full strength. Leaves and twigs whipped madly around her, stinging her face and arms.

The cloud hung heavily around the girl, not wanting to release its prey. But it was quickly realizing the whirlwind was too strong to withstand. The darkness began to lighten as the cloud was drawn up into the forceful wind. It twisted and writhed, moaning at the futility of its struggle. With a blast of blinding light the cloud released the last of its built up energy. With a final thunderous moan it was blown out of existence.

Much of the wind went off to play in the autumn leaves, a few wisps stayed behind to play in Brinn's hair. Cold and burned by the blasting dust, Brinn clung to the supporting apple tree, accepting its generous offer of energy.

Kaalla found Brinn still embracing the tree. Her hair was a tangled mess; the blue robe was in shreds, her skin raw and bleeding. The dragon immediately transported them both to the cottage.

"How long should we let her sleep?"

"The coach will be here tomorrow. She can sleep until then."

"How did you know to come? I didn't get a chance to call for help. It all happened too quickly."

"A passing cumulus thought there was something wrong with a small thunderhead out this way. I came out to take a look."

"If we stand around here talking we'll wake this poor girl."

It was still dark when Brinn opened her eyes, groaned and hid her face in the pillow. She felt sore all over, which meant she was alive. She knew she was lucky. With slow, painful movements, Brinn stood and put on a robe. She gingerly turned the doorknob. The light in the outer room made Brinn squint. Kaalla was dozing over her knitting and Loris was kneading dough at the table. Someone was sleeping in the corner on a thick, quilted pad.

Loris rushed over and helped Brinn to a soft chair. "Tea and scones?" she asked softly.

Brinn nodded and gratefully accepted the warm mug. She ate and drank in silence, not wanting to wake anyone. It was nice just to sit and watch the old woman shaping the bread as she, herself, had done for so many years. Her fingers itched to push into the warm, soft dough.

Loris placed the trays of bread by the fire to rise, and poured Brinn another cup of tea. "You gave us quite a scare." She picked up a knife and pulled over a bowl of apples.

"I'm sorry, I thought it would be better to stand and fight. I didn't know what that thing might do to your home."

Loris handed a slice of peeled apple to Brinn. "Of course you had to take that abomination on. But you were so covered with scratches and bruises...and we didn't know if you'd broken any bones, or what might be wrong with your innards." Loris continued to peel apples. "It was quite impressive to see a slip of a thing like you standing in the middle of that whirlwind. I'll never forget the sight of those lightning bolts coming down all around you. I would have been scared to death."

Brinn was embarrassed at the woman's praise. "I did what I had to do. Nothing heroic about it." She looked out the window; there was no sign of the sky lightening into morning. "How long have I been asleep?"

"Since yesterday. That worried me a bit, too, but Talon said it would be good for you." She indicated the sleeping form in the dark corner. "Funny, he didn't seem too surprised by the whole thing."

Brinn glanced at the sleeping wizard. "He was probably warned by Queen Ittra to keep an eye out for trouble." She tried to be vague, she and Kaalla had decided not to tell Loris about the scare they had had at the meadow.

Loris huffed, "Then they should have kept a closer eye on you. Leaving a young girl like you alone with powerful enemies around...irresponsible, I say."

Brinn took up an apple and began peeling. "Apple pie tonight?" she asked, trying to change the subject.

"No. I thought I'd make up some apple muffins to send along with you. Talon said the coach will be here for you in the morning."

Brinn nodded. She could pack her few belongings before she went to bed. "I wonder how long the trip will take."

"Two days," Talon said, walking into the light of the fire. "The coach is well cushioned so you'll travel straight through the night, only stopping to change horses." He took a scone from the plate. "It'll be best if you can get settled into your house as soon as possible. There are certain protections built in to your new home that will give Keldric second thoughts about bothering you there."

"So Keldric was responsible for that cloud?" Brinn groaned. "Why is he so obsessed with me?"

Talon thought it would be insensitive to tell her Keldric was probably trying to kill her to gain her power, so he shrugged. "Who knows what's in that dark pit of a mind." Talon ran a hand through his hair.

"Well, I'm glad you and the Queen were looking after me."

Talon smiled proudly. "Oh, you handled that cloud all by yourself. I didn't get here until Kaalla had brought you in and Loris cleaned you up. I would have loved to have seen that fight. I've never heard of a thunder cloud being used as a weapon before."

"Lucky me to be the first," Brinn said flatly. "With such a cunning enemy, I'm surprised you're sending me out on my own."

Talon caught the twinkle in Brinn's eyes. "Oh, who could every desert such a poor defenseless creature?" He sipped his tea. "Don't forget you can contact me mentally."

Brinn could not get used to someone else's words suddenly forming in her mind; it was more intimate than a whisper. She had never tried it herself. "How do you direct the thoughts?"

"Everyone who has spoken to you mentally has left a...an imprint with their thoughts. *Think* of that person. Along with the visual picture and memory of their voice you will find their mental imprint. Direct your thoughts through that imprint." When he saw Brinn's face screw up in thought, Talon cautioned: "Don't yell."

Brinn closed her eyes and thought of Talon. In her mind she saw him as she had that first day at the inn: dressed in black, hair in stark contrast, noble. Surrounding the dark figure was a dark green glow. "What's it like to have dragon memories in your head?" she mentally asked Talon.

"It was strange at first. I had a hard time separating the human thoughts and emotions from the dragon ones. I have learned to shut off random memories from both Olwin and Magrid."

"Will I be expected to follow in Fernley's footsteps?"

"No, of course not. Take what you want from his life and leave the rest."

Loris banged a spoon on the table. "Alright you two, I know what you're doing and it's rude!'"

Brinn opened her eyes. "Sorry."

Talon smiled sweetly and put his arm around the elderly woman. "We didn't want to disturb your delicate sensibilities with wizarding stuff."

Loris playfully jabbed Talon in the ribs. "Delicate sensibilities indeed. No chance of that after living with Kaalla for fifty years."

"You've never been delicate, hag." Kaalla grumbled from her chair.

"This coming from a monstrous beast."

"Behave you two," Talon scolded.

There were no short goodbyes the next morning. Loris refused to even step out of the cottage until every corner had been searched; she was sure Brinn had forgotten some small item or other. Talon and Borda, Fernley's coachman, had time for breakfast while cushions were looked under and cupboard doors flung open. Kaalla said little between blowing her nose and suffocating Brinn in massive hugs. Borda had told Talon the roads were clear and dry, so they should make good time. After long goodbyes with hugs and promises of visits, Talon helped Brinn into the coach. He had explained why he couldn't come with her, but promised to come and see her as soon as his schedule lightened. Brinn waved out the coach window with one hand while the other wiped away tears.

Without the least bump or jostle, the coach moved onto the main road and picked up speed. Brinn snuggled into the familiar cushions. Though she had never seen this coach before, Fernley's memory of it was strong. Brinn ran her hand over the plush tan velvet that lined the walls and the darker brown cushions. There was only one soft bench seat; the other side of the compartment was taken up by a beautiful oak desk with paper and quills. She knew one drawer held a deck of cards and an assortment of finger puzzles to while away the hours. A shelf for books as well as various food items took the place of the second door. Fernley had spent a lot of time in this coach. He had even magiked it so the ride would be smooth and quiet.

Brinn took off the beautiful muffler Kaalla had given her and hung it on a coat hook. The box of apple muffins was stored on the bookshelf along with a jar of chilled tea. For a while she looked at the scenery passing by the window. She smiled at the thought that only a few weeks ago she had never been farther away from home than the butcher's shop on the far end of the village. Most girls would be frightened at the prospect of going out into the world on their own, but Brinn was not like *most* girls. The knowledge that she was heading into the unfamiliar thrilled her. Up until now there had been someone close by to catch her if she fell.

Now she was on her own. Or at least as much as anyone could be with a head full of memories from a 260-year-old wizard. There were adventures ahead, and Brinn was heading toward them at a full gallop.

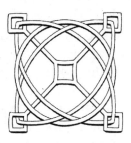

Chapter 14

It was nearing dusk on the second day when the coach slowed and mingled with the traffic entering the town of Enoa. Brinn looked out the window. She was a bit disappointed when she saw similar blacksmith and butcher shops as in her own village, though they were a bit better kept. As they moved further into town, Brinn saw others differences: more people, more buildings, and more traffic. They turned onto a side street and headed to the outskirts of town where the coach stopped in front of a beautiful mansion. Brinn stared at the neatly stacked stone wall, tidy rose bushes, lush green grass, and welcoming bay windows. This was *her* home!

Borda opened the door and stood aside. "Welcome home, Miss."

Brinn stepped out. She wanted to rub her numb bottom, but didn't think it appropriate at this moment. She shook out her cloak, stepped up to the door, and raised her hand to the knocker. Before she could lift the brass horse-head, the door opened and a tall, dark-clothed man stood in the entrance. Brinn instantly knew his name. "Good evening, Grindle. I'm Brinn."

The grim face smiled and the man stood regally aside. "Welcome, Young Miss. I have been expecting you."

Brinn stepped into the warm house and immediately felt at home. From the bright glow of the candles to the ornate rugs and gleaming wood floors, she instantly fell in love with the ordinariness of it. She had never lived in a *normal* house; her father had always run the inn. Talon's cave had been comfortable, but it was still stone and dirt. The widows' cottage had been cozy, but the conflicting sizes of everything had been hard on the eyes. This...Brinn touched the hall table...this was home.

Grindle quietly shut the door and Brinn followed him into the parlor. "I'm sorry I was not immediately able to welcome you to your new home when Master Fernley passed on. Pressing family matters took me away, as I explained to Master Talon."

Brinn wanted to touch each cushioned chair, pick up each knick-knack, and gaze at each painting. Fernley's memories of lounging in this chair, or purchasing that landscape, or receiving the porcelain rose from the Count of Reabone filled Brinn's mind. She purposely shoved the wizard's memories aside. She didn't want them intruding on her own impressions. She turned to Grindle. "There was no inconvenience. I had a nice visit with a pair of very interesting elderly widows but I would like to freshen up and have a bite to eat, if I may."

Grindle bowed. "This way, Miss." He led her back to the entryway and picked up her travel bag. "I have put you in the guestroom adjoining the master suite." They ascended the wide staircase. "I thought you would want to make any decisions on the redecoration of your rooms."

"Thank you." She followed behind the straight back.

The butler walked slowly down the hall past a number of doors. There was a large door at the end of the hall. Grindle opened a smaller one near it. He stepped aside to allow Brinn to enter first.

This was more than a simple guest room. There were signs that someone had spent a lot of time here. Perhaps a family member or a very close friend. Brinn did not search the wizard's memories. A door on the far side of the room connected to the master suite.

"Tea will be waiting for you in the study." Grindle quietly closed the door.

Brinn was glad to be out of her traveling clothes and slipped into one of the robes Talon had given her. She took a minute to look out the window at a small garden. She saw the ivy trellis needed some trimming and some weeds had grown between the paving stones. Fernley had tending this garden himself. She looked forward to repairing the neglect.

In the study, a tray of delicious-looking treats was set on a low table before a crackling fire. Brinn nibbled on a cookie while she wandered around. Clusters of cozy chairs were softly lit with small chandeliers. Among the chairs were low tables with curious knickknacks and interesting-looking books. A large desk dominated the room. Exploring it, she found the drawers were jammed with scraps of paper, scribbled notes, books, drawings, and a rainbow of inks and pens. Brinn smiled, you could tell a lot about someone by the condition of their desk. This desk was neatly arranged on the top but a disorganized muddle inside. Deep down, her predecessor was a slob and either he hid it well by being outwardly tidy or he had a very well trained staff. Brinn decided she needed to have a talk with Grindle. Seeing a bell pull near the fireplace, Brinn gave it a tug. In less than a minute of hearing a soft bell-tone, Grindle opened the study door.

"Yes, Miss?"

"Come in, please." Brinn sat down near the fire and motioned the butler to sit with her. "I think we should have a talk."

Grindle smiled and sat across from his new mistress. "Yes. How may I be of assistance?"

Brinn considered for a moment, trying to form her thoughts into words. "What do you know about me?" She knew it was a weak question.

The butler folded his hands. "Master Talon informed me of your ascension. I don't know much about you, personally, but I know what you *are*." He smiled, to Brinn's relief. "I have worked for Master Fernley my whole life, as did my father and his father.

170

My daughter will, if she pleases you, take over when I retire."

"Who else knew Fernley was a wizard?" Brinn wondered if all wizards were as open about their occupation as Talon obviously was.

"It would be hard to keep a secret like that for long. It's not openly talked about, but was known."

"And me?"

"That will be up to you, Miss. I have made it known around town that the Master has passed on, and his niece has come to take possession. I imagine that after a few decades you won't be able to hide the knowledge of what you are. If you choose to make your power public you will find most of the townsfolk will think nothing of it. Only the newcomers will come to bother you with petty requests. I can handle *them* for you."

Brinn nodded, she had decided to keep her abilities quiet for the time being. She inquired about the more mundane topics of the running of the house. Brinn was more than pleased to find out Grindle was in charge of all the household staff: a cook, maid, stableboy, and Grindle's daughter. She was just too young for that responsibility. Brinn thanked the butler for his help.

The rest of the evening was spent reading Fernley's diary. Brinn had found the book while rummaging through the desk. She much preferred reading through his written thoughts to having them pop into her head. Brinn discovered the old man spent much of his last days collecting nursery rhymes from small villages. He wrote about children coming to hear him tell stories and farmers coming to ask for help with infestations of mice or the sickliness of a prize sow. Brinn saw that this wizard's daily life was much the same as anyone else's. There were no great battles of good versus evil, no dramatic works of magic to save a damsel from being eaten by ogres, no earthly catastrophes averted. Much of his life was spent in the pursuit and telling of histories and legends. Brinn hoped her life would not be so dull.

The next few days were spent roaming through the house. There was a parlor for visitors, a library with walls of books, a huge dining room with sheets on the chairs and crystal chandeliers, a large hall where Fernley would read historic tales to small audiences, and a tidily kept kitchen and pantry.

In the attic, Brinn found an assortment of furniture. With the help of Grindle and the stableboy, she spent a whole day redecorating the master suite and adding her own touches to the study and library.

Brinn felt most at home in the cozy kitchen, sitting next to the large cooking fire. She spent many hours peeling carrots and listening to Cook's gossip. With Cook's permission, Brinn began to eat her meals at the well-scrubbed kitchen table.

When the weather permitted, Brinn enjoyed working in the garden. She spent hours clearing away the weeds, cutting back ivy, and preparing the flowerbeds for winter. One week after her arrival, while Brinn was carrying an armload of dead marigolds, her first visitor arrived.

Grindle politely cleared his throat and announced Mr. Martek Willit, Mayor of Enoa.

Brinn held back a grunt of frustration, she had been enjoying her peaceful pruning. She bowed politely and tossed her armload onto a smoldering pile. "Good afternoon, sir."

The fancy-dressed man bowed low. "I am very honored that you can take time out of your day to see me, Mistress Brinn."

Brinn motioned for the mayor to sit on a small stone bench. She knelt down next to her flowerbed. "How may I help you?"

Willit blew on his hands and rubbed them together as if he were feeling chilled. "Actually, Mistress, I have come to offer *my* assistance to *you*." He paused, waiting for that grateful look he had come to expect from his offers of help, but the silly girl kept pulling up dead flowers. "It must be a great sorrow to have lost such an influential uncle. At this time of uncertainty, I feel it my duty to offer my experience and support. As a newcomer to our town you will want to have a connection to the highest levels of society, to have someone who can introduce you into more elite gatherings. Since your uncle, all honor to his memory, cannot lead you through the quagmire of our society, I feel a responsibility to take up the task." The mayor puffed himself up. He was pleased with his little speech and expected the young girl to clutch him in gratitude. He was disappointed.

Brinn had a death-grip on the handful of daisy stems; she would have rather had her hands around the neck of the insufferable egotist. She contemplated lifting him into the air and shaking him mercilessly. Brinn took a deep breath. The idiot was waiting for her show of appreciation. She tilted her head and batted her eyelashes innocently. "Oh, you are too kind to a poor little orphan." Brinn threw her arms around the blue velvet shoulders. "I don't know what I would do without your generous support." She rubbed the browned flowers into the cringing back. "I'm just a poor country girl with no experience in the niceties of town life." Brinn kissed the mayor's cheek and stood up, scuffing mud on the glossy black shoes. "Thank you for your kind offer."

Willit stood, his hands longed to brush the dirt from his clothes but civility kept them still at his sides. He bowed slightly. "You have but to call upon me." He turned and escaped.

Brinn muffled her laughter. How long before the fool noticed the wilted flower in his hair?

The next day Brinn went to town with Grindle's daughter. Celisa drove the small horse cart at a steady, responsible pace. Goats and dogs seemed to have the right of way. If the girl wasn't so sweet, Brinn would have lost her temper and jerked the reins out of her hands. Only two years older than Brinn, Celisa had a serious, even-temperament and very little imagination. She would grow up to be just like her father.

Brinn had hoped to walk to town alone and roam around the shops but Grindle informed her that a respectable female would never go out unaccompanied. Celisa volunteered to be her escort. As they drove through the streets, Brinn did not see one 'lady' strolling the walkways on her own. There were the occasional maid, or shopkeeper's daughter walking alone but it was very evident that women here did not have the freedom Brinn was used to.

Celisa patiently followed along as Brinn browsed a few of the shops. Brinn didn't mind the company, but insisted on carrying her own packages. Too many times Brinn found herself the target of well-meaning, over-dressed dames of society who wanted to make her acquaintance. Like the Mayor, these ladies wanted to offer their sympathy and assistance in introducing her to society. They wanted to be on her good side in case she had her uncle's gift and could grant their wishes or curse their families. Brinn thought it best to humor them. Invitations for dances and recitals were extended and Brinn made vague promises to possibly accept. One very persistent dame cornered Brinn at the candlemaker's shop, intent on securing her as a guest at a formal dinner party. When Celisa caught Brinn's look of desperation the young lady created an excuse and politely rushed Brinn away.

"Thank you. I don't think I could stand hearing about one more luncheon party. Do those women think of anything but social events and who is wearing what?"

Celisa smiled; she liked this girl. "Just wait, when they get you alone they will fill your ears with the most dreadful gossip about everyone else's bad relations and marital strife."

Brinn linked her arm in Celisa's. "Maybe I should just snub them all and become an outcast."

The girls continued their shopping. Brinn found many shops she would like to return to when she had more time. One bookstore caught her attention. It was elaborately lit and had rows upon rows of high shelves filled with books of all shapes and colors. Plush chairs surrounded small tables where cocoa and cookies were served by a dour lady who picked up abandoned volumes. Brinn found another store she would come back to later that sold scented lotions and bath oils and a rainbow of candles. Somehow Brinn didn't think Celisa would approve of a long soak in lavender bubbles. There were more than a few doors Celisa steered Brinn away from; dark, mysterious shops a *respectable* girl would never enter. Brinn decided to return without her chaperone to explore their depraved depths.

Celisa returned them to the mansion before the sun set, as was proper and would please her father.

Brinn's days settled into a comfortable routine. Her mornings would be spent reading through Fernley's extensive library. Some books felt like old companions, others were stiff and unfriendly. She insisted on reshelving them herself rather than let Grindle pick up after her. After an informative lunch with Cook, Brinn went down into Fernley's workroom.

Brinn easily found the section of paneling that held the secret switch to open the hidden door. She didn't think she would ever get used to walking through the wall. Brinn enjoyed her hours of magical experimenting. She found the curved shape of the room was perfect for gathering energy. Each day Brinn chose one of the many spellbooks from the shelves or a scroll from one of the small cubbies along the walls.

She quickly learned that when she skimmed passed the tongue-twisting, antique words and studied the content and context of the spells, there was amazing power in the pages. There seemed to be no realm of magic that had not been studied in great detail by one wizard or another, from the mundane farm-related magic to the intricacies of emotional manipulation.

Brinn leaned toward the physical manipulation of energies. It was just too much fun to watch a bowl or book fly across the room. Through hours of concentration, Brinn learned how to keep a cup of tea floating near the ceiling while bringing a log from the pile outside to the fireplace, and sweeping broken glass from the floor.

After her experience with the storm cloud, Brinn thought it might be a good idea to study weather magic. She found numerous volumes dealing with moving clouds, coaxing rain, diverting snowstorms, and controlling winds. The garden offered her ample opportunity for experimentation. She was a bit surprised to find clouds gathering around the garden to see what was going on. One particularly black cloud took offense at having its moisture commandeered to water the ivy-covered trellis. It rumbled irritably and shot a small lightning bolt at the offending greenery before storming off. After a warm-air current objected to being diverted to keep some late blooming crocuses from freezing, twisting itself into a cyclone and breaking two windows, Brinn came to the decision that she needed to be more polite to the wind, the clouds and the sun, and not use with them to satisfy her curiosity.

As winter brought an end to lazy days in her garden, Brinn found herself trapped inside in the company of empty headed young women and unimaginative young men. It was beyond Brinn's comprehension as to what their parents wanted from her. She was being very careful to be non-influential in all matters. She even had the parlor redecorated in austere simplicity, to give the impression that she had not, in fact, inherited the supposed fortune that brought them calling.

One particular afternoon pushed Brinn to the brink of rudeness. She had been learning to handle fire when Grindle tapped apologetically on the paneling. Madam Vorcha had arrived for tea. Brinn had put the invitation out of her mind, and now it was too late to pretend she had come down with some contagious disease. The guests had been shown into a gloomy parlor. Brinn had taken great pains to decorate the room to be as unappealing as possible, thus encouraging unwanted visitors to take their leave as soon as civility would allow. When Brinn entered the chilly parlor, she really did feel sick. Madam Vorcha had five sons ranging in age from ten to twenty-five and they were all standing uncomfortably along one wall, as if waiting for execution.

The maid brought in the tea tray and quickly escaped. Brinn served the cloyingly sweet tea and plain cakes (Cook would not allow her new mistress to serve stale or bland cakes; she *did* have her reputation to think of, after all). The Vorcha sons looked awkward sipping from tiny teacups and handling the dainty forks. Brinn barely held back a giggle when the youngest made a face at the too-sweet tea (Momma was a bit lax in his training). Madam Vorcha made no attempt at small talk, to which Brinn was thankful; what response does one make to the comment that the new style of hats made one's head look like a menagerie? No, the stately dame got straight to the point of her visit. One by one the abilities and intelligence of each Vorcha son was cataloged. The boys shifted uneasily or rolled their eyes with each intimate detail.

No matter what Brinn did, the woman would not stop her recitation. Brinn wandered around the room, shifting oddities on their shelves, thumbing through dull histories, arranging wilted flowers.

Eventually Madam Vorcha came to the end of her monologue. Her next question startled Brinn, "Which one catches your fancy?"

Could it be that this over-dressed goose expected her to choose a husband from one of her sons? Brinn didn't know whether to laugh at the woman or slap her face. "I am not looking for a suitor, Madam Vorcha. I don't know how you came to that conclusion." Brinn said firmly, but the woman was oblivious.

"Of course you are, my dear. Every female past the age of five is looking for a husband." She waved away Brinn's astonished look. "I understand that you are still grieving for the loss of your dear uncle. I'm not implying that you should set a wedding date for anything earlier than six months, but these things take time to plan. So, if you don't mind some advice..."

"Oh, by all means."

Madam Vorcha didn't catch Brinn's sarcasm. "I think that Gollin would suit you just fine." She pointed to her third son, who was picking his teeth with the tea fork. "He's a well-behaved boy, not too controlling, and is competent at handling money matters."

Brinn looked at the skinny boy who couldn't be more than a year older than she. He smiled apologetically, his face a bright red. Brinn turned to confront the insufferable woman but the look on the pointy face showed she would not easily accept 'no' from Brinn. There would be no getting out of this situation without being rude. Brinn mentally scrambled for some way out. She could faint, or have a seizure, or create a cyclone to tear the house down, but Brinn had the uncomfortable feeling that these would not budge Madam Vorcha at all. Brinn did the only thing she could think of. She poured some tepid tea and offered another piece of cake to the skinny, offending woman.

Madam Vorcha picked up her plate and came face to face with a pair of pink eyes and long whiskers. The tiny creature let out a squeak, which was instantly drowned out by Madam's own shriek and the crashing shatter of the plate as it hit the floor. She picked up her teacup, hoping to steady her nerves, and found a little black mouse lapping from the rim. Another screech and the teacup joined the plate. Two more mice snuck out from under the couch to nibble on the fallen cake. Madam Vorcha scrambled away, clutching at Gollin. Brinn leaned down and picked up a stunned mouse, rubbing under its chin.

"I...have...NEVER..." Madam caught her breath. "I will not allow any son of MINE..." She reached for her hat and shook off the mouse chewing on the brim. "We are LEAVING," she announced to her sons.

The boys quickly followed after their indignant mother. The youngest boy remained behind for a moment. He pulled out a small brown mouse from his pocket and smiled knowingly. "My mouse's name is Nibblet. Can he have a piece of cake too?"

Brinn was pleased to see her social calendar clear.

Chapter 15

The entertainments of town and her studies should have been enough for Brinn. But she longed for the adventures she read about in so many of Fernley's books. There was only so much magic she could learn from books and scrolls. By the end of the year, Brinn believed she had reached her full strength and longed to get out in the world and see what it held for her.

Brinn wanted to visit with other wizards and to see the other dragon colonies Graldiss had talked about. She thought about going to see Ittra and Talon but during their long-distance talks Ittra told Brinn that Talon was seldom in the caves; his life as the Krrig Daa kept him busily moving between castles, cities, and colonies. Ittra discouraged Brinn from returning to Crinnelia, the heavy snows had driven most of the dragons to winter near the volcanic mountains across the ocean.

The answer to Brinn's boredom came in the form of a letter. A wizard named Barkin wrote that he would be honored if she would visit his estate. He had spoken to Talon and was fascinated by a female inheriting power and wanted to document her abilities. Brinn accepted his invitation with the promise of a visit when the snows melted.

The snow melted away two weeks later and the ground had thawed enough for the crocuses to peek through the mud. Brinn made plans for her trip, sending word that she would arrive within the week. Barkin provided directions and arrangements were made for the coach stops along the route.

Brinn was glad to be on her way. She imagined herself riding off to great adventure. Would the coach be stopped by robbers or break down and leave her stranded to be rescued by a dark-haired rogue? Would Keldric show up with some nefarious plot to steal her power? When the miles went by with never-ending drab, all hope for adventure faded. Brinn occupied the long, boring hours reading the books she'd chosen to bring along and floating quill pens around the coach compartment. The only excitement to break the boredom came when the coach wheel got stuck in the mud. Borda insisted that he could handle the problem if Mistress would just wait by side of the road for a few moments. It was on the fourth day of monotony that adventure found Brinn.

Just as the coach topped a hill, Brinn was thrown back against the cushions by a powerful emotional blast. She couldn't tell where it was coming from, the trees along the road, or further up the hill. Another wave of horror and mental anguish struck and Brinn screamed.

"Stop! Stop...pull over!" Frustration, anger, pain, terror! Brinn tried to take a breath. Borda pulled the coach door open and looked in on his mistress. Brinn grasped the doorframe and dragged herself out of the coach.

The coachman went to his mistress' side. "What's wrong? Are you ill? We will reach the nearest village in just a few hours."

"No, I'm not ill," Brinn said with false calmness. "I just need to stretch me legs. Please see to the horses, I'll be back shortly." She went into the woods next to the road.

Once hidden in the trees, Brinn grabbed her head, trying to shut out the mental screaming and think clearly. She staggered through the trees. Someone was in terrible danger, fighting for their life. Brinn fought to locate the injured party. She quickened her pace and the anguish grew and soon broke through the treeline. She leaned on a tree for a moment to take in the scene before her.

Three dragons hovered in the air above a large bear. Each dragon took turns swooping down on the poor beast, swerving away within inches of it. One vicious dragon dove down and singed the bear's fur. With so many attackers the bear was confused and stood paralyzed, howling helplessly.

Brinn relocated herself to the bear's side. "Go away!" she shouted to the dragons who hovered above, surprised at her appearance.

"Who is this?" one dragon asked.

"A little wizard," the second answered.

The third dragon swooped down. "This is *our* lunch, go find your own." His words were Humanish.

"You're not hunting this animal, you're terrorizing it," Brinn shouted back. "Go find lunch somewhere else."

"What did it say?" the first, sleek orange dragon asked the smaller blue one.

"I say we eat *it* first," said the second, a smooth red dragon.

"Go away," the blue said to Brinn. "You'll only get yourself hurt."

"You will not touch either of us!" Brinn pulled in energy and began to form a protective spell.

The orange dragon dove at Brinn. But instead of a soft, furless mouthful, he found himself chewing a thorn bush.

With a flick of her wrist, Brinn sent the attacking dragon to the other side of the field. While she wove thought and energy together the second dragon flew down, claws menacingly bared. Brinn spread her arms in a circle and an invisible bubble formed. The red dragon slammed into the barrier.

Again and again the two dragons tried to reach their prey. They could not believe that a *human* had outsmarted them. They clawed and flamed, and threw

185

themselves at the invisible wall. Brinn waited for the third dragon to attack but he drifted above, making no move to follow his companions.

The bear did not realize that it was safe from the horrendous flying beasts and panicked when it saw one attacking. Again it tried to run but found itself trapped. The bear turned and slashed out at the oncoming dragon, but it was Brinn who felt the sting of its blow. The smell of blood and fear was heavy within the enclosed space, and the bear went berserk, attacking Brinn.

From above, the small blue dragon saw the disaster and swooped down. He pushed away his companions, who thought the scene was entertaining. "Break the spell!" he shouted, but the girl was too far gone to hear him. He madly searched for some way to get through the bubble. His only hope was that the foolish young human had only drawn the spell down to the ground. He began to dig and found he could get under the invisible wall. He was amazed that even in her current state, this girl wizard was still holding the spell together. Luck was with him; the bubble was stiff and he easily flipped it over.

Brinn's mind was muddled. She hadn't been paying attention to the bear; she hadn't thought it would hurt her. She vaguely realized that the dragons had stopped trying to get through her protective shield, but no longer cared. Brinn could feel the grass delight at the gift of her energy flowing onto it, but the grass became greedy and wanted more than Brinn's blood. She was too weak to help herself. She didn't even notice when her shield was thrown off.

"Why did you have to do that, Agnar? It was just getting fun." The red dragon flew after the escaping bear.

Agnar paid no attention to Draega. He gently lifted the young girl and turned her over in his arms.

"What are you going to do with it?" the orange dragon asked. He tentatively licked the bloody grass. "Ick! Wizard blood; nasty stuff."

Agnar gently blew out a controlled flame and cauterized two bleeding gashes on the girl's arm. "And just how would you know the difference between human blood and wizard blood, Telis?"

The orange dragon spit to clear his mouth of the bad taste. "Just do, that's all. Wizard blood tastes sour. You know, like some of those nasty cheeses humans make. Bussil told me all about it. Her mother's uncle knew someone from Sturrik Colony who bit off a wizard's leg and almost died from stomach poisoning."

Brinn stirred weakly and Agnar held her close to keep her from falling. "Sure, whatever you say." He spread his wings and gently lifted into the air.

"Hey! Where are you taking that?" Telis launched into the air and caught up with Agnar. "You aren't thinking of bringing it back with us, are you? Because you can't. Besides, she'll probably die before we get home."

Agnar knew Telis was right. The girl was close to death but he couldn't just leave her there to die. There was something strange about this girl. She was a wizard, for one thing. He had never known a wizard who hadn't been a man. And there had been something about her courage had struck Agnar. He let some of his own energy flow into the limp body. Draega flew in front of Agnar making him swerve, trying to divert his attention away from the girl.

"You aren't going to keep it all to yourself, are you, Agnar? We always share our kill." Draega licked his lips.

"No," Telis answered, "Agnar's bringing it home to be a *pet*." Draega and Telis laughed and flew off ahead of Agnar and his burden.

Carefully but swiftly, Agnar flew toward the coastline.

Brinn woke to the sounds of ocean waves and seagulls. It was dark and cool. She sat up slowly, every muscle in her body was sore. With great effort she created a small ball of light. She was definitely in a cave, but it didn't seem to be naturally formed as the caves in Crinnelia had been. The stone walls bore signs of scraping. A distasteful odor hung in the air. Brinn enlarged the lightball. She saw that she was lying on a large pile of furs. There were two similar piles on the other side of the cave. A heap of ashes and charcoal near the opening of the cave indicated a firepit. Close to the pit lay a mound of bones and partially eaten carcasses. The smell of decaying flesh was almost too much for Brinn to handle. She moved her gaze to a dark area of the cave. A glint of metal caught her attention and she sent out the lightball to see what it was. Brinn screamed when the light revealed the mangled form of an armored knight. She hurried out from under the furs and vomited. Her light faded and she lay once again in the darkness.

Brinn's thoughts ran between terror and confusion. She tried to remember what had happened after she formed the protection barrier. She had felt superior. She had thwarted the dragons' cruel game but something went wrong. She hadn't been paying attention to the bear. It had pushed her to the ground and wouldn't let her up. Brinn reached back to touch her shoulder where she remembered feeling claws slash. She gasped at the dampness felt there. After a moment she calmed down. It was not the dampness of blood, but of salve she felt. She felt her leg and hip. More salve covered gashes from the attack. She tried to remember what happened after the bear had attacked her, but she could only recall glimpses of dragons. They weren't much taller than she was. A blue dragon had carried her away. Later a larger yellow dragon gave her something sweet to drink. The two other dragons from the clearing seemed to remain in the background.

Brinn heard voices and hid behind the furs. She recognized the voices as the three dragons who had attacked the bear. They were arguing about something but she couldn't understand their words. They did not speak in the dialect of Dragonese she had heard while living with Talon. They must have brought her to their cave. Did they intend the same fate for her as the ripening knight? No, if they had meant to kill her why, bring her here and heal her wounds? She heard them enter the cave and pulled some furs over herself.

"It smells in here." Telis put his paw over his nose. He waved a claw and several torches flared to life. "Couldn't you find somewhere else to keep it?"

Agnar paid no attention to his friend. Queen Betto had approved of his rescuing the girl and bringing her to the caves. He knew much of his friends' complaints were bluster. After they saw the attention the wizard got from their Queen, the two dragons were just as protective of the new pet as Agnar was.

"Ewww, it barfed!" Telis pointed toward Agnar's bed.

Agnar rushed to his fur pile. He panicked when he did not see Brinn.

"I'm not cleaning that up," Telis said, moving to the far side of the cave. He waved his wings to air out the stench.

"She's fallen off," Draega said, pointing to an exposed leg.

Agnar pulled aside the fallen furs, and saw the girl looking up at him. "Be calm," he said in Humanish. "We will not harm you."

Brinn sat up slowly. "Where am I?" she asked in the Dragonese dialect she knew.

"You are in the cliffs of Pallan." The blue dragon said softly. "You are safe."

"What happened to me?" Brinn gently touched her wounded arm.

"You were stupid and shut yourself in with a bear," Telis said with a smirk.

Brinn stood up shakily and boldly faced the dragons. "You were terrorizing the poor beast. I may have been foolish, but you left me little choice."

Draega dropped a fresh deer carcass on the fire pit. "You could have relocated the thing out of range," he said offhandedly. "You know, we *are* meat eaters."

"Does that include humans?" Brinn pointed to the armored corpse.

"This old thing?" Draega batted the suit of armor with his tail. The rusted metal hit the wall with a hollow clang. "It's just a little knick-knack Telis keeps around." He pulled off a moose hindquarter and placed it on the now lit fire. "But we *do* hunt live animals for our food."

Brinn's stomach rumbled at the smell of cooking meat. She sat down on the bed of furs and took a deep breath. "I don't call what you were doing to that bear *hunting*."

Telis grunted, "What's it to *you* how we hunt? So we were having a bit of fun. No one asked you to get involved."

Agnar put himself between Telis and Brinn. "How are you feeling? You've been unconscious for quite some time."

Brinn turned her gaze to the blue dragon, who was the smaller of the three. While the other two dragons

191

had intricately curled horns and smooth backs, the blue dragon had small back spines and was hornless. His ears were larger and frilled, not small and pointy. He resembled the dragons from Ittra's colony. "I'm a bit stiff, but my wounds seemed to have healed."

"Thanks to Livia's magic," Draega said flatly.

"Our healer is very skilled," Agnar explained. "She has studied with the wizard, Barkin, and understands human anatomy very well. She used a sleeping spell to help you to heal."

"And stopped your whimpering so we could get some sleep."

Agnar glared at Telis. The blue dragon opened his claws and an apple appeared in his palm. "You must be hungry." Brinn gratefully took the apple. "I am called Agnar, the rude one is Telis and the bottomless stomach is Draega."

Brinn watched Draega toss the roasted hindquarter into his mouth as if it were a mere tidbit. Telis was sulking on his bed. "I am Brinn. I can't thank you enough for saving me."

"Well, it was partly our fault," Agnar said.

"*Our* fault?!" Telis thundered. "She was the one who stuck her nose in where it wasn't wanted. If it had got chomped off, it wouldn't have been *my* fault." He bit off a chunk of meat.

"Oh, let it go, will ya," Draega said to Telis. "You've been complaining for a week. It's not like it's been a hardship on you. Agnar has done all the work."

Telis said something Brinn could not understand but it was very clear that the dragon did not approve of Brinn's presence. "The sooner she's out of here the better," he said and stormed out.

Draega brought a small chunk of meat to Brinn. "Don't pay any attention to Telis. He was caught by young humans when he was a hatchling. They tried to pull off his wings and tied him to a rope so he couldn't fly away. Of course it ended tragically with the accidental burning down of the boys' cottage. Telis hated humans ever since."

Brinn pictured the terrified young dragon, huddled in a crate with dirty boys poking it with sticks. She felt guilty for her whole species. "Then it would be best if I don't stay here long." She tried to stand but found her legs too shaky to hold her up and she sat heavily on the fur bed.

"I don't think you're ready to go anywhere." Agnar gently eased Brinn down into the furs and pulled one up around her chin. "Telis will have to put up with your presence a while longer or he can move out." The mess Brinn had made disappeared. "Livia would flay us if we let you out of this cave before you were fully healed." The lit torches dimmed. "Rest for now."

Agnar sat down by fire and the two dragons spoke quietly for a while before Draega left the cave. Agnar lay down near Brinn's bed and watched over her as she slept.

Brinn woke several times during the night. She heard the deep breathing of the dragons and decided not to make a lightball. She stared into the darkness, thinking about her hosts. Was this colony like the one she had stayed with before? Agnar was comfortable with a human around, and Draega at least tolerated her, but how many of the colony had the same feelings as Telis? Even in Ittra's colony there had been a number of dragons that objected to her presence.

Brinn also thought about how Grindle would take her disappearance. She was sure the butler was used to odd behavior from wizards, but he had kept such a close eye on her since she had arrived at Fernley's house, and he might be worried about her. And how long would Borda have waited for her? Did he search for her and panic when he saw the bloodstained grass? Or would he, too, expect odd behavior from his employer? Would Grindle try to contact Talon to let him know something had happened to her and would Talon come to rescue her? Brinn hoped she could get herself out of this mess before that happened.

Brinn woke quickly when she felt someone pull back the fur blankets. She looked up into the dark eyes of a large, yellow dragon. Brinn tried to move away from the massive jaws but a paw held her firmly.

"Be still," the dragon said in a calming voice. "You don't want to open your wounds." A nicely manicured claw probed for any tender areas on Brinn's arms and legs. "Agnar informed me that you had regained consciousness last night. I had hoped that you would stay asleep a few more days, but it seems you have a stronger will than most of my patients." The dragon rolled Brinn over and checked the wounds on her back.

Brinn didn't have a chance to speak.

"Queen Betto was quite surprised. She contacted the other queens to see if any of them knew about you." A gentle claw brushed a fresh scar.

Brinn felt an odd sensation of magic being used on her. She wanted to resist, but considered the size of the dragon healing her, and decided not to. Her arm felt hot but the ache eased.

"We received word this morning from Queen Ittra that you had been with them some months ago. I heard you had quite a bit of excite there." The furs were tucked firmly under Brinn's chin. "Now tell me, how are you feeling?"

For a moment Brinn didn't realize that she had been asked a question and didn't know what to answer. "I'm a bit sore," she said quietly, pulling down the furs that felt smothering.

"Yes, I can see how you would be. That will go away with time. Rest is the best medicine for healing." The dragon pulled the furs back around Brinn's neck. "I'll come tomorrow. Don't let those three beasts upset you." She turned to leave. "Try to drink a little broth tonight and perhaps a bit of toast in the morning." She ducked to get through the cave opening. "And rest," she added as her tail disappeared from sight.

Brinn pulled down the furs in defiance and sat up. When her head stopped spinning, Brinn tried to stand. She felt weaker now than she had the night before.

With effort, she staggered across the cave and dropped limply onto the rug by the firepit. Brinn was worried about the dragon's reference to Neesha. Would she become an oddity with this dragon colony as she had with the Crinnelian dragons? Brinn had hoped she could put that unpleasantness behind her at last, but here it was again. She wasn't anxious to have another mental examination like before. She brought the fire to a blaze and stared into its flames. She was so deep in thought that she did not hear the voices coming down the passage and she was unaware that she was no longer alone in the cave until Telis stood over her.

"What are you doing out of bed? Do you want to get us in trouble?" Telis picked Brinn up and dropped her back in bed. "Stay put."

Draega rushed to the bedside to see if Brinn was in one piece. He was relieved to find her glaring up at him. "Has Livia been by to look you over?"

Brinn nodded. "I'm afraid there's no chance of relieving you of my presence anytime soon." She smiled weakly.

Telis rolled his eyes and returned to his own corner of the cave.

Draega was relieved that the girl wasn't going to die in the next hour, and went about his own business.

Brinn watched the red dragon move around the cave. He picked up leftover bones and scraped the bloody dirt into a pile and sent it 'away'. After the cleaning was done, Draega made a table and stool appear on Agnar's side of the cave. Agnar came in much later. He dropped a large fish next to the fire and disappeared. When he returned a few minutes later his scales were shiny with water as if he had dove into the water to get their meal. Telis shook his head and mumbled something about Agnar catering to humans. Brinn drifted off after that, even the smell of roasting fish could not rouse her.

In the morning, Brinn was again left to herself. She felt a bit stronger and was able to stand and walk to the small table before her legs gave way. She was glad to find fruit and water had been left for her. As she consumed the meal, Brinn took a closer look at the cave. The walls had an odd glow as light seemed to travel into the cave through crystalline veins. The suit of armor (in the light it was clear there was no occupant) was posed in a ridiculous manner: one hand on the helmet, a foot in the face mask, the other sticking straight out to the side, and the other arm had been removed and placed so that it protruded from under the chest plate. Brinn smiled and wondered if the dragons played with this suit of armor like a doll. She was fascinated to see pictures stuck to the wall. Some were clearly masterpieces, slightly faded and torn; others were cruder, almost childlike, drawn with charcoal or brownish ink. Seashells, driftwood, and books were neatly stacked by Draega's bed. All in all, the cave looked quite homey.

While Brinn was finishing breakfast she heard a cheerful melody coming from the outer tunnel. Soon a dragon's form filled the entryway. Brinn immediately recognized it as the healer from the day before.

The dragon entered the cave and scowled at Brinn. "You shouldn't be out of bed."

A full stomach made Brinn brave. "I am feeling much better today, I'm sure a little exercise won't hurt."

The dragon did not get angry, as Brinn thought she might, but nodded. "Yes, you seem stronger, but do not over exert yourself." The dragon drew near and held out a paw. Brinn felt a numbing sensation. "Yes, your injuries are coming right along." She sat down next to Brinn. "I am Livia. You will be tender for some time, but everything seems to be working fine. I consulted Barkin to make sure your insides were arranged properly, and he is satisfied with your progress."

Brinn had forgotten about her expected visit with the wizard. "I was on my way to see Barkin when I stopped to save that bear. He must have been worried when I didn't arrive."

Livia shook her head. "He didn't know about you at all until we contacted him for help in healing you. If you were going to see *him* someone else must have arranged it."

Brinn frowned, puzzled, but was too tired to think about what that meant. "Thank you for your care. I was stupid to rush into the circumstance that brought me here."

Livia shook her head. "The Younglings should not have been terrorizing the bear in that manner. Queen

Betto was very displeased with them." She shook her head. "Younglings! They should be locked up in a deep pit until they get their permanent scales," she chuckled

Brinn thought Livia sounded a bit like Nethra after the stable boys had an egg fight and let all the chickens out of the yard. She smiled at the memory. "Is that what you call them, Younglings?"

"Yes. Dragons are called Hatchlings until their first molt, then Younglings until their permanent fangs and scales come in."

"Well they seem like nice dragons at heart. Agnar has taken very good care of me. Draega was nice enough to cook me a bit of meat last night. Telis..."

Livia smiled. "Telis hates humans," she said simply. She slowly got to her feet. "You should rest now."

Brinn was prepared to object, but realized the dragon was right and nodded.

"Your first duty is to take care of yourself. Listen to your body, and don't hesitate to have Agnar call for me if anything should go wrong." She turned and left.

Brinn returned slowly to her bed and slept soundly until the dragons returned.

It was several days before Brinn was strong enough to spend more than an hour out of bed. Her mornings were spent alone, with the dragons rising at dawn and not returning until later in the day. Telis usually returned grumbling. Brinn caught a few words referring to her. Draega paid little attention to her other than to pass some food along to her. Agnar spent the most time with Brinn. While she rested in bed, he taught her the Dragonese dialect of the Pallan colony. Brinn discovered Agnar had lived with Talon for many years.

"My hatchmates died in-shell," the dragon explained to her one day while Telis and Draega were out of the cave. "If Talon hadn't rescued me I would have died with them." He went on to explain that traditionally there were no orphan dragons; something about the mental state after being isolated. "Ittra went against that tradition and asked Talon to take care of me. Graldiss helped a lot. Most of the colony accepted me, I had the approval of the Queen after all, and living with the Krrig Daa clinched it."

Brinn sipped her tea and shifted her pillow. "But you're here now."

Agnar shrugged and looked away. "I guess you can't change some dragons' minds. It only took one accident, one misstep that injured another dragon and claws started pointing. Accusations of unsound mind were thrown at me. Ittra quieted the loudest protesters, but nothing could stop the rumors." Agnar frowned. "Talon was furious, of course. He threatened to curse the lot of them but instead brought me here to Betto's colony where there was no stigma of being a 'single'. Being the companion of the Chosen One I was accepted right away."

"And when Talon went back to Ittra's colony?"

"I had a place here and friends. Besides, Talon has too many responsibilities now. I didn't like being left alone so much."

During the quiet hours of the day, when the dragons were out of the cave, Brinn had a lot of time to think. She remembered what Livia said about Barkin not knowing of her coming to visit. If he hadn't sent those letters who had? Of course Keldric's name was the first one to pop into her head. Why wouldn't that wizard leave her alone? It should have sunk into his twisted mind that she would be strong enough and wise enough by now not to turn her life over to him. Was he still so irritated with her choice to go with Talon that he was interfering with her life out of spite? Or did he have more sinister plans for her? Brinn was irritated that he continued to interfere with her life. How long would it be until he found her here in these caves? And would she *ever* be free from his scheming?

These grim thoughts did Brinn's health no good. Livia noticed Brinn was carrying a heavy load on her mind. "You are spending too much time on your own," the dragon commented during one of her daily visits. "I think you are healthy enough for some short walks. I will tell Agnar to show you around the caverns tomorrow. I would take you myself, but a set of young clutchmates stayed too long in one of the sulfur pools and their scales are falling off by the handfuls." Livia didn't even poke Brinn's still-red scars. "In a day or two you may have some visitors. There are quite a few here who would like to talk with you about Neesha. Queen

Betto included. But be careful, there are some who do not approve of humans."

Brinn dreaded the thought of a crowd of dragons coming to see the oddity, probing her mind for some trace of the heroic dragon. But she *did* want to meet the queen. Agnar had not talked about her at all, and Brinn was curious to find out if she was like Ittra. "I would have thought Queen Betto would have heard the story from Ittra."

"Some of it, yes, but she would like to hear it first hand. Queen Ittra told us about the crowd that descended on you after Neesha was released. Don't worry about that happening here. I won't let them near you."

Brinn was relieved.

When Brinn woke the next morning she was surprised to see Draega still in the cave. He was sitting in his corner with a book in his paws. A page was turned carefully with his right pinkie claw. Brinn smothered her laugh when she saw a pair of glasses perched on his nose. She went about her morning routine: dressing, brushing her hair, warming bread and cider for breakfast. Draega paid no attention to her until she finished her meal.

"When you are ready, I have been asked to give you some exercise." He glanced back at his book for a second, then took off his glasses. "Do you feel up to it?"

"Oh yes, please," Brinn said eagerly. "I feel like I've been sitting around forever!"

Draega smiled. "I think Telis feels the same way. Agnar made me promise not to overtire you, so let me know when you want to come back."

Draega led Brinn slowly down a large hollowed out tunnel. There were very few caves opening off the artificially carved passageway. "All of your colony couldn't possibly live along this tunnel." Brinn commented.

The dragon turned his head back, checking to see that the girl was keeping up. "No, you're right. This passage is just one of many. This tunnel eventually leads to the Hatching Cave. I won't take you that far today."

Brinn was disappointed. "So we're just going to walk up and down this tunnel? Not very exciting."

"I'm not going to have Livia yelling at me because I've over-tired her favorite patient. A short walk now, and tomorrow Agnar may take you farther."

Brinn slowed a bit, breathed heavily for a moment, then caught up with Draega. It was hard to admit she really wasn't strong enough to walk long distances. "You know, I'm a bit surprised you are here instead of Agnar."

Draega stopped at a wide section of the passageway and turned around. He smiled down at the girl. It amazed him that a little bit of a thing was not afraid to be around dragons. "Actually, he would have been the one to take you on this walk, but Morisa, an elderly dragon, had some errands for him. I volunteered to take Agnar's place, but the smelly old goat doesn't like me."

Draega winked. "Lucky me." The dragon held out a paw, motioning for Brinn to walk ahead of him.

On the short walk back to the cave Brinn took her time, looking at the glow of the walls. There were more veins of clear crystal bringing light. The rock had been scraped out around the spidery seams to allow for maximum use of their luminosity. "These caves and tunnels aren't natural, are they?"

"No, they aren't. Our ancestors moved to these cliffs to save the colony from local knights." He spat on the ground. "They dug and scraped until they had a place large enough to live."

Brinn understood there had been some kind of war between humans and dragons, but still found it incredible it had gone on without everyone knowing about it. No one from her village knew dragons and wizards were *real*, or that knights slaughtering the beasts were more than tales for children. Sure, Brinn had read stories about dragons flying over towns, spitting flames from their hideous jaws and taking away young maidens, but they were just stories. Not one traveler who came through their town had mentioned any carnage left in the wake of such a monster's attack. The knights who had quenched their thirst at the inn's tavern had said nothing of the glorious crusade to rid the world of such vile creatures. "How could such a thing be kept silent for so long?" Brinn asked aloud.

Draega did not answer. They were soon back in their own cave. Brinn sat down on the smaller bed of furs Agnar had made for her. Draega did not seem in a hurry to escape Brinn's company. A partially eaten moose carcass was left in Telis' corner of the cave. Draega tossed it on the fire.

"Were they only stories?" Brinn asked. "Dragons burning towns and demanding virgin sacrifices?"

The seriousness of the girl's face drove away any anger Draega might have had about the accusations. "I can't speak for all dragons, but no one I know has ever burned down a village, though we might be tempted."

Brinn had already adjusted her perception of Dragonkind, but there were so many unanswered questions. "Still, *something* must have happened to keep so many of us from knowing about dragons. It's almost as if someone used magic to...hide that knowledge."

Draega laughed. "It would take a mighty powerful dragon to do that." He shook his head and answered more seriously, "No, that kind of magic is not within our power. I think the answer is that we became wise and stayed away from humans. We aren't stupid enough now to give humans any more reasons to kill us. Besides," he chuckled, "why would we want to capture a terrified human? Screaming and fainting everywhere? No thank you."

Brinn was glad to hear humor in the dragon's tone. "I suppose we would be good eating." She smiled at Draega's shocked look. "Well, not much hair, and we're a lot slower than a moose. No antlers either."

"But the antlers add fiber," the dragon added with a straight face. He looked down at Brinn. "You are an interesting human. You aren't afraid of us. I know you lived with the Krrig Daa for a while, but still, you seem so at ease. That can't be normal for a human."

Brinn didn't know how to answer. For the first time she realized that she had *never* been like other people. Now she had a reason to be different, and she *liked* that.

Chapter 16

Brinn began to look forward to her daily walks. Agnar was her guide most of the time, but Draega was also spending more time with the young wizard. For a time, they stayed away from other dragons. The Hatching Caves were off limits and many of the caves lining the tunnels were empty during the day.

"What do dragons do all day?" Brinn asked one afternoon.

Telis, who was lounging near the fire gnawing on a bone, scoffed. "What, you don't think dragons have important business? Do you think we spend our days flying over villages looking for houses to torch?"

Draega rolled his eyes. "Lighten up, will ya?" He turned to Brinn. "Raising and training of our hatchlings and providing for the colony take up a good part of our time. We hunt far from the caves so as not to frighten the nearby towns. We are constantly enlarging the caverns and visiting the elderly and infirm."

"Gosh, Draega, only you could make that sound so *boring.*" Telis had stayed out late the night before and was cranky.

"So you don't work with people at all?" Brinn asked. Telis snorted.

Draega nodded. "Some of our colony have joined the Krrig Daa in his fulfillment of the Prophecy of uniting dragons and humans."

Telis mumbled something under his breath.

"But there is very little interaction with humans here." Draega shrugged

"Our Queen shouldn't let humans tell her how to run a colony." Telis growled.

Brinn started to defended Talon but was silenced by the appearance of a small purple dragon. "Hold your tongue, youngling," the beautiful dragon scolded. "Your ignorance is an embarrassment."

Telis and Draega knelt and bowed their heads. Brinn followed suit. After a moment Brinn felt a claw under her chin. She lifted her head and looked into the small face. Two orange eyes stared into hers; the short, horned muzzle was wrinkled with age. Brinn had the sense of being in the presence of a dragon of great age. The dragon herself was not even as tall has Brinn.

"Leave us." The command was soft but final. The two young dragons disappeared. The beautiful dragon looked around the cave. "Someone needs to come in here and clean out this hole." She settled next to the fire.

Brinn sat at her table. She realized this small dragon was quite old, possibly older than Kaalla. There were scars on her muzzle and the tip of her tail was missing. Had she seen battle? She waited silently until the magnificent dragon spoke first.

The dragon looked Brinn over. "A wizard with black hair. That's unique," she said after a few minutes.

"I'm an oddity just being female, so I'm told."

The dragon laughed. "So you are, young Brinn." A bowl of plump berries appeared in front of the dragon, another one materialized on Brinn's table. "Livia says that you are almost healed."

"Yes, ma'am. Only a bit of stiffness in the mornings. I am grateful for her expertise." The dragon nodded but did not comment. Brinn braved a breech of etiquette, "Since you know my name, may I ask yours?"

"I am Betto, Queen of this colony."

"I am honored." Brinn bowed her head. "And I am indebted to your hospitality."

"Yes. Agnar has a soft spot for humans, naturally. Once you were here I couldn't just throw you out in the cold, could I?" The dragon smiled. "But what made you do such a silly thing as to put yourself between that bear and three dragons?"

Brinn had often wondered that herself these past few days. "I suppose I naively thought I could save it."

The queen shook her head. "Brave and foolish at the same time. An interesting character trait."

Brinn looked away sheepishly.

"A trait found in the best of humankind," Betto said gently. She cleared her throat. "Yes, well I promised Ittra to check on you myself and let her know how you are doing. She's quite attached to you, you know."

Brinn smiled. "Thank you. I didn't know if your caves would echo magic as the Crinnelian ones do, so I haven't tried to contact the queen, or Talon."

"Talon came shortly after Agnar brought you here. After he made sure you were going to survive he told me a bit about you. Quite a story."

Brinn moved to sit on the ground near the fire. "I didn't have much to say about any of it." She knew it sounded petulant, but she didn't want Betto to think she was something special.

Betto looked seriously at Brinn. "Destiny is never a clear path. Fate gives us a push, but it is our choices which define our future. Your choices have been exceptional."

Brinn blushed. "Please, I am nothing special."

"All extraordinary beings say that." Betto stood and stretched. "You are welcome to stay with us as long as you like. If these younglings aren't too much for you, I suggest you remain here. Not all in my colony would accept the presence of a wizard, even with my sanction. Agnar will be a good companion, and if you don't pay attention to Telis' rudeness, these three younglings are good at heart."

Brinn stood. "Thank you. Agnar and Draega have made me feel at home. I *would* like to stay for a while if I may."

The Queen nodded and turned to leave. Halfway through the entrance she stopped and looked back. "Neesha was a brave dragon, but should have accepted death rather than take the life of your mother. I am sorry for your loss. It could not have been easy for you." She turned and left before Brinn could say anything.

Brinn stood alone in the cave, tears stinging her eyes.

It was some time before Draega returned to the cave. He peeked his head around the cave entrance before walking in. He took a few steps but stopped, looking down at the ground. "Um, may I come in?"

Brinn could have laughed at the silly question, but the serious look on the dragon's face stopped her. "I think I need a cup of tea, would you mind filling up the kettle? I'll light the fire." She tried to be as nonchalant as possible.

The kettle appeared over her flames. When the water came to a boil Brinn scooped out enough fragrant leaves for two cups (or one cup and a large bucket). Draega was fiddling with something by his sleeping area. Brinn wanted to think of something to take his mind off his nervousness.

"Those glasses you wear, do you have trouble seeing?"

Draega pulled out the two large circles of glass held together with thick wire. "A friend of Agnar's got these for me." The dragon put them on and grinned. "They look silly, don't they? I only use them to read human books, the print is so small." He chuckled and took them off again. "I don't dare wear them around Telis, he'd laugh me out of the cave."

Brinn sipped her tea. "You like to read *our* books? Why?"

Draega sipped his own tea from the barrel-like cup. "I find it interesting to see how humans perceive the world." He pulled out a book and handed it to Brinn. It was a book of poetry. "'A cloud, a bee, a bird so free. Oh, to soar and fly with thee. So light the wind as through the tree. But here on land forever be. Cursed fate hear my plea. The cloud, the bee, the bird, and me.' Such sorrow."

Brinn read some of the poems. The author seemed to be full of regrets and forever cursing Fate. "Not everything we write is like this."

"Oh no, of course not," Draega said eagerly pulling out another book. "Ships of villainous pirates pillaging fishing villages, wicked kings sliced to ribbons, a sheep herder turned brave knight. You have such vivid imaginations." Dreaga became quiet again. He slowly put his books away. "You know," the dragon said quietly, "I've never been that close to her. And she came to see *you*."

Brinn didn't know what to say.

"Wow, were you nervous? What did you talk about? Is she mad at Telis? I can't believe she was in *this* cave!"

"What are you blabbing on about?" Telis sullenly walked into the cave.

Draega shot his friend a nasty look. "The Queen of course. I bet she's ready to turn you on a spit for that remark of yours."

Telis shrugged, but looked around warily. "Yeah, well...whatever. Are we going to sit around here? A pack of seals has been spotted up the coast. I just came back to get you. Are you going to stay here with...that," Telis waved his tail at Brinn, "or are you going to come and get an easy meal?" He stormed out.

Draega looked apologetically at Brinn. "Don't mind him. Do you mind if I take off? Agnar will be done with Morisa, one of the elderly dragons, in a few hours."

Brinn didn't want to keep the dragon from a fresh feast. "Go on. I'll just take a nap." She really did feel tired.

Draega smiled and followed quickly after his friend.

In the darkness under the fur covers Brinn thought about Betto. The dragon Queen didn't seem as friendly as Ittra had been but Ittra was young. Brinn wondered how old Betto was. Brinn was relieved beyond words that Betto held no ill feelings about a part of Neesha's spirit being held prisoner in her mind. And the Queen had been the first dragon to express regret about her mother's fate. In the dark Brinn again saw her mother's form being reshaped into that of a dragon. Was that new Neesha still out there? Could some small piece of her mother's spirit be trapped within the beast's mind as she had held the dragon's all those years? Brinn yawned and closed her eyes.

Just as Brinn felt herself relax and drop off to sleep a shout brought her awake with a shocks.

"Drae! Drae! Are you in here?! We want a story!"

Brinn groaned, threw back the furs and sat up. Before her, frozen in surprise, were four small dragons no taller than her knees. Two of the hatchlings screamed and ran from the cave, a third stood petrified staring at Brinn. A tiny paw reached around the cave entrance and grabbed the tail of the frightened dragon, pulling it free from the horrid monster's hypnotic stare. The fourth hatchling also seemed immobilized, not from dread but curiosity. The small brown head tilted slightly and thoughts raced behind the green eyes. He took a hesitant step forward and poked a claw at Brinn.

"You're one of those...humans Draega reads about, aren't you?" The baby dragon's voice was slow, as if considering every word.

Brinn smiled and nodded. "Yes, I am," she said in Pallanic Dragonese. "And who might you be?"

The little dragon giggled. "You just asked who my nose was. You don't speak very well."

"I'm sorry, I'm only just learning your language." Brinn changed to the Dragonese she had learned from Graldiss. "Do you understand when I speak this way?"

"Of course," a small paw waved in the air, "I'm not just out of the egg, you know." The hatching squinted its eyes. "You're glowing. Why?"

Brinn remembered Graldiss telling her that all wizards had a special aura. She didn't see the harm in telling the dragon-child the truth. "Wizards do that,

I'm told." She saw a bit of hesitation in the young eyes. "My name is Brinn. I'm staying with Agnar, Telis and Draega for a while."

The young dragon thought about this for a moment, then nodded. If Agnar wanted to keep a wizard as a pet it must be ok. "I'm Paygor. My clutchmates and I were coming to hear a story from Draega. He reads us human adventures from his...booooks."

"Well, I'm sorry, but Draega went out to hunt seals with Telis." Two heads peeked around the cave entrance. "You are very brave, Paygor, to face down such a terrible beast as myself."

The young dragon giggled. "You don't look very dangerous, even if you *are* a wizard."

"Apparently your friends think differently."

Paygor turned around and saw his clutchmates hiding. "Come on out, Yorel, it's not going to hurt us."

"Are you sure?" a small voice said from the passageway. "It might want to lure us all in and cook us for supper."

Brinn laughed. "My, you have been listening to some horrifying stories. I promise not to move from the bed, if that makes you feel safer."

Another small brown dragon entered the cave. "There are four of us, so don't try anything."

Brinn shook her head in mock seriousness. "But I only see two of you. Where are your friends?

A third brown dragon stepped forward. "Grissa will stay in the tunnel in case you attack."

Paygor groaned. "It's not going to do any such thing. It's Agnar's pet."

Brinn threw the covers back and stood up. "I am *not* a pet." Two of the hatchlings staggered back. "And I'm not an *it*, I'm a *she*."

"How does...she know how to talk like we do?" Yorel asked.

"She's a wizard," Paygor whispered. "She can probably read our minds."

"Now why would I want to do that?" Brinn waved her arms dramatically and the fire lit with a burst of flames. In the light she could see Yorel's brown scales were beginning to molt, revealing shiny red scales that matched the wings neatly folded on his back. Brinn pointed to the third dragon. "What's your friend's name?" she asked Paygor.

The small dragon puffed herself up proudly. "I am Mellisiannarita, the leader of our clutch. And you are..."

"I am Brinn, heir to the wizardry of Fernley the Storyteller." Brinn thought it would be a bit much to recite her full magical lineage.

Grissa peeked around the entrance. "Storyteller?" She came further into the cave. "We love to listen to stories! We were coming in to have Draega read us one of his human books. Do you know any stories?" The small dragon plopped down in front of Brinn.

Mellisiannarita rolled her eyes. "Some guard," she mumbled.

"Well, that's what we came for, Mell." Paygor pointed out. He sat next to Grissa and looked expectantly at Brinn.

Yorel shyly joined the other two. "Yes, please," he said quietly.

Mell huffed and grudgingly sat down. "So? Tell us a story."

Brinn looked down at the little dragons. What had she gotten herself into? She searched her memory for something that would interest dragons. After a moment she, too, sat down on the floor. She took a deep breath and lowered the fire to a glow. "This is the story of how wizards came to be."

"Many hundreds of years ago, when dragons roamed without fear across the world and man groveled in the dirt, an elderly Queen found two infant humans alone in the forest. The remains of the parents were in the possession of a pack of mountain wolves, not far away. Queen Gallia, that was her name, took pity on the helpless babes and carried them back to her den within her great jaws.

"At first Gallia only intended to look after the infants until she could find a human family with which to leave them. But she was lonely and the babes gave her days purpose so she kept them with her in her cave. Her colony thought the odd obsession would pass. Some even thought this would be a good chance to study the strange creatures. So Gallia and the colony raised the young humans. She named them Issic and

Tagga for the northernmost and southernmost peaks of their mountain range.

"The Queen was amazed at how helpless the infants were. They seemed to need constant attention. It took some days before they learned to accept the large face of they new parent. Of course they couldn't understand the language of dragons, so Gallia used thoughts to hush their cries and sang them lullabies. It was natural for Gallia to use magic to rock them to sleep, to clean their messes, to amuse them, and for the hundreds of little tasks it takes to raise a human child.

"Whether it was the daily use of magic or the ambient magic of the mountain caves, it is not known; but within the year the human babes were using magic themselves. They could easily express their needs mentally and their favorite toys were forever floating through the air. The two were also learning to speak in the tongue of their adopted race. No one thought it odd that the boys' hair had changed from midnight black to snow white.

"The years flew by. Issic and Tagga grew into healthy boys. There was little difference between the two young humans and the young hatchlings who played in the caves. They made up for the lack of wings and claws with strength and agility. Gallia even taught them how to lift themselves into the air for short periods of time. The boys made friends easily within the colony and there were few who would not give them a ride to the hunt.

"As they grew into young men, there was little that Issic and Tagga could not do. Their magical abilities grew along with their strength. They became also known for their wisdom and good nature. They never failed to lend a hand with some task that needed their smaller size and they were sometimes asked their opinion during council meetings. They had no knowledge of their own species. The colony itself dealt little with humans, who still roamed in small tribes following the grassbuck herds.

"But not every dragon in Gallia's colony had such high regard for the two humans. One fateful day, the two young men joined a hunting party that flew far over the mountains. Issic and Tagga were dropped into a thick forest and abandoned by their mounts. 'Don't try to come back,' one disgruntled dragon hissed, 'Gallia is old and can't protect you anymore.'"

Grissa growled.

"Be quiet." Paygor swiped at his clutchmate with his tail.

"What happened next?" Yorel asked anxiously.

"They starved to death, of course," Mell said matter-of-factly.

Grissa groaned. "No! That's not fair, they were part of the colony."

"That's not the way some dragons saw it," Brinn said quietly.

Paygor looked impatiently at Grissa. "They were wizards, stupid. They didn't die just because they were left in the woods. Now be quiet so Brinn can tell the rest of the story." Paygor turned back around. "That's not the end...is it?"

"No, that's not the end." Brinn waited for the dragons to settle down again.

"Issic and Tagga were shocked at the turn of events. Issic cried for his loss, Tagga raged and swore at the cruelty of those he had called brothers. The two spent the night in the forest. Of course they knew how to bring forth fire and they were excellent hunters, so they weren't uncomfortable. The next day the brothers made their way out of the forest. Tagga convinced Issic that returning to the caves was not a good idea. They found some human tracks and followed them to a small village. The villagers were wary of the strange men who spoke a foreign language and wore animal hide clothing. Tagga quickly saw these humans did not know about magic and began to plot to gain power among humans. Tagga was not evil, you understand, he felt that if he held enough power over humans they would not abandon him as the dragons had. Issic did not agree with Tagga, he did not care for the humans who were greedy and simpleminded. With a heavy heart, Issic left his brother with the humans and went off to live on his own." Brinn paused to drink some water.

The little dragons started chattering: "Is that all? Did Issic go back to live with dragons? Tagga shouldn't have let Issic go alone. Issic shouldn't have left Tagga."

"I will tell you more tomorrow," Brinn promised.

The four little dragons argued all the way to the cave entrance. Brinn would have thought they had forgotten about her but Yorel turned back and waved. "See you tomorrow!"

Agnar arrived just after the hatchlings disappeared. He laughed when he saw Brinn. "They didn't talk you into telling them a story, did they? Draega has been trying to get them off his back for months."

"Well, he can thank me when he gets back."

Word spread quickly and Brinn was soon surrounded daily by small dragons. It was fast becoming a problem to remember stories where the humans were defeated by dragons. Brinn had tried to tell the story of how Roga Mithus had bought a magic squirrel from a peddler and used his five wishes to create an island kingdom, but the complaints were loud and persistent. Brinn was left with tragedies and the few stories Fernley had collected from dragons. When she began to recite the Ballad of Vollin Ridge, where twenty valiant knights sacrificed their lives defending a poor village, Brinn had to change it to fifty vicious knights protecting a village full of egg stealing bandits. Pirates were hunted down after raiding coastal colonies, kings were defeated in bloody battles against outnumbered dragons, and villages were punished for offering innocent princesses as sacrifices. The only topic Brinn refused to fictionalize was the fights between dragons and wizards. She thought it would be best not to bring up that horrible period.

It wasn't long before older dragons started joining the group. It was clear these older dragons, most of them very old, were hoping to hear the story of Neesha's release. Brinn was becoming quickly overwhelmed. Livia stepped in and sent the adults away with strict orders not to pester Brinn.

Brinn noticed one of the little dragons had bright red scales, where most of the others still had their brown, hatching scales. She assumed it was a bit older than the others, though actually smaller in size, until the little dragon stayed behind one afternoon. The red youngling looked around to see if she was noticed by the others.

"The story's over, little one." Brinn was ready for a warm bowl of soup.

"I just wanted to ask you a question," the little dragon said in a childlike voice. The dragon was not looking at Brinn, but watching the last of the adult dragons exit the cave.

"A short one, please. I'm very tired."

After a moment the red dragon turned back to Brinn. "You seem like a person who cares about the plight of dragons, about the injustices that have plagued us these many centuries."

Brinn stared at the small dragon, who was no longer talking like a youngling, but like an adult. Cautiously she said, "There have been injustices on both sides."

"Yes, yes," the dragon waved the comment away with a paw. "But don't you agree these...conflicts could have been avoided by the simple elimination of contact between humans and dragons."

Brinn knew this was a simplistic assumption. She didn't know where this conversation was going. "I will accept that in many cases in the past dragons and humans have not benefited by close proximity." There, that was vague enough.

The dragon was pleased. This was easier than she thought it might be. "Many of us here feel we need a return to the old ways. A...separation from interaction with humans. If the object of hostility is removed then harmony can return."

Brinn didn't like the direction this conversation was taking. "I know you aren't as young as you first made out to be, and you are beating around the bush trying to get me to do something for you. Why don't you tell me who you are and just what it is you want me to do?"

The dragon looked around suspiciously and lowered her voice. "My name is not important. I am part of a growing group within the colony who feel the Krrig Daa is looking at dragon prophecy through human eyes. The balance of power is tipping dangerously toward the humans. You understand the need to force the scales toward the true dominant species."

Brinn wanted to grab the little dragon and shake her just before throwing her against the wall. Could she really believe Brinn would betray her own species! Brinn would have gladly told the beast off, but that would put the dragon on her guard. Brinn wanted a chance to alert Talon. She raced to think of what to say. She sagged slightly and put her hand on her head. "Please forgive me, I tire easily and my mind is muddled. I need to rest and consider your ideas with fresh perspective." Brinn turned toward her bed.

The self-assured dragon deflated a bit. "Yes, of course. Perhaps tomorrow." She sulked out of the cave.

Brinn heard the small dragon speak to someone in the passageway and a moment later Telis entered the cave. He glanced at Brinn before going to his own section of the cave.

Tensions that night were high. Telis kept staring at Brinn only to look away when she glanced at him. Brinn was preoccupied, going over the conversation with the small red dragon; she felt if she went over it enough times she would find some perfectly logical misunderstanding had been made. Draega was nursing a sore nose from a hunting accident and kept mumbling curses at walruses. Agnar was late arriving for dinner and threw a nasty look at Telis, daring him to make one comment about poor helpless old dragons. The surly bunch turned in early.

Brinn didn't sleep very well. The furs seemed to be launching a rebellion, repeatedly sliding off and leaving Brinn's feet icy cold. Her dreams were filled with dragons plotting in whispers. A rush of hot air was too much. Brinn threw back the furs in time to see a head-sized ball of fire arch over her head; she quickly opened both eyes but felt it safer not to move. As she watched, terrified, the flaming ball crisscrossed the cave. Brinn thought they might be under attack, though the laughter coming from the far side of the cave made her doubt that assumption. Brinn decided to risk turning her head.

A bright orange ball of fire flew straight at Draega's head, but instead of charring the dragon's face, the flaming ball was blown back across the cave. After slowly drifting toward Agnar the ball was magically pushed back toward Draega with a bit of spin on it. Draega batted the ball with his tail toward Telis who was waiting impatiently. With a wave of his claws the flame shot across toward Agnar at a frightening speed. The shouts and roars became increasingly louder until Brinn thought someone would come in and break up the game. No one came.

Back and forth the glowing sphere flew. A particularly loud whoop followed a shower of sparks when the ball smashed into Agnar's face. After seeing there was no harm to her friend's muzzle, Brinn relaxed, sure that the game was now over. She was wrong. Telis formed another red-hot ball. With a flick of his wrist, the orb flew across the cave to be bounced, and batted, and blown around. Sometimes the ball was stopped in mid air until the suspense drew a shout and it was sent flying again.

Brinn tried to cover her head and go back to sleep but the apprehension of getting scorched kept her on edge. When she was showered with debris from the ceiling after a wild shot, Brinn decided she had had enough. Using the water from the washbasin next to her bed, Brinn formed her own sphere. With a quick, but well aimed toss, Brinn's wet ball put a stop to the latest volley.

"Hey! What'ja do that for?!" Draega complained and formed another fireball.

"I am trying to sleep," Brinn said, emphasizing each word.

"Sorry," Agnar apologized.

"Wow, that was a great shot!" Telis said excitedly. "Can you do that again?"

Brinn glared at Telis, "It has got to be past midnight."

"It's more fun to play when it's dark." Draega tossed the ball.

Telis stopped the hot ball and let it float in the air near his belly. "You're a pretty good shot for a human. Betcha can't stop this one."

The flaming orb shot toward Brinn's head. Without thinking she deflected the ball to the fire pit where it exploded in a cloud of cinders. There was a lot of giggling in the dark before Agnar made another ball of fire. There was a shadowy grin on his face. Brinn saw a barrel of water had just been brought in and placed next to her bed.

"Since you're awake anyway, why don't you join in?" Draega suggested, pointing to the water.

Brinn looked at Telis, sure he would object to her inclusion. She was surprised to see his nodding head. Well, Draega was right, there was no chance Brinn was going to get back to sleep now. She shrugged and pulled a head-sized ball of water from the barrel. Elbows dripping, Brinn watched the flaming sphere weave through the air until the perfect shot revealed itself. With a quick flick of her wrist, Brinn sent the icy, wet ball toward the flames hovering in front of Agnar's face.

It took a very angry Morisa shouting complaints about ungrateful younglings to wake Brinn the next day. The furs were still damp and Brinn was thankful for a freshly lit fire.

Morisa stared when the young woman entered the firelight. He had never seen a human close up. "You're a...a...a"

"Human? Wizard? Girl?" Brinn supplied sleepily. "Yes, to all three. You must be Morisa." Brinn put a kettle on to boil. "Would you like a cup of tea?"

Morisa stammered and disappeared.

"It's worth keeping you around just to see the old bat's mouth hanging open like that." Draega joined Brinn at the fire. "Planning for more storytelling today?"

Brinn cringed. "I hope not. I'd like to get some fresh air today."

Telis came in from his morning trip outside. "If you go out for fresh air, you'll be getting wet as well. It's raining out there." He tossed Brinn a loaf of bread.

"Well, I won't melt." Brinn tore off a chunk of bread and speared it with a stick. "I will need some help, though. I may be a wizard, but I can't fly." She held the bread out over the flames to toast. "I've just got to get out of these caves."

Draega gulped a large cup of tea. "I'm sorry, but I have to help in the Hatching Cave this morning. I'm late as it is, so I can't fly you out. Agnar should be done in an hour or so."

Brinn sighed, she knew that within an hour she would be knee-deep in hatchlings and younglings. "Maybe later, then."

"I'll take you up." Brinn and Draega turned at Telis' words. "What? I don't have anything to do this morning."

Brinn smiled warmly. "I would like that very much."

Chapter 17

Brinn dressed quickly, throwing on her heavy brown cloak. She didn't want to keep Telis waiting and postponed brushing her hair and washing her face. She followed him down the passageway, squinting until her eyes got used to the increasing brightness from the outside.

On the wide outside ledge, Telis leaned down and held out a foreleg. Brinn climbed up. Telis was a lot smaller than Graldiss, so she couldn't sit astride his back, but instead laid down on his smooth back and held on to the muscled shoulders. The dragon spread his wings and with a mighty sweep they lifted off the ledge and into the air.

Brinn thrilled at being in the air again. She resisted screeching when the wind whipped them wildly. It took some concentration to stay balanced on the dragon's back and a bit of magic kept her from being blinded in the cutting rain. Within moments they were back on firm ground. Disappointedly, Brinn slid off Telis' back.

"Thank you. I'm sure you don't carry many humans." She took a few shaky steps.

"You're the first." Telis said simply.

"I am honored." She turned and looked out at the raging ocean. "What a magnificent view!" The top of the cliffs was covered with rough bushes and scrub grass both of which were white with salt. The edge of the cliff was a sheer drop so the honeycomb of entrances could not be seen from above. A gentle slope led away from the cliff's edge. Lifting her face to the falling rain, Brinn pulled the cloak tightly around her, breathed in the salty air.

Telis watched the odd girl. Until the day she barged onto that field to rescue the stupid bear he was prepared to hate all humans. This young wizard's bravery and calm acceptance of her confinement with dragons had shone a new light on the creatures. Brinn wasn't mean or spiteful, in fact, quite the opposite. She had not tried to act superior with her magic or undermine their lifestyle as Dee said humans would. Telis was confused.

Brinn sat down on the damp ground. She cleared her mind, brought up Talon's image and called his name. No answer came. Brinn tried again with Graldiss.

"Hello, Brinn. How are you feeling? All healed up?" The dragon's thoughts filled her head.

"Almost good as new, thanks. Where's Talon?"

"Some mines in the north. There was a cave-in and he took a dozen younglings to help dig them out. Did you need something?"

"Advice. Yesterday I was approached by one of the dragons here. I think she wants my help to...I don't know, put a stop to human/dragon interaction. I don't know if I should politely decline or just act stupid."

Graldiss laughed. "I think the stupid wizard bit is a stretch. I've met Betto, I know she accepts Talon's decisions on this matter, but I've heard she's having trouble with dissenters. You don't want to get mixed up with a revolution."

Brinn and Graldiss 'communicated' for a while longer. Telis occupied his time diving for lunch. He was just surfacing when Brinn finished her conversation and looked out over the cliff. A dragon bursting through the foamy waves with a fish in each claw is an amazing sight.

"Hope you're in the mood for fish." He landed on the cliff top. "Finished talking with whoever you were talking with?" He smiled. "I never knew how silly it looked to talk that way. Visiting with wizards?"

The rain had stopped and Brinn shook out her dripping cloak. "Dragon, actually. I promised to keep in touch with Graldiss."

Telis stared at Brinn. "You know Little Brother?" His voice held a note of respect.

Brinn was surprised he hadn't heard about her time with Ittra's colony. Agnar knew about her time in Crinnelia. Livia and Betto knew also. Brinn had assumed the rest of the colony knew. "Yes, I stayed with Ittra's colony just after I became a wizard. I needed time to adjust to my new abilities."

"Adjust?" Telis knelt down and Brinn climbed up. "I thought wizards trained for years before inheriting their power."

Brinn held tightly as the dragon leaped from the cliff. "I didn't get that opportunity." They swooped toward one of dozens of identical holes in the cliff face. "I barely knew Fernley before he died."

Telis landed lightly on the familiar ledge. Brinn slid off and straightened her cloak. "You didn't know he was a wizard?" He was stunned.

Brinn shook her head and walked into the darkness toward the cave. "I didn't even know *I* was a wizard until Talon came."

Telis stared at the disappearing girl. He ran after her. "Wait, how could you not know you were a wizard?"

Brinn easily found their cave. She took off her cloak and lit the fire. "Well, how was I supposed to tell? Things didn't start magically moving around, I didn't feel any different. I hardly even noticed that my hair changed from brown to black." Brinn saw Telis' shocked look. "Of course, I did finally have a talk with my predecessor and learned of my potential. With a bit of training from Graldiss, Talon and Kaalla, as well as Fernley's extensive library, I've come a long way."

"What about your training to kill dragons?"

Brinn turned and stared at Telis. "What are you talking about?"

"Wizards have always been behind the slaughter of our race," the dragon stated matter-of-factly.

Brinn laughed. "And you think I'm going to carry on the genocide? I'm sorry to disappoint you, but not all wizards are bloodthirsty killers. My predecessor was only interested in stories and histories. Personally, I'm rather partial to dragons." She didn't plan on telling him about her dragonslaying fantasies back at her father's inn. "Talon is changing the way wizards and humans think of dragons and vice versa."

"Maybe," Telis wasn't willing to give up his long-held beliefs. Draega and Agnar came in and the conversation ended.

The next morning Brinn prepared herself for her role as Storyteller. She walked down a wide side-passageway to the Meeting Cavern. Their small cave had quickly become overcrowded during the daily storytellings and the Queen allowed Brinn to use the larger cave. She had chosen the story of Prince Ah'sha and the Eagle King. She felt it was time to tell about human heroes. The cave was packed before long and Brinn took her usual place on a low stool. She was starting to be able to recognize many of the younger dragons seated before her. The small red dragon was in her usual spot at the edge of the hatchlings. She was starting to blend in more as the hatchlings began to molt. Brinn had been able to avoid any more personal conversations with the intense creature.

When Brinn began her story there were some whispers of dissatisfaction. Who wanted to hear about some armored thug chasing an oversized bird? But as the story progressed the whispers stopped and all eyes stared in anticipation. They growled when the fair maiden was snatched up in the mighty talons and groaned when the hero tore out the lion's heart to use as bait, there was even a slight cheer when Ah'sha slayed the Eagle King with a blow from his mighty battleaxe.

"Bravo!" Attention turned to someone clapping at the back of the cave. A hush fell over the crowd. Dragons moved aside for the Krrig Daa.

Brinn watched the hooded figure walk toward her. In her mind, Talon's words were quiet and earnest. "Kneel down and hold your arms out, don't look at me until I tell you to rise."

Brinn didn't question Talon's order, she stood as the wizard came close and knelt as he described. The dragons, young and old, stared as the young girl treated their Chosen One with the respect given only to their Queens. Talon stood before the prostrate girl. He placed his hand on her head and pushed. Brinn automatically resisted having her face pushed into the dirt. "Perfect," his words filled her mind. Aloud, his words filled the silence. "Blessings on you, young wizard. I am well pleased with you." Talon's hand lifted but he did not command her to stand, instead he turned to the gathered dragons and waited.

After a few tense minutes the older dragons knelt and held out their forelegs in supplication, the younger dragons followed suit. Talon held his arms over the bowed heads. "Blessings upon Pallan Colony and your Queen. Rise and be at ease." The dragons got to their feet in one wave. Talon leaned down and picked up a hatchling. "Hello, little one. When will you take your first flight?"

The small blue-winged hatchling gazed up in wonder. "Next month...sir." The tiny dragon looked at the older dragons who were staring at this human. He looked back at the wizard. "Pardon me, sir," he whispered, "but why do they look at you like that, you are human."

Talon smiled and spoke gently into the hatchling's mind. "They call me the Krrig Daa, young one. Do you know what that is?"

The bright green eyes widened and the little head nodded. "But you don't have two heads," the hatchling said, slipping a tiny paw inside the hood and touching the smooth cheek.

Talon laughed and kissed the bluish head. "Not today." He returned the hatchling to his gawking clutchmates. With a dramatic gesture, Talon disappeared.

In silence the cave began to empty. Brinn sat on her stool. Agnar, who hadn't been in the Meeting Cave, waded through the mass of exiting dragons. "He's here, isn't he?" He looked around expectantly. "Where did he go? Is Graldiss with him?"

Brinn looked at her friend. "I don't know where he went. Can we get out of here?"

It was almost an hour before Talon walked into Agnar's cave. Brinn was tossing a waterball to Draega, Agnar was pacing the cave, and Telis hadn't moved from in front of the fire since he heard of the holy arrivals.

When the robed figure entered, Agnar ran to the wizard and clutched him to his chest. "Oh it's good to see you again! Why haven't you come to visit? How is Silgaa?"

Talon squeezed the dragon tightly. "You are a welcome sight, Agnar." He looked the dragon over. "You've grown. You'll outsize these dragons soon. Silgaa is fine, he was promoted to clutch trainer last year. He sends his love. Now if you will introduce me to your cavemates, I'll let you know where you can find Graldiss."

Draega stepped forward and knelt. Talon put his hand between the curled horns. "Blessings, Youngling. If you freeze the core of your waterball you can get a wicked spin on it."

The dragon stood and grinned. "I'll remember that. I am Draega, we are honored to have your presence in our humble cave, Holy One."

Talon slapped Draega's back. "Call me Talon, please."

Agnar gestured toward the fire. "This is Telis."

Talon went to the orange dragon who had not taken his eyes from the flames. Talon laid his hand on Telis' head. Waves of sorrow and hatred flowed into the wizard's mind. Talon fell to his knees, clutching the dragon's head in both hands. After a few minutes Brinn caught Talon's whispered words: "All is forgiven." The wizard stood and helped Telis to his feet. "Graldiss is up on the cliff top. I'm sure he would like to meet all of you."

Telis smiled and nodded. The three dragons went to meet the legendary Little Brother. Talon sunk into a chair and gratefully took a cup of tea from Brinn. "He's a tortured soul."

Brinn nodded, but didn't ask what Talon had seen in the dragon's mind. "That was some entrance you made in the Meeting Cave."

Talon grinned. "It's always good to pop in unannounced."

"I didn't mean for you to physically come here when I talked to Graldiss. I'm sorry if I've inconvenienced you."

"It's always best to learn a new spell face to face," Talon said lightly, but the words in Brinn's mind were in a more serious tone: "You have a visitor. Let's play a little game until we can be alone." "I'm surprised Fernley didn't teach you this one," Talon said aloud. He began to chant a spell in ancient Valadian. Brinn's dress changed from red to green. "There, that was easy, wasn't it?"

"Thank you, I was so tired of that color," Brinn said happily. She repeated his words and her robe changed to yellow. "Wonderful!" Brinn took Talon's arm "I'd like to go see Graldiss, if you will take me."

Talon lifted his arms theatrically and the two of them relocated to the cliff top.

From a distance Brinn saw Agnar, Draega and Telis encircling the large dragon. She turned to Talon. "What was that all about?"

Talon pushed off his hood shook his hair in the breeze. Brinn noticed it had grown.

"A small dragon was hiding behind the suit of armor." Talon sat down on a rounded boulder. "I didn't think you'd want to talk about your problem around her."

Brinn had a good idea who it was. "That's the one I wanted to talk to you about." Brinn took off her cloak and spread it on the ground.

"I spoke to Queen Betto. The small dragon's name is Dee. Though she's small, Dee is a full-grown dragon...with aspirations of power. It seems she has begun to gather quite a following of disgruntled dragons."

"I wondered if it was something like that." Brinn was glad she hadn't committed to join forces. "What are you going to do about her?"

"I'm not going to do anything." Talon sent a stone flying over the cliff.

Brinn stared disbelievingly. "But she wants dragons to dominate humans again, and she's trying to get a wizard to help her achieve it."

"And my stepping in will only make her argument more potent." Talon stood and paced around the scrub bushes. "You saw them this morning; they do not willingly recognize my authority." He pointed to Graldiss. "He's the one they want to worship. Little Brother! To them the rest of the Prophecy doesn't matter as long as one of their own is glorified. Poor Gral, the whole affair of being shrunk was embarrassing for him, and that's all they want to hear about." He sat back down. "I don't want to be worshiped, but it's hard enough convincing humans to accept the need for equality between the two races. It should be easier with dragons. This Prophecy belongs to the dragons, they should be willing to accept and follow it."

"Are there really that many dragons fighting against the reuniting?"

"Fighting or ignoring, enough to make my job difficult."

Brinn laughed. "Did you really think fulfilling prophecy was supposed to be easy?" Brinn thought about Dee sneaking into the cave and listening to their conversation. "If you aren't going to interfere here, why did you come?"

"Betto wanted to speak to me."

"She wanted your help?"

"Quite the opposite. She wanted to make sure I would stay out of what ever happens. She said: 'This is not the time for you to intervene. This is a dragon matter. The river must follow its course.'"

Brinn was surprised. "What does she mean by that? Is she just going to let this happen?"

Talon shrugged. "Dragons can be very mystical when they want to be. She is the Queen; I won't step in unless she asks."

Brinn felt frustration at Talon's words but said nothing. Instead, Brinn brought up her concerns about the letter she had received from Barkin.

"I'm sure you've come to the same conclusion about that as I have. I can't prove it, but I'm sure Keldric was up to his old tricks." He tossed another rock. "That was a very silly and dangerous thing you did with that bear."

Brinn opened her mouth to defend herself but instead she laughed. "Alright, I guess it *was* pretty stupid. But it seemed like the thing to do at the time."

Talon continued to scold, "Borda waited *three* days for you. He was frantic when I found him. It took an hour to convince him you were still alive and another to get him to return home. I'm sure you'll see that his loyalty is amply rewarded."

Brinn felt guilty at her thoughtless behavior.

Agnar joined them. Talon stood and turned his mind to happier thoughts. "The Hatching Festival will take place next week."

"What are you going to bring me?" Agnar asked Talon.

"That is a secret, Youngling." Talon put his arm around the dragon's shoulders. "How have you been? I've missed you."

"You could have come to visit," Agnar said petulantly.

"My presence would have made your life more difficult, you know that. Besides, we've spoken together often enough for you not to be homesick."

"What's the Hatching Festival?" Brinn asked.

"It's a yearly gathering of all the colonies to unite and celebrate." Graldiss explained.

"And to compete," Draega added. "We're going to enter the relay race," he told Brinn, "and Fireball Elimination; you've been helping with our training."

"I'm large enough this year to compete in Cloud Soaring," Telis said proudly.

"Will you come?" Agnar asked Brinn.

Talon shook his head slowly. "I'm afraid that's not possible."

Brinn tried not to feel hurt, the look of disappointment from her cavemates helped. "I'll get some needed rest. Just be sure to tell me all about it."

The sun was beginning to set and Graldiss motioned to Talon. "We need to go."

"Yes." Talon hugged Agnar. "I'll see you again soon. I like your friends." He took Brinn aside. "Betto has granted you shelter indefinitely in her colony, but with the way things are going, you might consider returning home. Speaking of home, Grindle wanted me to bring you these." Talon picked up a package from between two boulders. "Take care of yourself." He put his arms around the small shoulders. "Trust your instincts. I know you want to help here but remember...you're a human and a wizard, twice the enemy in the minds of many." He kissed Brinn's forehead as he would a child's. "Contact me if you need help." Talon waved jauntily and climbed onto Graldiss' back.

The large dragon winked at Brinn before spreading his wings and lifting into the sky. They faded quickly from view. Telis gave Brinn a ride back to the ledge.

The rest of the night was filled with excited chatter and quiet contemplation. The dragons had a number of visitors eager to hear about their time with Little Brother. Happily Brinn was left out of the discussions. She sat quietly by the fire, considering what she would do in the next few weeks. Returning to Enoa seemed like the only thing to do. She had grown used to living with dragons; did she really want to live around humans again? But how could she stand by and watch a sneaky little revolutionist cause trouble.

Brinn picked up the package Talon brought her. She was glad to find it contained an assortment of clothes. She went behind her dressing screen she had asked Agnar to set up and changed into her favorite robe and furred slippers. With a sign of contentment Brinn curled up next to the fire and opened a book from Draega's library. She only got through a few pages before she was unpleasantly interrupted.

Dee asked to speak to Brinn. Seeing no way to decline, Brinn invited the small red dragon to join her by the fire.

"They'll go on like that all night." Dee said sourly.

"Like what?" Brinn desperately wished the small dragon would go away.

"Younglings are so impressionable. They will babble all night about their Krrig Daa." Dee's annoyance was obvious.

"Actually I think they're talking about Little Brother." Brinn looked down at her book.

"He didn't stay long, did he," the dragon said thoughtfully.

"Well, Talon *did* need transportation back to the mountain." Brinn noisily turned a page.

"I meant the Krrig Daa. He didn't stay very long. I wonder what he was doing here," Dee asked pointedly.

Brinn remembered Dee had been eavesdropping earlier. "Talon came to help me out with a spell."

"And he had a long discussion with the Queen." Dee didn't believe for one minute Talon had come here for so silly a reason. "Any idea what they were discussing?"

"It would have been impolite for him not to visit the Queen while he was here," Brinn said in a light, naive tone. "He told me he spoke to Betto about the Hatching Festival."

Dee waved the excuse away. "He didn't have to make an appearance for that." The dark eyes became slits. "No, he was here to confer with Betto on something more important. What is he planning to do?"

Brinn had had enough, she slammed her book down on the table and bent her face down to Dee's. "You would be advised to keep such questions to yourself and leave the affairs of the colony to someone more qualified."

Dee got to her feet and glared up at Brinn. "You would be wise not to meddle in the affairs of dragons," she hissed, then disappeared.

Brinn sank into her chair and took a deep breath. She was surprised that the other dragons had not been aware of the incident by the fire, only Telis glanced her way for a moment before rejoining the heated conversation about their colony's chance at winning the relay flight at the Festival. She put a log on the fire and began to plan. Brinn knew she was not going to stand by and watch this vile creature poison the colony.

Brinn had more time to herself as the day of the Hatching Festival neared. Telis spent his days in high-altitude soaring, Draega searched through his books for the perfect story to tell during the Bonfire, Agnar was finishing work on a leather-bound book for Talon. Fewer and fewer dragons came to hear stories until the day before the festival when only the first clutch of four dragons came to listen.

"What story will you tell at the Bonfire?" Grissa asked after Brinn finished telling the story of Tiggat, The Wizard of Calippa.

"I told you," Mell whispered harshly into the greenish dragon's ear, "She can't come, she's a human."

Yorel huffed at Mell. "You don't know everything. The Krrig Daa is a human."

"The Krrig Daa is special," Brinn said firmly. "I will spend the day here, in peace and quiet."

"I can't wait to see the races." Paygor flapped his small wings and was able to lift off the ground a few feet. "Kedri will win for sure."

Yorel jumped up and down in excitement. "The Air Dancing!"

"The food!" Grissa licked his lips in anticipation.

Mell shook her head. "Hatchlings! I will spend the day listening to the elders discuss affairs of the day." She reached behind a horn-bud and scratched a new yellow scale.

Brinn watched as the clutch argued over which event would be more exciting. She had an urge to grab them all up in her arms and hug them to her. In the few weeks since they had entered the cave looking for Draega, the hatchlings had grown many inches and begun to lose their hatching scales. She couldn't wait to see them make their first flight.

"I have a gift for you." Brinn brought out small packages.

"Hatching gifts!" Grissa clutched the package to her chest. "We didn't bring you anything."

"She didn't *hatch*," Mell said under her breath while she eagerly ripped open the colored wrapping.

The hatchlings oohed and aahed over the brightly colored ribbons decorated with bells and beads. Yorel tied his to the tip of his tail and gave it a jingle, Grissa tied hers into a pretty bow around her neck, and Paygor wrapped his forearm in the shimmering blue material. Mell held hers up carefully, the firelight playing on the shining beads; tears filled her eyes. The tiny dragon threw her arms around Brinn. "It's beautiful!"

Brinn smiled and wiped a tear from her cheek. "Now run along, it's almost time for supper." She chased the hatchlings out of the cave.

Just after breakfast the next day, Agnar and Telis began to prepare for the outing. Brinn reassured Agnar she wasn't disappointed at not accompanying them. "I'll spend the day roaming the cliff top, gathering flowers. A quiet cup of cider and a good book in the evening. I'll have as much fun as you."

Brinn chose not to accompany her friends to the Hatching Cave where Betto would transport large groups of her colony to the festival grounds. She felt the powerful surges of magic as she pulled on her walking shoes. When the surges ended, Brinn felt it was safe to transport herself to the cliff top. Brinn was working on her second armload of flowers when she heard voices.

Brinn dropped to the ground and searched the skyline. Two figures were coming toward her. She willed herself invisible. A pack of dogs started barking,

Brinn watched them bound over the brush and rush in her direction. They were halted by the length of their leash. One of the figures stopped, holding tightly to the ropes, the other walked up to the dogs and looked in the direction they were barking.

"I know you're there, wizard. You can't hide from the dogs. Best come out before they break free and tear you apart."

Brinn stared at the horrible gnashing teeth only a few feet away and at the scruffy man looking through her. The dogs leaped ahead another foot and Brinn screamed. She let loose of her energy and became visible.

"That's it. No need to come to any harm, at least not yet anyway." The awful man laughed.

A third figure appeared over the ridge. "Come, come, Sencha, that's no way to talk to a powerful wizard."

Brinn got to her feet and faced her enemy. "Keldric."

Chapter 18

Talon stood against the wall of a large meeting hall. He had made a point of attending these yearly gatherings but rarely enjoyed them. This year was especially tiresome because it was scheduled for the same day as the Hatching Festival. He would much rather be in the open fields watching Air Dancing than standing around with a bunch of self-centered old men in a smoky, gaudily decorated room.

Barkin made his way to Talon's side. "Big crowd this year," he said conversationally. "Must mean Garsun isn't providing the refreshments." Talon smiled. "Are you sure you should be here? You know what they're going to be discussing."

"That's why it's important for me to be here." Talon looked at his friend. "Someone has to object."

"You know I'll support you. But I don't know the girl, don't know what the power will do to her." Barkin was honest enough to look guilty.

Talon knew if someone as educated as Barkin still held on to the antiquated prejudice against female wizards, there was no way the others would accept Brinn. With the sounding of the gong, Talon took his place around the great table. He looked at the worn and cynical faces around him. Many of these men had seen several centuries.

Talon searched for Keldric in the crowd, but in a sea of snowy heads there was no sight of the black-haired wizard. When he commented about the absence to Barkin, his friend smiled slyly. "I heard the Council banned the snake. He's made a lot of enemies while regaining his power."

The meeting was called to order by a portly, elaborately dressed wizard named Nymna. "Welcome Brothers! We are glad so many could attend this year's gathering. You will be pleased to know that this year Brother Peasoh has graciously taken on the duty of arranging the refreshments for us." Nymna looked at a neatly written scroll. "This year we are saddened by the loss of Fernley the Bard." Talon noticed that Nymna didn't mention Fernley's successor, as was customary. "Four of our number have begun the training of their apprentices; please sign up to help with their passing-on parties before you leave. There have been requests by Rolloon, Frittik, and Marchal to relocate their territory. If you know of a suitable cave or cottage available, please pass that along. The rotation of High Council members will take place during the full moon next month; candidates are requested to turn in scrolls of application before they leave today. Leog the Mild has asked for help with the translation of the Drallian

Tablets; he needs three volunteers to spend the summer conjugating verbs; meet with him later to make arrangements. We are still asking for any information you might have on the whereabouts of five missing Brothers: Momett, Tristo, Riddliak, Bassal, and Onial." Talon could hear Keldric's name being whispered around the table. Nymna looked over his notes and put the scroll down. "Well, that's all of the announcements, unless someone has anything to add." No one did. "Then let's move on to the principal purpose of this meeting." He looked seriously at the wizards seated around him. "A female inherited power."

It was clear that most of the wizards were unaware of this bit of news. The room broke out in outraged shouts, table banging and arm waving. Talon never believed the reaction would be this bad. He was well aware of the reaction most men had at the inclusion of women in previously male-only institutions such as armies, sovereignty, and child rearing. It took only one vicious female army slaughtering their way through the Rint Valley before generals started taking a second look at some of the girls laboring in the fields as possible recruits. A doddering old king had allowed his daughter to succeed him and the prosperity of her realm was unparalleled. The growing number of widows raising children had made many change their ideas of parental roles. If these fundamental changes were being accepted, why couldn't Brinn's existence also be accepted.

"This is an outrage!" One ancient wizard shouted. "How could it have happened?"

Nymna looked at Talon, but did not ask him to explain. The wizard leader had the power to see into the past, and he knew very well what had occurred at the inn. "With little regard to protocol, Fernley did not arrange for an apprentice when his time was near its end. With his last breath he transferred his being to the innkeep's daughter, though there were ample male candidates available."

"And did the girl lose her mind at the moment of transference?" Drees asked with morbid curiosity.

Talon wanted to tell them of Brinn's courage and clear-headed actions but he knew it would make no difference. Though Talon was accepted as Olwin's successor, the wizards were still suspicious of what mental instabilities might have arisen with his receiving a dragon spirit. No, they would not listen to his opinions.

"As far as we can tell, she retains her sanity, but we can only guess at the misery she must be going through." Nymna looked around the table. "We feel that under these circumstances it is up to us to do what is necessary to correct Fernley's error. The floor is open to comments." Nymna sat down.

A storm of shouting filled the room. Talon picked up the phrases: waste of power, can't think clearly enough, too emotional, can never make up their minds, easily controlled, and it's just not done. Talon looked around for some supporters. He found Nymna looking straight at him, a sly smile on his face.

Talon's anger would not allow him to sit quietly by any longer. He stood and in a voice that quieted all the others, he said: "I'm appalled!" All heads turned to stare. "Here you sit, making irrelevant remarks of someone you know nothing about! And all of those judgments can be said against any number of you." Talon pointed a finger at a wizard halfway down the table. "Grollar, last month you got so angry at a tree that wouldn't flower at just the right moment that you blew up a whole orchard, wasn't that a bit emotional? And you, Karrag, it took you fifty years to decide between two apprentices. Vyssa, you let King Murtis decide every move you make. I could name a dozen wizards who were imbeciles or who have wasted their power on trivialities. What makes you think the mere fact of being a woman would make a difference in how a person handles the power?"

Embarrassed mumbles and defensive grunts were all that answered Talon. After a moment, Nymna stood and cleared his throat. "Honorable sentiments, Talon, but I don't think we are ready for any more of your radical ideas." The old man stood and raised his hands. "Shall we have a show of fire from those in favor of removing the problem?" The room lit up with pillars of flame above the wizards in agreement. Talon sat down slowly. "Opposed?" Four pillars of smoke. "The majority has spoken." Again Nymna looked directly at

Talon. "Now we must consider how the deed should be done."

Forrit cleared his throat. "Whatever the method, I believe the power this girl carries should not be transferred, but rather dispersed. There's no telling what... contamination has taken place." Muttered agreement spread around the table.

"Very well, let her spirit be released." Nymna was able to sound magnanimous about the whole event.

Talon sat, stone-faced, as his fellow wizards discussed quick, painless, quiet, isolated methods of killing his friend. After agonizing minutes, Barkin stood and made a suggestion. "You have decided on a course of elimination, but have you considered removing the power and not the girl?" The room was silent with bewilderment. Talon could have groaned. "Some of you have witnessed this process when one of our own tried to kill Talon." Oret and Poldrun nodded, having been at Talon's Rite of Transference and seen Keldric's powers removed.

Eyes turned again to Talon. "Yes, what Barkin has suggested can be done." He looked apologetically at Barkin. "But it will not be done by me. I know the girl you are discussing so cold-bloodedly. She is worthy of the power she carries. I will have nothing to do with *any* actions taken against her." He stepped away from the table and disappeared.

Nymna was unmoved. "Then that decides our choice, now how shall it be carried out?"

***

Brinn shifted uncomfortably on the rocky ground and pulled the thin blanket over her shoulder. The chain around her ankles made movement difficult. Her body was already sore from the day's ride on a horse, now she had rocks the size of apples boring into her back. Her anger and frustration had been bumped out on the back of the packhorse and now she was just tired. She was hungry, too. When Keldric offered her a bowl of soup Brinn had rejected it out of spite. Now she wished she hadn't. Tomorrow she would have to swallow her pride, tonight she would have to listen to her growling stomach. She relocated one of the larger stones from under her hip. A low, menacing growl answered her action. Brinn didn't know which was the bigger threat, the dogs or Keldric.

In the light of the fire, Brinn watched the two men in charge of the horrid dogs. Sencha and Krillik were dirty and crude. They were perfectly comfortable sitting in the mud next to their dogs. They even ate and scratched like their dogs. The dogs themselves did not look different or special. Brinn could only imagine the training they had been put through to be so sensitive to magic.

Just how sensitive were they? Brinn began experimenting with different levels of energy drawn in and released. Even the slightest surge brought forth a growl. Brinn quickly discovered that using even the smallest amount of magic against the chains was futile, they resisted any spell. It didn't take long before Keldric stomped across the camp and threatened to knock Brinn unconscious if she continued to play with the dogs. Keldric was clearly uncomfortable around the beasts. He had stayed well ahead of them during the day and far outside the firelight at night.

At sunrise, they mounted and traveled steadily toward the forested mountains. Brinn figured Keldric was trying to hide from the dragons. Brinn had hoped to learn what the wizard's plans for her were, and how he had found her again, but Keldric was not in a talkative mood. Brinn was left to assume the monster was planning on killing her for her power. Brinn imagined a host of horrible tortures for both Keldric and the dogs. They would only be fantasies if she couldn't get out of the magic-resistant chains. To this end, Brinn began hardening a twig she picked up. Small bursts of magic brought growls from the dogs but Keldric was too far ahead to hear. Krillik soon ignored his dog, swatting at him from time to time.

Keldric was pleased when Brinn had given up testing her magic. What he didn't see was that she was concentrating on a single link in the chain around her ankles. Brinn had been able to harden her twig enough to use it as a lever, prying apart the ends of one silvery link. Brinn also changed her demeanor to one of helpless female to slow them down. She asked the dirty men to perform trivial chores for her: warming her shoes, straining the leaves from her tea, smoothing out the ground under her bedroll. Krillik did not want to incur the great wizard's wrath and grudgingly saw to Brinn's needs. Brinn also took frequent pardon-me-but-

I-have-to-step-behind-a-tree breaks, prudishly asking the men to turn their backs. These seemed to work as the men slowed their pace and left her alone at night, happy to get away from her petty requests.

In the heat of the fourth day, Brinn felt a glimmer of hope as her link budged. As Sencha prepared the noon meal, Brinn silently put her whole strength into the hardened twig. With one final twist the link bent just far enough to slide off the next link. The chain fell to the ground. Brinn stood and took a few short steps as if her feet were still bound. She waited until the men's attention returned to the boiling pot then went behind a wide tree. Brinn tore the hood from her robe and hooked it on a low limb in hopes the men would think she was squatting behind the tree. Without looking back, Brinn headed upward into the thick of the forest.

Brinn sacrificed speed for stealth, avoiding piles of crunching leaves and slapping branches. It was some time before she heard any sounds of pursuit. The angry voices of Sencha and Krillik drifted up the hill and Keldric's could be heard even over the howling dogs. It appeared the dogs were not bred for chasing prey who weren't using magic and they were being dragged up the hill. Brinn just had to resist the temptation to use magic. Now that she was being followed, Brinn gave up all pretence of stealth and ran.

Keldric's frustration overpowered his self-control and he blasted a small stand of trees. The dogs went crazy, deserting the smell of girl and lunging at the wizard. Krillik swore and beat the dogs with sticks.

Sencha had to brace himself against a tree to keep the dogs from pulling him over in their desire to tear Keldric to pieces.

Brinn stumbled onto an overgrown path and veered to the south. It soon became evident that the path was not going to make her escape easier. Roots and branches seemed to bend to block her way, rocks and bushes appeared to move to intercept her. She fell frequently and tears were making it hard to see. The dogs must have picked up her scent; Brinn could hear their barking getting closer. She climbed faster, angrily pushing branches aside and stumbling over stones.

Blood oozed from wounds in her palms, Brinn held them tightly to her thighs, cringing at the stinging pain. She couldn't stop now, continuing was the only option. Frustration spurred her to anger. "Move!" she shouted at a branch that crooked down to block her path. Brinn had not expected her words to be anything more than a venting of her anger, but to her surprise the brambles shook slightly and pulled away from the path. Without questioning, Brinn moved on. When a root unearthed itself to catch her foot, Brinn shouted angrily and it slipped back under the dirt. At first Brinn thought she might be using magic unconsciously but the dogs didn't seem to pick up any magic surges. The path's irritating foliage seemed to be cooperating on their own.

When Brinn thought she could go no further, the path widened into a clearing on the hilltop. She stood breathless and bleeding next to an enormous oak tree.

She leaned on it and looked around while she caught her breath. The clearing was larger than she originally thought. There was a garden and a small pond filled with birds. Sheets and towels fluttered on a clothesline. Rather than the weeds and scrub grass Brinn had seen on the path, there was a brilliantly green carpet of grass. The sound of someone humming reminded Brinn that it was not safe to stop for long. She hid behind the tree when an old woman stepped through the bushes.

The woman hummed a lively tune as she bent down and pulled radishes from the garden; carrots and beets followed. Soon her basket was filled with vegetables. She pulled the sheets off the line, folded them neatly and put them on the top of the carrots. "I don't suppose you would help me carrying this in, Missy, it's a bit more than I can handle."

Brinn cringed at being discovered, and slowly came out into the open. "It wouldn't be so heavy if you put less in," she commented, pointing to the heap of vegetables.

"No need to sass, Missy. You don't expect me to entertain guests with just a loaf of bread now do you?" The old woman collected the armload of flowers she had set down to harvest lunch. "Bring it along," she ordered, walking around the oak tree.

Brinn felt surprised at the woman's assumption she was staying, but she didn't want to be rude. She picked up the overloaded basket and walked after the old woman.

On the far side of the tree Brinn saw a door built into its trunk. The old woman disappeared through the door. Brinn stood for a moment, looking into the tree. It appeared to be hollow inside, even furnished. She went inside. It took a minute for Brinn to recover her sense of dimension. The inside of the hollowed out tree was three or four times as large as the outside, and there were doors leading to other rooms.

"Bring that to the kitchen." The old woman took off her shawl and threw it over a chair. She busied herself with arranging her flowers.

Brinn put the basket on the kitchen table. Her attention was drawn to the glowing torches; they didn't smoke at all, in fact, the glow wasn't from a flame. "You're using magic!"

The old woman chuckled and wiped her wet hands on a towel. "Well, of course, Missy, isn't that why you came here?" She took Brinn's hands and clucked at the wounds. Bandages appeared on the table; with quick movements they were wrapped around the cuts and scratches. "The path would not let you through if your quest wasn't worthy."

"I didn't give it a chance. You're a wizard."

"A wizard?" the woman laughed. "Heavens no. I'm a witch, my name is Shawni." The old woman unloaded the basket and began to wash the vegetables.

"A witch?" Brinn searched her memory and Fernley's for any reference to witches. Sure, Brinn had heard fairytales, but she had never heard of any real witches. Fernley's memories only supplied rumors and legends of townsfolk accusing women of being witches, blaming them when the crops failed or for a series of unfortunate coincidences. But no one had actually stood up and claimed they were witches. "Interesting. I found your path by accident. I must say, your plants are very persistent."

Shawni handed Brinn an onion and a knife. "Finely sliced, please. The forest is very protective. Too many villagers were coming up and ruining the forest, so the trees and shrubs started to discourage them. And they are very efficient at keeping out witch-hunters."

Brinn suspected it was really Shawni's influence creating the interfering plant-life. She was glad the native animals hadn't gotten the same protective ideas. "Interesting home you have. Is it natural?"

"What a silly question. Have you ever seen a five-room tree? No, I slept under this tree for a few months before I came up with the idea." Shawni finished preparing the salad and took two potatoes out of the cooking fire.

While she set the table, Shawni spoke to a large grey cat that lounged on the bench. Brinn poured out two mugs of apple cider and sliced the still warm bread. The two ate their meal in silence. Shawni seemed to prefer a one-sided conversation with her cat, and Brinn was still too cautious to make small talk.

After the meal was finished and the table cleared away, Shawni put a kettle on to boil and sat down in a well-worn rocking chair. Brinn had followed her into the central room and was sitting on a couch with lots of multi-colored cushions. With the setting of the sun, a number of birds, large and small, took up perches around the room.

Shawni intertwined her fingers and placed them on her lap. "You may begin," she said.

Brinn stared for a moment. "Begin? Begin what?"

"Your request. You need my assistance; anyone who is desperate enough to make it through the obstacles of the forest is worthy of asking for my help." Shawni sat quietly, waiting.

Brinn didn't know what to say. "I don't think you understand. I didn't come here for your help. As I said, I came upon the path by accident. I am not one of your villagers looking for a potion or magical spell."

Shawni said nothing. Brinn noticed the old woman's fingers unfold and begin to move in a rhythmical fashion on her lap. From across the room there was an odd clicking sound. The clicking had a soothing effect and Brinn felt herself relaxing. She did not expect the gentle push of a mind reaching into hers. Brinn gently shut out the intruding inquiry. She decided it would be easiest to find a problem for Shawni to fix than to try to deter the old woman. "Well, actually I do have a problem."

A smile of 'I knew it' appeared on Shawni's face. People only came when they wanted something from her. She nodded her head, but said nothing, waiting for Brinn to reveal her need. Her fingers stilled, the clicking ceased.

"I need sanctuary."

Shawni's head stopped in mid-nod, she had not expected this type of request. She squinted her eyes and looked more closely at the young woman sitting before her. This little bit of a thing had resisted her mind reading and had not been intimidated by her use of magic. Something was wrong. "Who *are* you?"

It was Brinn's turn to smile with superiority. "My name is Brinn, and I'm a wizard."

Shawni stood up quickly, startling a nearby hawk. She spoke a protective spell and edged away from Brinn.

"Don't worry, I'm not here to harm you. What I said was true: I need a place to hide for a few days."

The old woman moved to the kitchen, making sure the knives were within reach. "Who are you hiding from?" She looked at the door nervously as if expecting something dangerous to come through.

Brinn didn't want to reveal everything, and Shawni looked too frightened to know the whole truth. "A man is looking for me. He thinks I took something of his, something valuable, and he's very persistent. I came upon your path while trying to escape his hounds."

Shawni relaxed. She knew what it was like to be hunted; but the girl was still hiding something, she was sure of it. "What did you take?" she asked.

"A...an amulet." Brinn fell back on her vivid imagination. "It belonged to my father. Keldric stole it from Father's dying hands. My brother was killed trying to recover the heirloom, so it became my quest to regain that which was ours."

Shawni didn't believe a word of Brinn's story, but there was a ring of truth in her request for shelter. "Where is this man now?"

"He was less than an hour behind me. I'm hoping your helpful plants will steer him away from this direction."

Shawni considered for a moment. She even consulted the cat. "You may stay," she said solemnly. "If you will excuse me, I will see to our safety." Shawni left the house.

Brinn walked to the door and looked out. What would this woman do to protect them? As she watched, Brinn heard Shawni speak in a foreign language, something guttural. Within moments a wolf entered the clearing. They looked at each other for a while, then the wolf left. Shawni returned to the tree. "Will she help us?" Brinn asked.

Shawni was pleased Brinn understood what had just taken place. "Yes, she will bring her pack here. Some will stay the night, others will find your pursuer." She went to a cupboard and pulled out a woven blanket. "I'm not accustomed to over-night guests; you will have to make do with the couch."

Brinn gratefully took the blanket. "Thank you. The couch will be fine. It is quite comfortable."

Shawni poured herself a glass of water and retreated to her room. "Good night." The grey cat followed close behind.

Brinn hadn't realized just how tired she was until she pulled the blanket over her shoulders. After one deep breath she fell asleep.

A fresh breeze roused Brinn from a thankfully dreamless sleep, but she didn't feel like getting up, so she pulled the blanket over her face and rolled over. She didn't go back to sleep, but took the time to assess the events of the previous day. Keldric would not easily give up his search for her, and though the protective spell around this glen was strong, he would eventually find his way in. Brinn knew she needed to find a permanent escape, but for the day she should be safe here. She wondered how strong Shawni was, and marveled at the way the old woman had protected herself so perfectly. Brinn considered whether *she* could do the same somewhere. No, Brinn had no desire to become a hermit.

Brinn's thoughts were interrupted by the pressure of a cat climbing on her back. "We're not exactly hermits," the cat said, fitting itself into the gap between Brinn's hip and the couch. "Quite a lot of visitors, if you include the animals along with the few humans that make it up here."

Brinn wondered if she were still dreaming. She was used to talking to dragons, but a cat?

"Got a problem with cats?" A pink tongue went to work on a paw. "Every animal can talk, though most of them don't have anything important to say," he said smugly

"And you do?" Brinn asked.

"Of course. You want to know about Shawni, don't you? Well, I'm the one to ask since I'm the wizard who's power she holds."

Brinn was stunned by this revelation. Nothing in Fernley's library had mentioned the possibility of a wizard inhabiting an animal after transferring his power. "How can you be a cat and your power be in Shawni?"

"It was the only way I could keep her sane. She wasn't ready to have my thoughts and memories in her head, and she couldn't handle the power without my help. It's amazing what you can do if you don't have any preconceived notions. Now I mostly lounge around. I let Shawni run her life, and am here if she needs any help."

Brinn remembered the old woman talking to the cat last night. She decided it was time to get up and find out more about this *witch*. Brinn slipped on her dress and followed the sound of whistling outside.

Shawni was tossing crumbs into the pond. A variety of birds, deer, and small animals surrounded her. "Don't crowd me," she scolded. "Line up." To Brinn's amazement the animals scrambled to form a line, some of the smaller animals sneaking in front of taller ones. A black wolf stood guard by the path. Sensing Brinn's presence, Shawni waved a carrot. "Good morning. I hope you're hungry; I have fresh fruit, apple muffins and blueberry pancakes."

Brinn found that she was, indeed, very hungry. She followed Shawni to an outside table and accepted a cup of tea. The cat jumped onto the table and started in on a saucer of milk. "Does your cat have a name?" she asked.

Shawni poured batter onto a hot skillet. "Riddliak. I call him Riddle; he *is* a bit of one, you know." She passed Brinn a plate of muffins and fresh butter. "Blackflank said that the party following you was camped below the path last night. The dogs with them are anxious."

"Probably having a difficult time with so much magic in the area. These dogs can sense magic."

Shawni grinned. "The wolves will see that the beasts get a good run today." She bit off a chunk of muffin. "You were dead to the world this morning, Missy, they must have run you ragged yesterday." Brinn nodded, her mouth too full to speak. "Best to rest yourself today."

Brinn took a plate of fluffy pancakes. "Thank you again for allowing me to stay. I know it was an odd request."

Shawni laughed. "Folks don't usually want to spend a lot of time with a witch."

Brinn looked at the old woman. "You weren't always a witch, any more than I have been a wizard all my life."

"True." The old woman gave the cat a piece of muffin.

"Will you tell me how it happened?" Brinn didn't know how much Riddliak had told the woman about wizards. She would have to be careful about how much of her own story she told Shawni.

Shawni put two pancakes on a plate and poured herself another cup of tea. "No, I wasn't always a witch. In fact, it's only been the last five years, maybe six, it's hard to keep track of time up here. I used to live in a small village below the forest." She paused for a moment, remembering days gone by. "My husband died and left me a small shop. I bought wool and wove the softest blankets for miles around. They sold very well. My children married. My son took over the shop and my daughters moved to big towns. I was told that Delia had a baby last winter, a little red-haired girl." Her gaze was far away for a moment, saddened.

"Six years ago a young boy wandered into the village. He was covered with scratches, clothes torn, hair matted. He looked like he'd crawled through the woods on his hand and knees. His eyes were wild, terrified. He babbled incoherently. My daughter-in-law knew some healing, so he was brought to our shop and laid on a cot in the back room. He wouldn't eat or drink, and kept trying to get up and run away. We made him drink a cup of comfrey tea. The Healer was sent for, a mistake of course. The old fool immediately declared the boy to be possessed by a demon. He said it would be safer if we didn't go near the boy. It took two days for the poor thing to die. I was wiping his brow when he took his last breath."

"Within the hour I began to hear the voice. At first I refused to listen to the gibberish, but when it started making sense I became scared. I didn't dare tell anyone; I still had nightmares about how they had let that boy die. Day by day I became more certain that the demon who possessed the boy had entered my body. Strange things started happening around me. Objects began to move on their own, small things that I wanted to happen magically happened. Meals cooked in half the time, the goats stopped straying into the neighbor's garden, the looms practically ran by themselves, the die lots were perfect, and mean old Olivian's hair began to fall out.

"I couldn't hide my secret for long. My family discovered it first and tried to protect me, but it was no use. The villagers were an ignorant and frightened lot. The town leaders easily stirred them into a frenzy. I even agreed with them; I thought I was a witch. They felt it was bad luck to have a witch in the village, even suggesting that I be purged. I didn't stick around to let them give it a try."

It was clear by the look on the old woman's face that she still resented the village. "After many days of wandering and nights of listening to the voice in my mind, I found this clearing. Riddliak, after he left me to become a cat, talked to the forest animals who agreed to protect me, and later he showed me how to get the forest itself to keep out all but the most desperate of customers. I get a couple dozen visitors a year who find their way up here to request favors. They keep me supplied with yarn and sugar."

Brinn knew her own story would have been similar if Talon hadn't rescued her, or worse, she would have ended up with someone like Keldric. She was intrigued by Shawni's description of Riddliak 's possession of her mind. Fernley had barely made himself known to her until Talon freed him and then he faded into memory after their initial encounter. Brinn couldn't fathom what it must have been like to have another person living within her head. "But the cat...he's..."

"Interesting, isn't it?" The grey cat snatched the last bite of pancake from Brinn's plate. "Can you imagine the shock I had finding myself inside the mind of a *woman*?"

Brinn glared at the cat and pulled her plate away. "Fernley didn't seem to have any trouble with it." Her curiosity got the better of her. "There are no records of a wizard ever separating himself after the Rite of Transference."

"It took some doing, I can tell you. I gave Shawni such power as she could handle and kept the rest for myself. I mean, you've never seen a cat talk, have you? One of my predecessors came across the spell a century ago. It required the new wizard to accept the split. Once I taught her how to use the power I gave her, Shawni released me into this cat. It took some time to get used to this body, and the feline mind, but its temperament suited me."

"And I was glad of the company." Shawni sat back and looked at Brinn. "Now you said you were a wizard. I think it's time for you to tell *your* story."

Brinn nodded and poured herself a cup of juice. "Up until a few months ago I worked for my father at his inn. When one of the guests, later identified as a wizard, became ill I took care of him. As he died, he transferred his power to me. I was lucky, I didn't find out about my new abilities until after another wizard came to give me the news." Brinn decided not to tell Shawni and Riddle about Talon or the dragons; that was just too complicated.

"And why is a wizard chasing you?" the cat asked.

Brinn looked at the wizard-cat and gave him the best excuse she could think of. "You, of all people should know how wizards feel about my sex having power." She turned to Shawni. "It seems this is a very exclusive guild. No women allowed." Brinn laughed to herself. "I wonder what they would do if they found out there are *two* of us."

Shawni shook her head. "I'm not like you. A witch, that's all I am."

"I'm sorry to break it to you...but you are a lot more powerful than you think." The cat pawed Brinn's arm, so she didn't say anything further.

Shawni kept Brinn busy during the day weeding the garden, preparing meals, and caring for an injured sparrow. After lunch Brinn reached out her mind for Talon. He was quite worried about her. He had detected the dogs and hadn't dared to contact her.

"I will send someone for you immediately. Do you know where you are?" Brinn described the direction they had taken after leaving the cliffs as best she could.

The cat was watching Brinn converse mentally with Talon. When she finished he curled up on her lap. "I have been out of contact with other wizards for quite some time, never really cared for the lot. Tell me a bit of what's been going on." He tilted his head and allowed Brinn to scratch his neck.

Brinn saw no harm in telling the cat everything she knew. She delved into some of Fernley's memories for information about the wizards she'd had no contact with. She was glad of something to fill the time.

As the sun began to set, a figure appeared in the sky above the clearing. Shawni was intrigued. "I've seen a lot of birds in my time, but that one is the biggest...doesn't fly like any bird I've ever seen."

"It looks like a vulture. A very large vulture." The cat decided it would be safer to be in the tree house.

Brinn watched the bird fly overhead. She felt an oppressive weight as it descended. Squinting, she saw a rider astride the giant bird. Brinn reeled as a powerful blast struck her.

"What's happening?" Shawni asked, helping to steady Brinn.

Brinn pointed to the bird. "My pursuer, Keldric, is riding that thing."

"Well, it's awfully rude of him to come crashing in on us." With a surge of energy the trees stretched up

271

and swiped at the bird, flinging out vines and pinecones.

The vulture rose out of range. Keldric began to form a ball of flames. But before the sphere was fully formed another giant bird swooped toward the vulture. Keldric's ball slipped and singed his bird's wings. With an agonized cry the bird twisted, dumping Keldric from its back. The wizard disappeared from the sky. The vulture wanted no part of a battle with the intruder and flew off.

As the second 'bird' began to spiral down, the setting sun glinted on scales. Shawni could not take her eyes from the descending creature. A host of birds escorted the dragon to the clearing. Shawni backed away, lifting the cat that had come out of hiding. The birds flocked around the dragon as if it were one of their own. Agnar beamed with delight.

Brinn broke into the festive scene. "You are a welcome sight! It didn't take you long to find me."

Agnar gently shook off most of the birds. "Not after Talon told us where to look for you." He peered at Shawni and the cat then back to Brinn. "The cat is glowing," he remarked.

"I imagine both of them are. I'll explain it to you later." Brinn turned to Shawni. "This is my friend, Agnar of the Pallan Cliff colony. Agnar, this is Shawni the Witch, and Riddliak, the Wizard."

Agnar bowed. "Pleased to meet you."

Shawni stepped forward. "Never seen anything quite like you, but I'm pleased to make your acquaintance." Riddle wasn't so pleased and remained aloof. "Come into the house, I'll make us up some..." The witch looked curiously at the dragon.

"Tea and toast and perhaps a few of those muffins would be wonderful."

Shawni grinned. "Blackberry jam?"

Agnar eagerly followed Shawni into the tree, ducking his head to fit inside. Brinn scanned the sky for a moment. Would Keldric give up now that Agnar was here? Riddle decided he would rather be in the company of wolves than dragons and remained outside.

Chapter 19

Shawni left the dinner dishes in the sink and went to bed early. Brinn and Agnar went out into the warm night and sat under the stars. Brinn noticed Blackflank no longer guarded the glen. Agnar made himself comfortable on the grass, shifting to accommodate the ducks, geese, sparrows and a crow.

"Is that normal?" Brinn pointed to the flock. She hadn't seen Graldiss collect birds like this.

Agnar shrugged. "I don't know, this is a strange place." He liked this new attention he was getting. "That is *some* tree. There's even a fireplace! And did you notice the moss on the floor? I should see if we can get it to grow on our cave floor. I would like to have her show me how she makes those knitting needles work, I can't get my paws around those tiny needles. That woman is quite a powerful wizard. Everything around her goes out of its way to please her. I've never seen that before."

Brinn explained Shawni's background to Agnar. "I don't think any of the other wizards knows she's up here."

"That's probably for the best. With such magical protection as she has, who knows *what* would happen to someone trying to do her harm."

Brinn recalled how the trees fought off the large vulture. She told Agnar about the forest path. Eventually she told him everything that had happened to her the past few days. They decided it would be best if they left the next morning before Keldric had time to try anything more.

Brinn returned to the tree and left Agnar to sleep with the birds.

Shawni was sad to see her company leave but understood their haste. She also hadn't liked Keldric intruding and Riddle had been on edge since the dragon appeared, so it was best for life to get back to normal, or at least what *she* considered normal. Shawni gave Brinn a knitted blanket and placed a charm around Agnar's neck that would keep his scales shiny. Brinn promised to write down Shawni's story and come back to visit when she could.

Brinn slid onto Agnar's back and they leapt into the air. Birds trailed after them for a while, dropping back one-by-one as the dragon out flew them.

"Are we going back to the cliffs?" Brinn shouted against the wind.

"No, Talon wants us in Crinnelia." With a surge of energy they blinked away from Shawni's mountain and reappeared in cooler skies. Brinn was surprised when they didn't veer toward the cave openings in Ittra's mountain but down to a large stone cottage in the middle of a field. "Talon will meet us here tonight."

Brinn slid from Agnar's back and followed him to the cottage. The door was wide enough for a large dragon to pass through. The inside looked very much like the inside of a cave, there was only one room, sparsely furnished but comfortable. It didn't look like a powerful wizard lived here. There were no book-filled shelves or potions bubbling in pots. The only oddity Brinn could see was a stack of rolled, woven sleeping mats along one wall; then she remembered Talon talking to Ittra about a group of younglings living in his cottage.

Agnar made himself comfortable, pulling knitting needles and yarn from a bag Shawni had given him. From a comfortable chair Brinn watched as the dragon practiced making the needles move in mid-air. When the yarn persisted in knotting up she offered to help cast-on. By the time Talon and Graldiss arrived that evening Agnar had three inches of lumpy scarf to show off. Graldiss thought the whole thing was silly.

Brinn had hoped to have a leisurely supper and catch up on events, but Talon informed them that Queen Py was expecting them within the hour. After a quick meal of bread and cheese, Talon and Brinn climbed astride Graldiss and vaulted into the sky, Agnar close behind.

After an hour of leaping from landmark to landmark Brinn caught her first glimpse of Tor Akkra. She tried to grasp the idea that a mountain could have exploded in such a way that it looked like a jagged-edged bowl. As they neared, Brinn could make out rows of caves cut into the steep walls, a lake of deep blue filled the basin floor. It wasn't until they began the descent into the mountain's gaping maw that Brinn grasped the immensity of this dragon-city. There was no doubt that the enormous size of the community was necessary, the dragons who circled the lake and flew into, or out-of, the caves were twice the size of Graldiss.

She felt very small as they headed into one of the largest openings. Graldiss flew through the twisting tunnel with ease. Brinn was suddenly blinded when the passageway opened onto a brightly lit cavern. After her eyes became accustomed to the light, Brinn saw there were few actual torches but their light was reflected on the glassy surface of the walls. Brinn saw a number of dragons washing and grooming themselves. Graldiss landed gently near a waiting dragon.

The bronze dragon bustled around Brinn. "You are late!" he scolded Graldiss. "No time for a bath, and she smells like dirt!"

Before Brinn knew what was happening she was engulfed in a torrent of energy. Her body tingled and her hair untangled itself and formed a neat twist. In a quick jerk her dirty robe was replaced with a simple blue wool cloak over a white dress. An apple, shined to gleaming, appeared in her hand. With a gentle push Brinn found herself relocated in front of a large oak door. Talon soon joined her looking equally cleaned-up, though his robes were much more elegant than Brinn's.

"That was interesting." Brinn gently touched her hair.

Talon smiled at Brinn's sarcastic tone. "Rartha was actually very gentle. He doesn't like humans much. I think our lowliness upsets his delicate sensibilities. It was months before I came out of his ministrations without a bruise."

Brinn rubbed her arm absently. "Why are we waiting out here?" She began to pace. "I don't even understand what we're doing here. What does this queen want with me?"

Talon leaned casually against the tunnel wall. "Why don't you eat that apple. You'll need your strength. We are here because Py told us to come, and you never ignore a summons from Py. There is no ultimate Queen among dragons but Py comes close. She is the most respected of all dragons."

Brinn felt ashamed of her outburst. She quietly ate her apple. When Brinn had taken her last bite the core suddenly vanished and the oak door silently opened. Talon grinned and led Brinn into Py's private chamber.

It took a lot of self-control for Brinn not to stare at the opulent surroundings she walked into. Gems sparkled on the floor, gold and silver statues of various dragons lined the walls, intricate tapestries hung from the high ceiling to the glassy floor, velvet cushions large enough for the massive dragons were set before an ornate fireplace. Brinn expected to see an equally opulent dragon holding court but the bright blue cushion where the Queen would have sat was empty. A smallish dragon stood by the fire. She turned when the door closed.

"Thank the Ancestors you're all right!" Betto went to Brinn's side. "I am so sorry that you were tangled up in this unhappy affair. I feel responsible."

Brinn bowed to the queen but was puzzled. "How could you feel responsible? It was Keldric who kidnapped me."

Betto slowly shook her head. "He had some help. I can't prove it, but I'm fairly sure Dee was involved. She wasn't at the Festival and we now know she's made a pact with Keldric."

Brinn was stunned by this revelation. "Excuse me, I don't mean to be rude, but if Dee is conspiring with Keldric why are you here and not at the cliffs?"

Betto smiled grimly. "Ah, you see the danger of those two combining forces." The queen nodded thoughtfully and returned to the warmth of the fire.

Talon put his arm around Brinn's shoulders. "A lot has happened since you disappeared." He led her to a cushion by the fire.

After a few moments Betto turned her gaze from the fire and looked sadly at Brinn. "I am here as an exile. Py has granted me sanctuary."

Brinn didn't know what to say. How could the queen give up her colony? What had Dee done to make her leave? "I don't understand."

"Dee had convinced enough of the elders that I was dangerously close to allowing humans to control our future. She even had a human prisoner who said Talon was preparing to install human regents within each colony with the plan to reduce dragons to slaves."

Brinn laughed. "How could they believe such a thing?"

"Ignorance and fear. Once Dee had a sizable following she made her move. She knew her position would be shaky if I died mysteriously, so she claimed the Right of Challenge. I had the choice to fight or go into exile."

"But I thought dragons never fought each other." Brinn was trying to take in everything she was being told.

"Yes, normally that is correct. But the Right of Challenge has been a way for colonies to rid themselves of bad queens. I think I surprised Dee by taking exile." Betto patted Brinn's arm when she saw the battle of emotions on the young woman's face. "You think I deserted my colony, but, in fact, I saved it by choosing to leave them for a time."

Now Brinn was really confused.

"You see, I knew something most of Dee's followers didn't, Dee has no magical power." Betto grinned. "A birth defect of sorts. She has hid it very well. If there was even the slightest chance she could kill me and take my power I had to keep it from happening."

"And good thing you did." An enormous blue dragon entered the cave from between two tapestries. "If that *toad* had gotten the knowledge and power of a queen she would be unstoppable."

Talon bowed low, Brinn followed. The large dragon touched her head to Talon's then turned and placed her paw on Brinn's. With a quick gentle brush the dragon touched Brinn's mind with her own. She liked what she saw.

Brinn wanted to weep and laugh at the same time. She had never felt such vastness in another's mind. She fell to her knees. A great claw lifted her chin. "Greetings, Brinn. I have long wanted to meet you." Py's voice was soft and gentle.

"I am honored," Brinn stammered and got to her feet.

The dragon grinned. An enormous kettle appeared on the fire and a plate of fruit floated through the air, settling on a low table. "Betto was very brave and selfless. We have no doubt her colony will see that *lizard* for what she really is." Py served up plates of fruit and poured tea.

To break the uncomfortable silence Brinn told the story of Shawni. Py was interested to hear about Riddliak, as the concept of transferring power into an animal was unique. Talon seemed unusually pleased when Brinn described Shawni's protective glen. After the meal was finished Py stood and looked seriously at

Brinn. "Are you strong enough to go through a bit of an ordeal? There's a ceremony I would like you to take part in."

Brinn was feeling cozy and a bit sleepy by the fire. She would have loved to say 'No, I've had enough ceremonies' but she found she could not resist the gentle giant. She stood and brushed off her dress. "I won't have to do anything strenuous, will I?"

Py laughed. "No battles today. Talon will bring you in." The two queens disappeared from the room.

Brinn waited silently until she felt a tingle and Talon got to his feet. "It's time."

Talon led Brinn between two tapestries and down a short pathway to a cliff face. Graldiss was waiting and flew them to a ledge overlooking the immense crater, then led the way back to the Meeting Cave. Brinn paused at the cave entrance for a moment.

"Nervous?" Talon asked.

Brinn nodded. She took a deep breath, and adjusted her cloak, pulling the hood up as Talon had. She squared her shoulders, held her head high and followed Talon. The first steps were slow and uneasy but when Brinn caught sight of Agnar next to the entrance ready to accompany her she gained confidence and strode purposefully forward.

The rumble of conversation died down as the Chosen One led Brinn through the crowd. They stopped below the steps leading up to the Queen's dais. At Talon's direction, Brinn climbed the steps alone. Py was seated regally at the top, Betto at her side. Brinn knelt low before the queen, holding her arms wide in submission.

Py rose and placed her forefoot on the covered head. The queen's mind touched Brinn's for a moment. "Just be yourself," she whispered in the young wizard's mind. The clawed foot was removed. "Welcome Brinn of Enoa. We are honored to have you here with us today."

Brinn turned and looked out at a sea of colors and horns and wings. Hatchlings and Younglings were seated closest to the steps. Py gestured and Brinn sat on a low stool and slowly pulled back her hood. It was evident from the murmuring that many of those gathered were surprised to see a young woman's face.

Py spread her wings for silence. "Hundreds of years before the oldest of you were born, we lived in a time of great fear. This was not the fear of knights and wizards hunting us down to rid the world of our race, but the terror inflicted by a single deranged wizard. Targis Orlag." The hisses and growls were overwhelming.

"No one knew where Orlag's hatred of us came from. If he explained it to his victims they took it to their grave. We might have understood had he fed off our power, but that was not his desire, nor did he crave the notoriety of being a dragonslayer. This not knowing only added to the terror Orlag held over this colony." Py closed her eyes and took a deep breath, telling this story was clearly difficult for her.

"The horror began suddenly with the murder of a youngling who was hunting unaccompanied." The name Chandri was wailed by every dragon present. "Precautions were taken but everyday there were signs of a menace aimed against our colony. Threatening messages scrawled in the tunnels, disemboweled animals in caves, tainted food, and other vandalism, traps...and killings. We could not defend ourselves against an enemy we could not see. We lived everyday in fear. Then came the horrible day when our most sacred of places was violated. Orlag sneaked into our Hatching Cave and destroyed one egg from every clutch." The moans and cries were soft and heart wrenching.

"So terrified was the queen that she placed her newly birthed egg into a tiny cave hidden deep within the mountain and sealed it both physically and magically. When I was safely hidden, my mother confronted Orlag. The battle was fierce, not even the old magic could destroy the monster. The queen returned mortally wounded. So grieved was her council that they risked their own lives to defeat Orlag. They devised a plot where four of the five would physically and magically attack the wizard while the fifth gathered enough energy to bind the wizard to her. The four died of their wounds." The names of the Honored Four were spoken with reverence. "Grasping Orlag in her claws the fifth rose high into the air." Neesha's name was chanted. "In a death dive the two plummeted to the craggy peaks." Brinn had to hold her hands over her ears as the chant grew louder. "Just as death reached up to clutch them, Neesha disappeared." The cave went silent. "Targis Orlag's crushed and bloody body was found on an icy, jagged peak." A cheer rang out. "But Neesha's body was never found, her fate was never known." Py motioned for Brinn to come forward. "Until now."

The crowd went silent. Brinn looked fearfully at the mass of gigantic dragons. What would they do to her if she told them the whole story? She turned to Talon who nodded. She took a breath, closed her eyes. She was startled when the voice that came forth was not her own. "As we spun in our death spiral the profanity that was Orlag hung limp in my grasp. Thinking he might already be dead I loosened my mental grip and prepared myself for death. In that moment the *Filth* cast a spell. I was flung away into a dark, glassy pit that was sealed with his dying breath. The pit sustained me so that I could not die from starvation. It was many years before my body faded but my mind lived on. At first it fed on hatred and revenge, but was tempered through the centuries until my only desire was to see the sunlight on the mountain peaks again. One day a tiny human child unknowingly lifted the stone that sealed my prison. With a rush of joy my spirit entered the young girl. Finding only fear and ignorance, I left the girl and entered into her mother. In an instant I saw a longing for excitement and freedom the woman did not have in her life. I offered the woman a chance for both. The woman offered me her body to house my spirit, not knowing of the change that would take place. In my thrill at being given a second chance I transformed the woman into my image before she could kiss her daughter goodbye. For that I am truly sorry. Since that day I have lived high on the peaks of the mountains I knew as a child." Brinn dropped to the ground. She had not thought to tell the dragon's story in first person but something inside had taken over.

After a silent moment a cheer went up. Brinn was pulled from the platform. A pair of clawed paws raised her in the air and passed her from dragon to dragon. With each paw that touched her, a jolt of pure joy entered her until she was laughing with the exhilaration. It was long minutes before she was brought back to the dais.

Brinn fell to her knees. She felt lightheaded both from the experience with the dragons and with the revelation of Neesha's story, from Py's lips and her own. She no longer hated the dragon that had taken her mother. Agnar went to Brinn's side and helped her to her feet. With a reassuring smile, Brinn let her friend lead her to the queen. Brinn knelt at Py's feet and touched her head to the massive front paws. "Thank you," she whispered.

Py leaned down and touched her head to the wizard's. "Thank *you*." She stood tall and unfolded her wings. The crowd fell quiet. "Today we gather for more than a telling of histories. Winter has come unto our garden. Many plots and connivings are riding on the breeze." A fair amount of rumbling ran through the crowd. "We must face this ill wind and do what we can to stand against it. But we do not have to stand alone."

The queen turned to Brinn. "Your involvement with dragons is not by chance. Prophesies are not always clear, and they are rarely complete. It would seem you are meant to take some part in our destiny. Our seer finds that your fate is intertwined with Dragonkind. Freeing Neesha was no coincidence; there is something more you are to do. But it remains hidden to us. We may not demand your involvement. It must be of your own free will. We tell you this only that you may understand the choice when it arises. You will not be judged harshly if you do not choose the path that might put you in harm's way." Py looked down at the young wizard, waiting.

It was evident the queen and every dragon in the hall was waiting for her answer. She knew what she *should* answer but was it the right answer for *her*. For the first time in her life Brinn had to decide what she wanted her future to be. Before Fernley came to the inn her father controlled her life completely and after... Had Brinn had any control since? Yes, the brief months she had lived in Enoa. Brinn mentally slapped herself out of the self-centered reflections. She was being asked to take part in one of the most important events in history. Brinn stood tall and looked into Py's deep brown eyes. "When the time comes I will stand with dragons."

A deafening cheer rose up. Py leaned down and kissed Brinn's forehead. "And we will stand with you, young one." Py stepped back, again spreading out her wings. The hall became silent. She held out her paw and two large gold rings appeared. "Behold the Rings of Ko-Mon Po. The Rings that aided in the extermination of thousands. Given to Dragonkind by our Krrig Daa as a token of the union between our two species. But the Rings were never meant for dragons. They were created to protect, not to be held out of fear. This young wizard is in need of that protection. Shall we give her the power to defeat her enemies?"

Another deafening cheer filled the cavern. A look of surprise appeared on Talon's face. Py grinned. "Destiny has a few twists," she said to Talon.

The Queen held out the gold bands to Brinn. "Take these as a gift of trust. Wear them and learn to use the magic they possess."

Brinn took the Rings and slid them onto the middle finger of each hand. For a moment she thought they would be too large for her fingers but they seemed to shrink to fit snuggly. The gold was warm against her chilled skin but other than that they didn't seem very magical. She raised up her hands for all to see. When the crowd went silent instead of cheering, Brinn was confused, then she looked up. Golden flames engulfed her hands. Without thinking she clapped her hands together and held them out straight to the gathered dragons. A flash of yellow light shot out over the surprised heads. Brinn felt her own energy stream out to the dragons. At first there was a collective gasp then chaos broke out. Some dragons took to the air, soaring and spinning. Others were grabbed in massive hugs by their neighbors. Hatchlings and younglings were tossed into the air, bouncing from paw to paw. Shouting and laughter filled the air. Brinn looked at Talon who just shrugged. From the center of the mob came a single, clear note. The singer slowly rose into the air. As the note grew in volume the surrounding commotion decreased until all the dragons stood silent, listening to the beautiful sound. Slowly other dragons took up the note, also rising in the air, heads tilted upward. Brinn wanted to cry from the beauty of it. The note faded and the dragons settled back to the ground.

With no warning, the dragons began to disappear. Brinn turned to look at Py, concerned that she had done something wrong. "What happened? Where did they go?"

"They went back to their caves. It's quicker to relocate than to use the tunnels." Py instantly moved them all back to her chamber. The queen sat down on her cushion. "You did better than I expected. You honored them by giving them your energy. They accepted it, with joy and celebration. Then they honored you with the purest note they could sing. Quite amazing."

"They went away without letting me thank them."

"But they were thanking *you*. I wasn't sure if they would accept my giving the Rings to you. I am very proud of my colony...and you."

Brinn remembered the importance of the Rings from Fernley's memories. "Why did you give them to me? What are they supposed to protect me from? Keldric?"

Py and Betto looked at Talon. Brinn turned to the wizard. Talon took a breath, he didn't want to tell Brinn about the decision made by the Wizards Council. "During the recent meeting of wizards it was decided by majority, with dissenting votes registered by less than one fifth of those present, that a gender restriction handed down from the dark generation should be upheld."

Py smacked Talon with her wing. "Spit it out."

Brinn didn't need clarification. "What are they planning to do with me?"

Talon looked away. "Kill you."

Rather than falling to pieces as Talon thought she would, Brinn laughed. "That would indeed eliminate their problem. Do they have a deadline." She laughed again. "Oh, that was a good one. Come on, why are you so serious? I'm not dead yet. And if Keldric couldn't manage it, I'd like to see what the others can do. Is that why Keldric kidnapped me?"

Talon shook his head. "He wasn't at the meeting. Keldric was acting for his own benefit. The council decided that your power would not be transferred. I wouldn't be too flippant about their decision if I were you. There are a lot of very powerful wizards out there looking to improve their status by removing an embarrassing mistake."

Brinn didn't like being called a mistake. She looked down at the Rings. "That's why you gave these to me," she said to Py. Brinn wanted to pull the gold bands off and throw them at the dragon. She was no longer a simple maid with no means to protect herself. They didn't think she could take care of herself!

Betto read Brinn's thoughts and gently thumped the girl on the head. "Don't be a stubborn youngling. Be wise enough to take help when it's offered."

Brinn rubbed her head and looked apologetically at Py. "Thank you."

"They won't be asking permission to exterminate you. These Rings were created for just this very task. But don't rely on them to keep you safe. They will only protect you against magical attacks, a knife will still draw blood." The queen yawned. "It's late. We will talk more tomorrow."

Brinn walked beside Talon down the dim passageway. "Did you know about these Rings?"

"I know about them, yes. I had retrieved them for my mentor, Olwin. I wore them for a while when I first became aware of the possibility of magic. When Olwin died I kept them for a while before passing them to Py. Before my time they were worn by knights questing for dragons. The Rings protected the knights against harm from dragons because dragons are magic personified. For Py to give them to you is a great show of trust."

Brinn looked at the golden bands and suddenly felt the weight of their true value. She didn't feel worthy of possessing them and tried to pull them off.

"Don't bother. You are the Wearer of the Rings. They won't come off until they want to. Self-centered little things."

Brinn hid her hands in her robe sleeves. A hundred other questions raced through her mind. But one question refused to be pushed aside. "Who dissented?"

Talon stopped for a minute then caught up with Brinn's train of thought. "Barkin, Trissa, Oret and myself."

"So few. The others don't know anything about me, yet they're willing to kill me. You'd think we were back in the dark ages."

Talon agreed. He couldn't think of any way to justify their decision. "I told you it wouldn't be easy."

"But they're going to *kill* me."

"Not if *I* have anything to do about it." Talon drew aside a dark tapestry and led Brinn into a side cave. It wasn't nearly as large as the queen's but it was comfortably furnished with a number of thick cushions and low tables. A fire had been lit. As Brinn walked in she was assaulted by two dragons.

"Wow, that was fantastic!" Draega grabbed Brinn's hand and dragged her to the fire.

"Did you see that silver dragon's spiral dive? And that light! Those rings must really be something special!" Agnar sat close to Brinn. Draega spread his forearms in dramatic measurement. "I wish I could be that big."

"That's silly Draega, you wouldn't be able to fit into our cave."

"Yeah, but Lorindi wouldn't tease me about being so small."

"No, she'd tease you about being too big." Agnar smacked Draega with his tail.

Brinn was glad to be back among friends. "Draega, what are you doing here?"

Draega puffed himself up proudly. "I followed my queen. A lot of us did."

"It was awful. Dee ordered all Humanish things to be destroyed as they were abominations to Dragonkind. All of Draega's books and paintings, Morisa's rugs, Livia's books and lotions, every ribbon, cup, blanket, table. Anything that had been made by human hands.

"Even my suit of armor." Telis grumbled as he came into the cave.

Brinn was surprised to see Telis. She thought he would have been against humans. She thought he had been one of the dragons mixed up with Dee's ideas to take over the colony. She ran and hugged him.

Telis smiled at Brinn. He knew what she was thinking. "I may not like humans, not *all* of them anyway, but it is un-dragonish to revolt against the queen. You should have seen the look on Dee's face when I walked out." He joined the three by the fire. "I'd like to see Queen Betto scratch that sneer from the horrid little lizard's face."

Talon left the four to their reunion and went to consult with Betto and Py.

Chapter 20

Brinn looked back one more time before Graldiss flew her out of range. The wind whipped her tears from her eyes. Last night she had agreed to Talon's advice that she return home. Saying goodbye her friends had been harder than she ever thought possible. Only the promise that she could return in a few months made the parting bearable. She traded thoughts with her three cavemates so she could keep in contact with them while she was away. Py gave Brinn a gold necklace with a dragon pendant. Talon spent more time on his goodbye than usual. He wanted to make sure Brinn was aware of the dangers that would be heading her way and to let her know which wizards she could trust (there weren't many). He promised to check in on her as often as he could. Though Brinn knew he would be busier than ever if Keldric had indeed joined forces with Dee.

Graldiss made a couple of 'leaps' before he was stuck with straight flying. Brinn was glad of the extra padding that was added to the saddle.

"We just weren't built for passengers," Graldiss commented after Brinn shifted for the fiftieth time.

"That's obvious." Hours of sitting between two spines was taking its toll. Before, she had been able to lean against Talon when she got tired, and with Agnar and Telis she had to lie down. "A back rest would be a pleasant addition to his saddle."

"Why don't we take a break?" Graldiss drifted down to a grassy clearing. Brinn slid gratefully to the stationary ground and loosened a bag from the saddle. "I'm going to find something to drink. Will you be all right?" the dragon asked.

Brinn waved him away as she gulped her own chilled juice. After the dragon flew off she found a comfortable boulder to lean against and closed her eyes. She pulled the cloak around her chin to keep out the cool breeze and drew the over-large hood over her eyes to keep out the light. The soft hum of bees lulled her to sleep.

"What on earth happened?!"

Brinn pushed back her hood and squinted sleepily at the anxious dragon. "What?"

"Are you ok? I'm sorry, I didn't think I was gone that long. Are you hurt?"

Brinn rubbed her eyes. The Rings seemed to be warmer than usual. "I don't know what you are talking about. I'm fine, just dozed off." As she got shakily to her feet Brinn noticed a bit of red fabric flapping in the grass. On second glance she saw it was the hem of a robe, the wearer was lying immobile in the tall grass.

"That's not the only one," Graldiss said slowly, looking behind Brinn.

With confusion and horror Brinn climbed onto her boulder and looked around the meadow. At least seven bodies lay scattered behind rocks and were hidden in the grass. "Who are they?"

"Wizards," the dragon said tensely.

"What happened to them? Why aren't they moving?" Brinn climbed down from her boulder and cautiously walked to the closest body. Frost edged the robe hood and white beard. A look of shock was frozen on the ancient face. "They aren't...dead, are they?"

Graldiss kicked a nearby singed leg and was answered with a grunt. "Well, this one isn't. A bit charred around the edges, but still breathing." Checking the other bodies Brinn and Graldiss found a total of nine wizards, all barely breathing.

One greenish-looking wizard babbled deliriously: "The Rings, the Rings."

Graldiss laughed. "They were zapped by their own spells! Look at this one, he still has his arm out as if he were trying to blast you with...ugh, something sticky. This is just too funny!"

Brinn did not see the humor in the situation. "They tried to *kill* me! With no warning! While I was sleeping!"

"Did you expect them to ask permission? You're lucky they didn't come at you with knives and arrows, you'd be dead." Graldiss bent down. "Come on, let's get out of here."

"And just leave them like this?"

"Do *you* want to wake them? I'd rather get you home, if you don't mind."

Brinn looked at one slowly melting wizard. "You're right." She settled into the saddle. As they climbed into the air Brinn looked back at the clearing. Some of the bodies were beginning to move. "Will they come after me again?" she asked mentally.

"Probably not, but there will be others." Graldiss decided not to give Brinn any false hope. "They'll find out about the Rings eventually. That's when things will get really dangerous. If they don't try to kill you themselves they'll send assassins, who won't be effected by the Rings."

Brinn wasn't frightened by the dragon's grim predictions. "Then I'll just have to find a way to get them to change their minds."

Graldiss laughed. "Wizards? Most of their minds are more unyielding than a mountain."

"Then I'll have to try harder. I'm not about to let them win."

Graldiss smiled.

It was late evening before they approached the outskirts of Enoa. Brinn felt a surge of energy from Graldiss. They landed next to the main road but the dragon did not lean down to allow Brinn to slide off. "I promised Talon to see you to your front door. Lie as flat as you can."

Brinn would have liked to stride through the streets with her head held high but decided that such arrogance could get her killed. She leaned around a low spine. Graldiss walked toward the city gates. Strange, no one on the road noticed a nine-foot dragon walking alongside them.

"Why don't they see you?" Brinn asked mentally.

"Oh, there are ways to keep humans from seeing what they don't want to see." Graldiss smiled, hadn't he had this same conversation with Talon decades ago?

There was some difficulty at the gate. The wagon entrance had been closed, leaving only a small entrance for foot travelers. Graldiss leapt gracefully onto the high narrow wall, balancing on his hind legs until he spotted a large enough space to land. With a daintiness Brinn didn't think possible of a large dragon, Graldiss touched down next to the town fountain. Luckily the streets were set up for two-way carriage travel and were wide enough for the dragon.

They had navigated through the shops and were almost to Brinn's home when a knife bounced off Graldiss' shoulder. "How can they see us now?" Brinn asked.

Graldiss just shrugged. "They are seeing you, not me." He picked up his pace, not bothering to avoid apple carts and awnings. Many people were strangely 'pushed' aside. Oddly shaped indentations in the street and wall were left to be puzzled over.

Without further incident, dragon and passenger arrived at the neat stone wall that surrounded her home. After a serious look around, Graldiss bent his knee and let Brinn down. "I'll let you work out personal protection, but I'm going to set up something special."

"Talon said there were protective spells on the house already."

Graldiss squinted up at the house. "Not enough, I bet."

Brinn felt the dragon draw in energy. He stood on his hind legs, and began to walk around the stone wall, tracing the mortar. Grindle appeared and bowed to his mistress. "Welcome home, Miss."

Brinn put a grateful hand on the butler's arm. "Thank you."

"Will the dragon be staying for supper?" the butler asked in a matter-of-fact tone.

Brinn smiled, this was not something one heard a butler ask everyday. "No, Grindle, I'm sure he has other plans."

Graldiss completed the tracing of the wall and stood before the entrance. He touched the ground and raised his paws up and out, encompassing the breadth of the mansion. He motioned for the butler to step forward. With perfectly somber calmness Grindle stood nose to chest with the dragon. Graldiss held his paws over the neatly groomed man and released a second wave of energy. The butler grinned at the unique sensation.

"There," he said, turning to Brinn, "you'll be safer now. I've placed a *tresh*...a circle of protection, around the house. No one of magic besides you will be able to cross this wall. And no one else may enter your home without permission from the butler. That should keep sneaky wizards and assassins at bay." Graldiss leaned over and put his forehead on Brinn's. "Take care of yourself, you are a very special human," he whispered to her mind.

Brinn flung her arms around the dragon's neck. She had said too many goodbyes today and wasn't up to another one. With a heavy heart she watched Graldiss blink out of sight.

"Come inside, Miss," Grindle said gently, "There's a bit of a chill this evening."

Brinn was glad to sink into a soft chair in front of the fire. After a cup of hot cider and a bowl of Cook's delicious stew, she had begun to feel like herself again. With a second cup of cider she began to plan how she was going to keep herself alive until something could be done about the other wizards. No clear plan came to mind and Brinn went to bed early. It was refreshing to have her own clothes and familiar things around her. She slept soundly knowing that Graldiss' magic would keep out unwanted intruders.

The next morning Brinn thought it best not to go into town. She spent the day in her hidden study reading up on numerous ways to protect herself. Some books described potions she could rub on her body to keep poison darts from penetrating the skin. She read how to strengthen fabric and make it impenetrable, how to give the appearance of standing a foot to the left of her real position, how to amplify her senses to be able to detect threatening actions, and how to read people's minds to find out if they were planning an attack. She even found references to the Rings Py had given her. The only thing she found truly useful was a smaller version of the protective shield she had put around the bear months ago. If she concentrated hard enough she could bring it tight against her skin, allowing for her to interact with people, but she could only keep it up for short periods. She decided her best bet was to find a way to fix her problem at its source. She somehow had to convince the other wizards that she was not a threat to them. That would not be an easy task but it seemed the only solution.

Grindle was finding his new job as house guard more work than just answering the door, as was his usual job. He now had to admit the various deliverymen and servants who made the household run smoothly. He was pleased to find that once he had admitted someone he did not have to be present as they came and went over the course of the day.

In the following days, Brinn ventured out for short walks and trips to town, accompanied by Celisa of course. There were very few incidences of physical attacks but Brinn felt the Rings become hot on a number of occasions. Delivery boys brought stories to the house of strangers falling ill with mysterious ailments and there seemed to be an influx of shifty characters hiding in alleys. Apparently no one had linked these curious events to Brinn's return.

Brinn was in daily contact with Talon and Agnar; however, they could not give her any specifics about Dee's manipulations or Keldric's intentions. She had read dozens of books on Wizard History but could come up with no reference to female wizards. Why did Fernley decide she had to be the first! In a last effort to find an alternative to being killed, Brinn went into a deep trance and searched through the memories stashed deep in her mind of all the previous wizards. It took many hours and she learned many interesting and peculiar things, but nothing with which to fight the council's decision. It was beginning to look like she would have to follow Shawni's example and hide away from the world. It was during these grim thoughts that she had an unexpected visitor.

"Excuse me! Is anyone home?" A familiar voice called cordially from the opening in the stone wall.

Brinn closed her book and rose from her comfortable seat under a peach tree. She wondered why the visitor wasn't being brought around by Grindle. When she came around the front of the house she understood, leaning against the invisible *tresh* was Keldric. Brinn wished she had some vicious guard dogs to set loose on him. She stood defiantly within a few feet of her enemy. "What can you say that will keep me from blasting you into the next county?"

"I can save your life," he said smoothly.

Brinn didn't believe him for a minute and she made no move to let him get any closer. "Try again."

Keldric was a bit shaken that his offer was brushed aside so casually. He made another attempt at crossing the wall's threshold and felt the strength of the magic that held him back. "I know we've had our differences in the past. I've made mistakes in judgment. I apologize. But I really can help. I have some influence with the Wizard's Council."

"Which you didn't use at the time because you were in the middle of kidnapping me."

"But which I can now use to get them to reconsider their grave mistake and welcome you wholeheartedly." Keldric's cajoling tone was incredibly self-assured.

"And how would you accomplish this amazing feat?"

Keldric smiled to convince the girl of his sincerity. "The head of the Council, a powerful wizard named Nymna has joined me in a great cause. He has assured me that if you would join us he would use his vast influence to rescind the death sentence placed on you by those wizards with little foresight."

Brinn wanted to laugh at Keldric's proposal. Talon had told her about the assembly and how Nymna had led the vote against her. Could Keldric really think she was so desperate for his help or just stupid? But Brinn decided to get as much information from Keldric as possible. "Why would this...Nymna need me to join his 'cause'?"

The wizard's smile deepened, his voice no longer needed to be persuasive. "A turning point is approaching where men—people of power can attain their final destiny as rulers of the world. Join us and take your rightful place in the new order of life!"

Brinn felt ill at Keldric's words. Rather than argue or play stupid anymore, she simply chose to turn and enter the house, leaving Keldric seething and pushing vainly at the invisible wall. She was especially glad now of Graldiss' protections.

The rest of Brinn's evening was spent thinking up various uncomfortable things she could do to Keldric and this Nymna character. She hoped she would get a chance to use them some time soon.

As the sun rose the next morning Brinn tried to contact Talon. When she could not reach his mind, Brinn tried Graldiss but with no success. She could not reach Agnar or Py either. As panic began to set in, Brinn tried Ittra.

"Good morning, Brinn. How are you doing?" the young Queen asked.

Brinn sobbed with relief. She told the queen everything Keldric had said. "I tried to reach Talon and warn him."

Ittra sent a mental wave of soothing comfort. "You did right to contact me. Talon and the dragons are deep within Py's mountain conferring on what to do about the upcoming war."

304

"That's what Keldric was talking about then: a war." Brinn understood Keldric's meaning now. "Between wizards and dragons."

Ittra was surprised at Brinn's assumption. "No, between dragons. Dee's might be recruiting wizards to fight on her side."

Brinn couldn't hide her confusion. "But her goal is to *remove* human influence on dragon society, to return to dragon superiority. Keldric is working toward the exact opposite."

"Hmm. Py and Talon will have a lot to consider with your news."

"But is the war inevitable?" Brinn couldn't imagine what such a battle would be like.

"If we can't find a way to stop it, yes. I'll pass along your information to Py immediately."

"I want to help. I want to be there."

"Not yet, child. Now don't be upset, we will need you later. Right now we need you to stay put. Let Keldric think you're not getting involved. Try to keep your regular patterns, don't hide away. But if he gets too close stay within the protection of your house."

Brinn felt she was being treated like a child but didn't dare go against the queen's command. They talked for a bit longer. Ittra told Brinn to be brave and patient and gave her a mental hug.

Brinn moped around the house the rest of the day, napping in the garden, having a simple lunch in the kitchen with Cook. In the afternoon, Brinn retired to her workshop. She had collected an armload of chipped pottery from Cook. With great pleasure Brinn spent the afternoon releasing pent-up frustrations by blasting the crockery to bits.

The frustration and anger came to a head a few days later as Brinn and Celisa were coming home from their daily walk to town. Brinn was complaining about the lack of sweet pickles at the grocer's when a green-clad body dropped from an overhanging branch. Celisa leapt forward to protect her mistress. Brinn didn't wait for the would-be assassin to pronounce sentence upon her, with a wave of her hand she relocated him to a very damp manure pile behind the town stables. Another wave brought down two other ambushers from the trees. She set their voluminous cloaks ablaze and dangled them over the millpond before dropping them into the murky water. With a smile of satisfaction Brinn continued down the lane. "Do you think Cook has some pickles hidden away in her pantry?"

Most of the assassins left town the next day.

Just before dawn, a week after she contacted Ittra, Talon's thoughts woke Brinn. "Are you going to sleep all morning?"

Brinn wasn't sure if she was still dreaming or not. "Is there something else I should be doing?" she mumbled into her pillow.

"Be ready in an hour. We've decided you should join us."

When Brinn only answered in a moan, Talon sent a sharp rap on her drowsy mind. "Ok, I'm awake!" Brinn sat up.

"One hour."

Brinn tried to clear her mind. Did Talon say where she was going or which dragon was going to pick her up? Did it really matter? She didn't have to sit around doing nothing anymore. She was going to join the battle. Brinn tossed back the covers and instantly set all the candles in her room alight. Excitement surged through her veins. Battle! She couldn't wait to go head-to-head with some of those wizards who thought she wasn't good enough for them. What did one wear to a war? Brinn put on a pair of loose fitting pants and a matching shirt. The ground might be muddy, Brinn thought, so she chose a pair of low-heeled boots she had worn for walks in the woods. She tied her hair back and threw on a blue cloak.

She left a note for Grindle and sat by the fire to wait for Talon. While she watched the flickering flames Brinn imagined what it would be like to go into battle. She thought she might swoop down at the enemy on the back of a mighty dragon, blasting them with her Rings.

"They don't work that way." Talon's thought intruded on Brinn.

"But you saw what they did at the mountain, and what about the wizards in the meadow?" Brinn asked. "They must have a lot of power."

"Actually, they have very little. They were created to keep Ko-Mon Po safe from another vengeful wizard. They keep you safe from harmful magic, your own as well as other's, nothing more. I'm not sure what happened at Py's mountain, you might have a common lineage to Po and the Rings recognized that, or it came purely from within yourself. You have a lot of untapped power, you know."

Brinn didn't know. Sometimes the amount of power she wielded frightened her.

"Are you ready?"

"Yes, but the dragon isn't here." Brinn looked out the window.

"There won't be one. I want you to sit as still as you can in the middle of the floor." He waited for a moment. "A few others will join me in your mind. It's going to get crowded so try to clear your mind of unnecessary thoughts."

Brinn did has she was told. Within a few minutes she was aware of other minds entering her own. Each mental projection bowed and spoke their name in greeting: Poldrun, Tellyanar, Fredik, and Barkin. Brinn acknowledged each one. She felt the five minds link together, like holding hands, then a sensation of being pulled away from where she was. She closed her eyes against the dizzying blur of motion. After what seemed an eternity but was only seconds, Brinn felt herself land on solid ground. She sat motionless for a moment and waited for the world to hold still before she slowly opened her eyes.

Talon knelt beside Brinn, smiling at her. "Welcome! Glad to have you here."

Barkin was on her other side, he looked younger than his thought image. He lifted her arm and put his fingers on her wrist. Brinn felt the warm tingling from his fingers move up her arm. Soon the chill from the relocation eased. With help Brinn stood up. She looked around at the other men standing near her. She recognized some of them, though there were slight differences in their appearance. There was no doubt that the well-dressed wizard with the pointy beard was Poldrun, while the one in tight leather pants and jacket with tightly curled white hair was Fredik, Tellyanar had an extraordinarily long hair and beard and wore an ornately embroidered black robe. Two other wizards were unknown to her and she looked to Talon to introduce them.

Talon helped Brinn to her feet. "This is Oret and Larn. They were the anchors for your retrieval."

Brinn glanced at Talon in amazement, realizing now what he and the other six had done. "That wasn't possible!"

"Well, you're here, aren't you?" Fredik said with mock sarcasm.

Poldrun offered Brinn a cup of hot tea. "Talon used some of that Dragon Magic of his."

Oret grunted and sat down next to the fire.

"It was rather like catching a fish," Fredik explained. "The five of us hooked you with our minds and the other two reeled us in. Quite an extraordinary experience."

"Unnatural, if you ask me," Oret grumbled.

Brinn looked at the short wizard. She knew that he was one of the few wizards who had come out against her 'removal' but she found that she could not immediately like him. He was a scruffy looking man, dressed in a bearskin, his hair was twisted in a long braid down his back and his beard was in two braids that brushed his knees when he sat, and he wore no shoes on his feet. Brinn watched as he wiggled his fingers rhythmically and a mug appeared next to him on the bench. "You don't like dragons?" she asked.

Oret drained the mug in one long swallow. "It's not a matter of liking or disliking. They are and we are," he said vaguely.

"Oret feels that dragons and humans should not mix," Poldrun explained.

The dirty wizard scowled at Poldrun. "Like unto like."

"I think Oret's been living on his own too long," Fredik teased. "He's forgotten how to carry on a simple conversation."

Oret conjured up another mug. "The people I know aren't interested in conversation but in giving orders." He looked at Brinn. "Dragons ruled the land for centuries, now it's our turn. They should step aside and leave it to us. None of this working together or mingling of powers." He glared at Talon.

Brinn asked Oret why he was here if he disliked dragons so much.

"I'm not here to get involved with warring dragons. I'm here to stop those beasts from killing innocent people in that village."

Brinn didn't understand and turned to Talon for explanation.

"There's been a new development since Ittra spoke to you." He pointed to the valley below the cliff.

Dee's army was gathering along the western curve of the wide valley but rather than seeing a second army led by Py, Brinn saw plowed farmlands straddling the riverbed that led to a fair sized town. "Dee's planning to attack the town?"

"So it would seem." Talon was definitely not happy with this turn of events. "We didn't think she would involve humans in this conflict."

"That's why we're all here," Larn said firmly. "And I think it's time we started doing something more than just sitting here."

Everyone looked at Talon. The young wizard joined the others around the fire. He considered what he should say for a few minutes. "I have spoken to Py, who is gathering an army to intercept Dee's dragons before they attack the town. She has chosen me to be her spokesman." He paused, listening to the voice in his mind. "She understands your concern about the lives of the townspeople and assures me that every effort will be made to ensure their safety. If at all possible they won't even realize what is happening around them. The true battle will be dragon against dragon. Queen Py humbly asks that we not interfere in that battle."

The wizards nodded, dragons were a proud breed and this was their fight. "Py requests that we act as defenders for the town by countering whatever magic might be used against it by Dee's dragons."

Barkin stood. "If that's to be our role I think we should start devising a course of action." He was answered with nods of agreement, and an intense discussion began on methods of defensive magic.

Chapter 21

Brinn became quickly bored by the strategy discussions. In her heart she wanted to be with Agnar and Graldiss, preparing for battle against Dee. This frustration was increased by the continual dismissal of her suggestions on defensive techniques. It didn't take more than an hour before Brinn no longer joined the heated debates over the virtues of one spell over another. She spent her time watching the gathering army from the safety of their cliff top camp.

The sun was high in the sky but the air was chilly on the grassy cliff top when Talon joined Brinn at the cliff's edge.

"Why did you bring me here?" Brinn asked as Dee's army took up position along a steep riverbank.

"I know it's been hard for you to just wait here but it's important that you do so. Things aren't all they seem here." Talon looked down at the gathering army. "What do you see down there?"

Brinn drew in energy from the grass and magnified her vision of the valley floor. "Four or five dragons are flying surveillance but the townspeople don't seem to notice. Dee is shouting orders. It looks a bit chaotic."

Talon nodded. "What can you deduce from this picture?"

Brinn looked at Talon. She hadn't taken part in the strategy sessions with the others so didn't know what assumptions had been made already. "Their presence is hidden from the town, so it will not be prepared for the attack that's coming. From the look of it, I'd say Dee is trying to run the battle by herself. No one else is giving orders."

Talon smiled, he had come to the same conclusion. "Anything else?"

Encouraged by Talon's tone Brinn brought up something that had bothered her. "Why isn't Keldric there, and the other wizards? If he's working *with* Dee, where is he?"

Talon's smile widened. This girl had a quick mind. "He's in the town, along with Nymna."

"What is he doing? Is he organizing a counter attack?"

Talon shook his head. "He is hiding his actions. We don't think the townsfolk know he is even there."

Brinn was shocked. "That's insane. Is Keldric going to protect them? What is his role in Dee's plan? This doesn't make any sense."

Talon turned from the edge of the cliff. "It's odd, though, he is projecting the image of an armed camp. Apparently for the benefit of the scout dragons." Talon chuckled, "Dee hasn't thought to check it out more closely."

"What about us?" Brinn asked. "Don't they know we're up here?"

"Oh, I'm sure they do. But Dee doesn't want to pick a fight with us. Fighting against normal humans is a lot easier than fighting against a pack of angry wizards." Talon walked back to the fire.

Brinn looked back down at the dragons. She wondered where Py and her dragons were.

When the sun went down with no sign of imminent attack the war council on the cliff took a rest. Oret retired to his tent as did Poldrun and Larn. Barkin unrolled a leather mat and laid out an assortment of ivory playing pieces. Fredik sat down across from him and pulled out his own pieces. Talon said he needed to talk with Py and disappeared. Tellyanar was the only one left sitting at the fire; he waved Brinn over.

"Come and warm yourself." A tray of curiously shaped rolls and balls of meat appeared in his hands. "You must be hungry. These young men seem to have lost their manners."

Brinn smiled and joined him by the fire. She took one of the offered balls and hesitantly nibbled then popped it into her mouth. With a smile she took another. Between bites of savory meat balls and flaky rolls, Brinn filled in some of her background for the elderly wizard and in exchange Tellyanar told her wonderful stories. He was much older than even his long beard and wrinkled face indicated. He told the story of an ancient civilization that had built a magnificent city-state called Gundrim. Warring merchants broke Gundrim apart and divided it up into a collection of little kingdoms. After centuries of squabbling the land was ripe for conquest and was swallowed up by merciless warlords. They used up the land and its people until nothing grew. In an act of desperation the people rose up and overthrew their oppressors. "So deep was the hatred for authority that even to this day no king or lord has been able to demand fealty in the Wastes of Gundrim."

"But Gundrim isn't a wasteland," Brinn had always looked forward to the wagonloads of fresh fruits and vegetables when winter snows had melted from the roads. "It's one of the most prosperous farming communities in the world."

"And such is the reward for the determination of free, independent, hardworking people. But for centuries outsiders would see it as a desolate land of poisoned lakes and rocky fields." There was a wily grin on the old man's face.

Brinn saw that smile and grinned. "You were there, the whole time. Why didn't you do something to stop the merchants or kings or warlords?"

Tellyanar shrugged. "In the beginning, as a young magician, I was as fascinated as the rest of them with the growing cultural center we were becoming. When I saw the increasing power of a handful of merchants I tried to warn the people, but no one wanted the advice from a peddler of potions. Of course all the bickering kings wanted me to take their side in their petty wars and the people blamed me for not solving all their problems. During the centuries of persecution I went into seclusion, helping where I could to ease the plight of the people but being careful not to come to the notice of the warlords. Later my role as protector was forgotten and the people were too suspicious of anyone with power to accept my help. So I put a small spell over the land and left them to find their own destiny."

"A spell on the land? Is that why it's so rich and plentiful?"

"No, I take no credit for that. I just planted a feeling of distaste to overcome anyone who thought to try and take control. Amazing that it's still working after all this time." A second tray of sweetcakes and fruit appeared. "So tell me, little one, will you continue with Fernley's work after this mess is over?"

Brinn tossed the crust from a berry tart into the fire. "I don't know, I'm tired of fighting for my life. I might just find a nice secluded forest to disappear into."

"Like the old witch and her cat?" Tellyanar moved his finger along the outside of an apple and its peel dropped neatly to the ground.

Brinn stared at the old wizard. "You know about Shawni?"

"Is that her name? I've never actually met the lady, just saw her while I was having a look around a few years ago." Brinn's confusion was clear. "Every few decades I like to find out who my comrades have passed their power on to. It's really the only way I can keep track of them all. I never liked going to those council meetings. Damned silly notion to have wizards making group decisions."

This was news to Brinn. "How do you do it? Seeing wizards."

"Oh it's easy, really. I find a nice high mountain, get cozy, close my eyes and look for power auras. Sometimes I watch for weeks."

"You see the auras? Like dragons do?"

"I don't know about dragons. I never saw one of the beasties before Talon and his friend landed in front of my house a few days ago. I know the old stories, of course, but never got the chance to come face to face with one. Do they see power auras, too? Interesting. I imagine it's one of the lost talents. All wizards could see auras in the beginning, when our power was pure. It's gotten thinned and diluted over the centuries." He scowled at a roll, picking off the raisins. "I suppose that's why Talon is so powerful, he was born with pure power. Besides having inherited that dragon's power along with Olwin's. You can imagine my surprise when *he* showed up during one of my viewings." He laughed. "I bet Olwin was floored when he first came across the boy." The old wizard looked at Brinn. "As surprised as Talon was to find you, no doubt."

Brinn nodded. "Just not *done*." Brinn puffed herself up like disgruntled old wizard, "'We don't allow *women* to be wizards!'" She smiled. "I was pleased to find that I wasn't the only one."

"There are more of you than you think." Tellyanar winked. "Many more." He stood and walked to his tent, leaving a surprised Brinn staring after him.

Brinn developed a headache trying to comprehend everything Tellyanar had said, and went to bed.

Brinn looked down at the bloody battlefield, seething at the helplessness imposed upon them by Py. What use were they up here while dragons and humans were being slaughtered. Cries of anger and agony rose through the haze. Brinn covered her ears and turned away. A sudden rush of air turned her attention back to the cliff face. A blackened dragon shot up from the valley floor. Brinn pulled in energy to blast the attacking dragon but let it go when she recognized Agnar.

"I thought you might want to get in on the action." He folded his singed wings.

Brinn grabbed her sword and leapt onto the dragon's back before the other wizards could stop her. "Py will be furious."

"Not if you help us win."

Agnar dove down into the battle. Brinn slid off his back just as a lightning bolt shot toward them.

"I'm going for Keldric," Brinn shouted.

Agnar nodded and the two of them fought their way through the swords and claws until they reached the red-flagged pavilion where the two Nymna and

Keldric directed their soldiers and threw magic around like spears. Fireballs, lightning bolts, ice sheets all flew from within the pavilion at the attacking dragons. With speed and surprise Brinn was able to get within sword range of Keldric. The shock on his face as her blade cut deep was sweet revenge. But the element of surprise did not last long. Nymna stood over Agnar's body, laughing. Brinn dropped her sword and pulled in the power draining from her friend's lifeless body. She drew back her arm, preparing a blast that would send the wizard deep into the cliff face. But as the words of the spell formed on her lips Brinn was hit with a very strong and very real need to...pee. She sat up and found herself looking into Oret's face.

"Awake now? Good." The wizard left Brinn's tent.

After relieving herself and putting on a robe Brinn joined the others. "Sorry if I slept in. I was in the middle of a dream."

Talon handed Brinn a mug of tea. "We all were, magically. I don't know which side did the deed, but it was very effective."

"It didn't have the smell of dragon to it," Oret commented from the fire.

"If Oret hadn't been keeping guard we might have all slept through the fight. The spell was quite powerful; no shaking or shouting could rouse us. Oret was quite inventive in his method of waking us."

Brinn remembered the intense feeling and smiled at the wizard's ingenuity. "What's happening down there?"

"Nothing," Oret grumbled.

"Dee's dragons are taking up defensive positions. They're expecting something." Barkin handed Brinn a sausage roll.

Brinn looked down at the valley floor. "Is Py nearby?"

"She will bring her dragons here when they are needed," Talon said. "She is watching the situation here."

"Wait, something is happening," Poldrun said from the cliff face.

The wizards felt a great surge of power. As the rising sun slid over the eastern mountains, dark clouds moved swiftly from the north. Brinn remembered the storm-cloud attack some months earlier. Before she got a chance to bring up a strong wind to counter the storm Oret waved his arm and the clouds dissipated.

"It has started." Larn stated coldly.

The wizards spread themselves out along the cliff face, sitting or standing, and prepared themselves. Brinn sat cross-legged near a rocky outcrop and began to pull in energy from the plants around her. She watched the sky for signs of magical attacks. Barkin, Tellyanar, and Oret watched the town while Fredik and Larn watched the valley floor and nearby mountain ranges. Talon stayed in touch with Py.

The next attack came from the sky as large balls of flame began to rain down on the town. Brinn and Larn easily diverted them to the snowy mountain peaks.

The townsfolk were oblivious to the danger around them. "Keldric must have put together quite a spell to dull their minds." Fredik diverted a rockslide.

"Py is handling that part," Talon said proudly. "It would appear that Keldric and his companions are being kept busy with little disasters all around town."

"This is an odd sort of fight," Barkin remarked as he melted hailstones the size of melons. "With all these dragons why doesn't Dee just attack the town physically?"

Oret waved away a dozen horrendous apparitions like wisps of smoke. "Good question. Anyone got an answer?"

The others were too busy to guess why the bulk of Dee's dragons were just standing around, waiting. Dust storms had to be stilled. Swarms of bees, bats, and snakes were relocated. Levitated farmers were eased back to earth. By mid-afternoon the dragons seemed to be out of ideas and with the exception of the occasional unusual weather phenomenon, the evening was quiet.

That night the wizards ate in silence and turned in early. They slept unaided but uneasy. Larn took first watch.

There was little change when Poldrun woke the rest of the wizards the next morning. Dee's dragons looked restless but were still making no move to physically attack the town. Dee, herself, was visibly furious. Brinn enjoyed seeing her short-temperedness and tantrums. Not much magic was used that morning so the wizards on the cliff top had little to do but watch and wait.

Early in the afternoon Keldric's charade of an army disappeared. When the scout dragons rushed back with the news that no human soldiers were present in the town Dee's scream could be heard for miles. The dragons became confused and disorganized. An angry shout brought the dragons back to order. Dee began barking orders. Multiple magical disturbances rose up around the town. Fifty to sixty dragons took to the air while the rest spread out over the valley floor in preparation for the attack.

The wizards were hard pressed to keep up with the dust storms, locust swarms, smoke clouds, ghostly apparitions, and angry thunder clouds. There was noticeably no action coming from the town. If Keldric intended to make a move there was no evidence of it.

As one the dragons advanced as if still expecting a counter attack from the town. Brinn held her breath as they drew nearer and nearer to the defenseless town. When Dee's army reached the edges of the farmland, hundreds of huge dragons appeared on the ground and in the air to block their path. Brinn cheered out loud. The other wizards on the cliff stared in awe. The valley was filled with a rainbow of color. The town went still. The residents slumped in sleep.

Brinn, not taking her eyes from the amazing site below, moved next to Talon. "Will they really fight each other? Ittra said dragons never attack each other."

Talon sighed, a terrible sadness in his eyes. "There are times when the unthinkable was inevitable. If Dee's influence is strong, dragon blood will stain the ground before nightfall."

Brinn's heart sank.

The two sides faced each other tensely. Suddenly Py appeared between the two armies. A moment later Dee stood next to the immense Queen. The difference in the two dragons' size would have been comical at any other time.

"You will go no further," Py said in a voice loud enough for the whole valley to hear.

"We have a right to defend ourselves." Dee's voice was filled with passion.

Py didn't bother to look around. "I don't see your aggressors."

Dee pointed past the line of defense before her. "That village houses an army of violent humans preparing to attack."

"I'm sure your scouts have told you that any such army has vanished. You might want to talk to your wizard about it." There was a chuckle behind the large queen. "You might have wanted there to be an army here, and I'm sure it was a big disappointment when it did not materialize, but we both know you are attacking a defenseless village."

The dragons behind Dee began to shift uncomfortably. Dee flew a few feet off the ground. "There are no innocent humans." Dragons on both sides nodded.

"Just as there are no innocent dragons. We are all responsible for how we walk The Pattern. But innocent or not, you will not attack that village." The line of dragons behind Py came to attention.

Dee was visibly infuriated. "It is not for *you* to decide what *my* colony will do." The small dragon turned and gave orders to a green dragon on the front line. "Our dispute is not with you. Move aside and let us pass."

The large dragons took a step forward, Py held up her wing to still them. "Your behavior has made it necessary for us to become part of this so-called dispute."

"So be it." Dee flew back to her command post. Quick words to a pair of larger dragons and the order to attack was given.

The wizards on the cliff watched in horror as the two armies came together in a clash of claws, teeth, and tails. The difference in size didn't seem to make any difference in the viciousness of attack. Poldrun, who had seen many battles in his years as an advisor to kings, was fascinated with the methods of dragon combat. Magic mixed with physical assaults in quick exchanges. An opponent might disappear one second while another appeared from behind. Dragons were surprisingly agile. While in mid-air combat they would twist and dodge in unthinkable ways. Less magic was used in the air, while that seemed to be the main method of combat on the ground. Boulders and thorn bushes appeared in front of and on top of an opponent.

And of course the physical attacks were as artistic as they were vicious.

Brinn didn't see the battle with as analytical an eye as Poldrun. She saw flesh rending and blood splattering. Dragons from both sides, that she knew personally, lay wounded on the ground. Eventually she joined Talon who had retreated to the main tent when the fighting started.

When dusk fell the armies withdrew to heal and rest. Talon left to consult with Py and Betto. Brinn did not join the others by the fire. She did not care to listen to their study of the varied tactics the dragons were using.

"Did you notice they aren't trying to actually kill each other?" Barkin noted. "They aren't even aiming to maim or mortally wound."

"It looks more a test of skill," Oret commented.

"They are quite fast for their size," Larn said with awe "I don't know how knights could have killed so many."

"Did you see the array of colors?" Tellyanar asked. "So many different sizes and shapes."

"They were tossing around magic like...like...well it was really amazing to see," Fredik said with amazement. "It's second nature to them."

"Yes," Oret said with some pleasure, "At this rate we'll be through here by tomorrow."

Brinn shivered. These men didn't care about the pain and horror the dragons down below must have felt. She longed to go down to find out if Agnar, Telis, or Draega were among the wounded. Brinn knew that Talon would have said something if Graldiss had been hurt. She anxiously waited for Talon to return with news of her friends.

Chapter 22

Brinn woke early. Talon hadn't returned and Brinn hadn't slept much. The other wizards were still sleeping off their late night fireside chat. She poured a cup of cold tea and went to the edge of the cliff. The cup bounced once before shattering on an outcrop. The battle was well underway and Graldiss was leading the charge against Dee's army.

"He insisted." Talon hung in the air a few feet from the cliff top then floated to the ground next to Brinn. "Stubborn goat. He thinks that being 'Little Brother' might put some doubt in the rightness of the opposition's cause." Talon looked tired.

"There are so few left." Brinn looked back down at the battle. "Were there so many injured yesterday?"

Talon turned away from the cliff. "Too many. The ranks are smaller because many have chosen not to fight today."

"On Dee's side?" Brinn asked hopefully.

"On both, actually."

Brinn turned to look at Talon. "They deserted? Py's dragons? But how could they?" Brinn couldn't believe it.

Talon knelt down and picked up a handful of dirt and let it sift through his fingers. "Dragons aren't like humans, Brinn. Their idea of wrong and right isn't always clear, even from one moment to the next. Their lives are run by a vision of Destiny mixed with a surety of free will." He sifted another handful of dirt. "To many, being here, at this moment and place, would have been foretold centuries ago but whether they fight or not is their personal choice. There are no recriminations for their choice either way. There would have been no shame if Dee had chosen not to lead her dragons into battle yesterday, or today. She believes this is her Destiny and has made her choice."

This idea was completely alien to Brinn. "But they should fight for what is right."

"What *is* right?" Talon asked. "Who is to say which side is following the true path of Destiny, if there is such a thing."

"Here," Brinn said angrily, tapped her chest, "I know what is right and wrong."

Talon smiled parentally. "Was it right to leave your father? He is without family now, perhaps grieving for his loss, not understanding why you deserted him. Was it right to interfere with the life of that bear? It might have been its time to die and take its place in the food chain. Destiny brought you to the point where you chose to leave the inn. Destiny took you to that field where you chose to save that bear. Your choices have allowed Destiny to bring you to this place."

Brinn looked down at the savagery below. "Destiny has brought me here," she said sullenly. She didn't want to be here, didn't want to know that some dragons would kill humans for no reason, didn't want to see dragons fighting dragons, didn't want to know that some wizards hated dragons enough to watch them hurt each other, and she didn't want to just stand here and do nothing. Brinn squared her shoulders. "Now I'm going to make a choice." Brinn disappeared from the cliff top.

The sudden appearance of a human in the middle of the battlefield had the exact effect Brinn wanted. The dragons were stunned into immobility. That gave Brinn just enough time to put her hastily-made plan into action. Quickly sucking up energy, she put up a barrier between the bulk of the two armies. Within minutes Dee pushed between two dragons. "Leave human! This is not your fight. You defile us with your presence."

Brinn looked down at the red dragon. "You have made it my fight by attempting to slaughter members of my species." She enhanced her voice so that all could hear. "There is no solution to this fight. Dee wants to eliminate humans and their influence. But that is never going to happen. You lifted our ancestors out of the mud, but we have taken that mud and built cities. We are not going away."

Brinn turned to face the large queen, and she bowed with respect. "Queen Py, though you are here to protect humans you are also fighting against change. A group of dragons have chosen a life outside the rule of a queen. You see this as a threat against all you hold dear. Who is to say if they are right or wrong? It is their choice. Even if their method of secession is a bit rough. Using strength to force your views will only reinforce their determination to rebel.

"You are both fighting against that which you can not control. Have the courage to accept it. Think of the welfare of your armies and end this battle."

Py silently looked back at the dragons who had fought with her then turned back to face the small human. "There is truth in your words. I cannot deny we...I...am fighting for my way of life. Change is part of The Pattern and I...admit I may have entered into this fight to stop that change." The Queen turned to Dee's dragons. "Forgive me."

After a stunned moment a cheer rose up from Dee's army. Dee saw her control slipping away with the simple apology. She flew into the air and addressed her dragons. "We have won a great victory here today, but the battle is not over! We will never be free when there are humans hunting us down and where wizards are leading the extermination!"

Brinn held up her hands to try and quiet the building rage. "We are not trying to exterminate you! Humans and dragons *can* live together. Look at the work the Krrig Daa has made toward stabilizing relations between our species. Don't destroy everything he, and you, have worked for. End this fight."

Enraged, Dee flung herself at Brinn. She struck the invisible barrier and dropped to the ground. Panting, the small dragon got shakily to her feet. "This fight will *never* be over. You speak as if you were an equal," she hissed at Brinn, "but you are just a *human* . You will never understand what it means to be Dragon." Dee turned and began to walk away.

"Is that what it takes to be heard? So be it." Brinn dropped the barrier, took a deep breath and began pulling in energy, more than she'd ever taken in before. She was not picky about where it came from. Dragons began to back away when they felt their own power being drawn in by the young wizard.

Talon was watching the amazing scene with pride from the cliff top. He rushed to Brinn's side when he realized what she was doing. "Let it go, you can't hold that much energy."

Brinn gritted her teeth, she could not control the energy and speak. She sent a mental message to Talon. "I can't stand by and let this happen. Help me...I need Agnar...I need more energy."

Talon called Graldiss over. "Get Agnar."

The dragon stared at Brinn. "What is she doing?"

"I don't know, but she's taking in a lot of energy, so it's going to be big." Talon called for the other wizards. "Create a circle, put your hands on her and feed her all the energy you can."

"What's happening?" Barkin asked. "Did you put a stop to the fighting?"

"Whoa!" Larn pulled his hands away after touching Brinn. "Where is she putting all this energy?"

Oret stood apart, not sure he wanted to be a part of whatever Brinn was planning. It must have something to do with these dragons and he didn't want anything to do with them.

Graldiss and Agnar came through the crowd of dragons. Agnar went to Brinn who leaned against him, clutching his neck. His eyes opened wide when she revealed what she was doing. Agnar quickly passed on the information to Graldiss.

The dragon stared at the young girl. Talon had to shake him to get his attention. "She's going to change," Graldiss said with awe.

"What does that mean?" Fredik asked putting his hand on Brinn's arm.

Word spread quickly and the circle around Brinn became tightly packed.

"You can't do this, it's crazy!" Agnar tried hard not to panic for fear he would break Brinn's concentration.

Brinn mentally leaned on her friend as she shifted the flow of energy into every cell of her body. "I have to," she whispered into his thoughts, unable to form her lips to speak. "If it will keep you all alive." Brinn was finding it hard to think about more than one thing at a time.

A reassuring voice intruded on the conversation. "You don't have to do this," Py said gently. "There are other solutions. Dee is only one dragon with her own opinions. We are not lost yet."

"There will be others. If they can see what a human is willing to do to bridge the gap, maybe it will save some lives...on both sides."

"Perhaps, but it is a big risk for you to take."

"I'm willing to take it."

"Fair enough. This is what you have to do." Py explained the process of permanently changing shape to Brinn. "You won't have to remember every detail once you've studied it, your mind will take care of that. Don't make the change until you are completely ready. It must be done in one burst of power, not easing into it by pieces. If anything were to happen to stop you half-way through it would mean your death. You can stop at anytime before the change. I cannot help you further, it is up to you now. Good luck."

Brinn felt more determined than ever. "I'm sorry, Agnar, this might be hard for you."

"I can take it. Do what you have to."

Brinn left Agnar's mind and began to study his body. First the outside; the scales: how they were layered, the thickness, their makeup, and how they attached; the head: shape and proportions, placement of the ears and their movement, horns and muzzle; the body: tail, spines, legs, feet, claws. Brinn spent a long time studying the wings, each vein, fold and ridge. How long would it take to learn how to fly? She began to delve into the inner working of Agnar's body.

When she finished her study, Brinn rested. She felt the pressure of many hands on her, energy flowing into her, renewing her strength. For a second she opened her eyes. She saw Talon, eyes closed in concentration. His hand was on her right shoulder. Graldiss' large paw was on the other. Barkin, Larn and Tellyanar were at her right side; Telis, Draega and Betto were on her left. Hands and claws pressed gently at her back. The watching dragons were as still at statues, waiting.

She saw Dee step forward, nervous. "It won't matter if she changes her body, her spirit will still be *human*."

Py turned on the small dragon. "Then I will share some of my own spirit with her." Dragons from both sides shouted that they would do the same. Dee slunk back.

Brinn felt overwhelmed. She closed her eyes and began the final steps for her transformation. She formed a picture of herself as a dragon, adjusting color, height, and gender. The excitement from the energy surging through her whole being and the event that she was about to undertake made her giddy. She wished she could hold on to it forever. She prepared for the release and change.

Chapter 23

"NO!"

Brinn's eyes shot open. She followed everyone's gaze upward. A dark shadow plunged from the sky. The circle of dragons pulled back to let a tremendous black dragon land.

"STOP!" A vicious claw pointed at Brinn.

The energy within Brinn burst from her. Dragons and humans were thrown yards away by the blast. Brinn clutched her arms around her chest, weeping from the sudden loss of the energy that had been ripped from her. When her vision cleared, Brinn focused on the giant before her and was astounded.

When the wizards and dragons got to their feet they stared at the huge dragon confronting the young wizard.

The black dragon turned to Py. "Why were you going to allow this girl to risk her life?"

The powerful Queen hung her head in shame. "It was her choice and I agreed that it would be good for..."

"Shame on you for taking the easy way out." The large dragon scolded.

Dragons from both armies were shocked at the superior manner of the unknown dragon.

Brinn staggered forward. "Don't you dare speak to the queen in that manner. It was my choice to make."

The dragon looked down at Brinn. "You have grown up, child. I can see you have become a very strong wizard. But the change you were attempting is not in your power." She gazed out over the two armies, now enlarged by the wounded and those who had chosen not to fight that morning. "This a sad day. Never in our history have we come to a point where dragon must fight dragon. What has brought us to this point?"

Dee boldly stepped forward. "You speak with wisdom, Great One. It is not ourselves but humans who are our mortal enemies. Before us stands a town which houses two vile wizards who have plotted toward our downfall, nay our very extermination!"

Brinn moved toward Dee, her hands itching to strangle the lying beast. But Py motioned her to remain still.

The black dragon leaned down her mighty head to the small, earnest dragon and said with a sly smile: "Please, tell me more."

Dee was bolstered by the large dragon's interest. "We had information that a large army had been gathered with the sole purpose of striking out against Dragonkind, ravaging colonies across the land. My dragons and I came to prevent this tragedy from occurring."

"*Your* dragons?" She put her head on her paw and listened intently.

"Yes. And we were barred from our duty by Queen Py, whom I believe to be under the influence, unwittingly, of course, of wizards with questionable motives."

"*These* wizards?" An arcing tail indicated the wizards standing next to Brinn.

"Yes. They have blocked our attempts to use magic as a means of disabling the town and its vicious army. Now this girl-wizard is seeking to trick us by taking the shape of a dragon to gain our confidence."

"She's such a small girl."

"But devious beyond her years. It is rumored she held a dragon's spirit trapped within her mind," Dee said viciously.

"A horrible fate indeed." There was no anger in the calm voice. "But tell me more of those vile wizards building an army to exterminate Dragonkind."

"A treacherous wizard by the name of Keldric who is joined by the Wizard King. Keldric is notorious for stealing a queen egg. He is reviled among his own kind for killing wizards to gain increased power."

"Yet *these* wizards are defending the villains." The black dragon waved a paw again at Talon and the others.

"A ploy to gain Py's confidence, no doubt."

The great dragon stood. "Let us have this unpleasant beast and his cohort brought before us to answer for their crimes." In the blink of an eye a sleeping Keldric and Nymna stood before them.

The two wizards awoke with a start, surprised at their change in location. Keldric quickly recovered and stood with his head held high. Nymna took one look at all the terrible beasts around him and slunk back behind Keldric. Keldric glanced at Dee, then faced the largest dragon, assuming it was in charge. "What right have you to bring us here against our will?"

"I am Neesha, oldest of dragons, and I bring you here to answer for your crimes against Dragonkind."

The revelation of the black dragon's identity brought loud murmurs of awe from all the gathered dragons. This disclosure boosted Dee's confidence, here was a dragon who had reason to hate wizards.

Keldric did not grasp the significance. "I do not recognize your authority to judge my actions. As a wizard I answer to no one, especially to a dragon."

"Such arrogance. Do you deny gathering an army with the intention of exterminating our species?" Neesha looked directly into the wizard's eyes with a power that demanded the truth.

"I would like nothing better than to see all of you rot in the hot sun." The ferocity of Keldric's words brought shouts of rage from the dragons, and a smile on Dee's face. "But that was not my purpose in being here."

Dee's smile vanished, replaced with panic. "He has admitted truthfully to wanting to destroy us all, what more do you need to prove his guilt? Kill him!" she shouted desperately.

"My purpose in being here," Keldric said firmly, "was to provide a reason to reignite the war between our species. I was asked to bring together an army that, with the aid of my accomplice, would overpower a dragon army and thus enflame Dragonkind into retaliation." Keldric turned and looked coldly at Dee. "Wasn't that the plan?"

With no warning Dee launched herself at Keldric, claws bared. So quick was the attack that only the target knew it was coming, because he suspected this statement might draw such a reaction. Dee's slashing claws missed Keldric only by inches as he shifted to the left. But an attack of such hatred is not easily halted and the small dragon's new victim stood just behind where Keldric had been.

Nymna didn't understand why he was suddenly on the ground, unable to breathe. Something was on top of him. Something wet ran down his cheek. When the weight was lifted from his chest the wizard sat up. A small wild-eyed red dragon was being held aloft by two claws belonging to the black beast. Blood dripped from the tiny claws! Panic stricken, Nymna put his hands to his cheeks. When he drew them back they were covered with blood! He shrieked and patted his face to discover the extent of his disfigurement. He felt only smooth skin and beard. Nymna let out a sigh of great personal relief when he saw Talon wrapping a piece of torn robe around the bloody sleeve of a young girl he did not know.

Barkin rushed to Brinn's side but she waved him away. She begged the dragons around her to calm down.

Keldric straightened his robe and grinned evilly at Dee. "You see, she would rather kill me than let her plans be revealed."

Neesha glanced at Brinn before turning back to the loathsome wizard. "I gather you did not follow through with this plan."

Keldric laughed. "I am not a pawn to be played by power-hungry dragons."

Dee made one last effort to save herself. "This human...this *wizard* is clearly lying to save himself! How can anyone believe such a preposterous story?"

Shouts of agreement came from Dee's steadfast supporters.

Neesha nodded. "Quite a knot we have before us. I think we need to hear from someone unbiased." She turned to Talon.

"I object! He's a wizard! Do you honestly expect him to be impartial?" Dee could feel her downfall closing in.

"I will not be judged by the likes of *him!*" Keldric stormed.

Neesha paid no attention to either argument. "Can you give me an honest account of the events that transpired these last few days?"

Talon stood before the great dragon. He bowed low on bended knee and spread his arms. A large paw settled on his head and Neesha read his thoughts. Before she left his mind Talon also showed Neesha the pain he had seen within Brinn's mind from the memory of losing her mother.

Neesha slowly nodded. After a moment she raised her head and spoke to the waiting dragons. "The wizard Keldric has spoken the truth."

The silence condemned Dee.

"But only in part," Neesha continued. "It seems this man led Dee's colony to believe there was, in fact, an army ready to attack. At the same time hiding the knowledge of the approaching dragons from the townspeople. It would appear he had his own plans for rousing humans to take revenge."

There was a long silence before calls of retribution began to circulate through the crowd.

Neesha held up her wings. "Before you are quick to pass judgment, consider your own part in these events. You, who were quick to follow the decisions of your leader without question, were ready to attack a human town without provocation." Dee's colony looked away in shame. "You, who felt that your responsibility to defend humanity was so important, sacrificed the single most fundamental rule of our species, dragons never attack dragons." Py and her army hung their heads in disgrace. "You wizards played it safe by following orders not to interfere in the battle, only one of you had the courage to disobey." Barkin and the others were surprised to be included in Neesha's scolding, but knew they deserved it. "And Brinn," Neesha said, looking down at the girl. "you were willing to give up your humanity for these silly, bickering beasts."

Brinn had had enough. "Who are you to swoop down and judge our actions? Who made you Queen of the World? You refused to accept the end of your life and the dissipation of your spirit. You chose to take over the body of another without thought of the effect it would have. I'd say you were in no position to wave our mistakes in our faces."

Neesha stared for a moment at the young girl. "You are right. I have made my share of mistakes." She blinked a few times and straightened. "But this cannot be left unresolved."

Brinn had to agree, and so did everyone else.

Neesha turned to Talon. "You have accepted the role of Krrig Daa. You should be the one we turn to for a solution here today."

Talon cringed at the idea.

"But if you will allow me to take on this burden..."

Talon was glad to accept. "As you are the elder most dragon, I feel obligated to defer to you on such matters."

"Never!" Keldric screamed and blinked out of sight, only to be brought back the next instant. "You can't do this to me! I'm a WIZARD!"

"You wouldn't hurt your own kind, would you?" Dee said in her most convincing innocent voice. "Remember, dragons never attack dragons."

Neesha roared and the two were silenced. "The two of you have shown a lack of respect for authority, for the rules of decent behavior, and of life. You are incapable of accepting the responsibility of your actions or even accept that you have done anything wrong at all. You are uncaring, manipulative, liars and are a shame upon your species. You have wasted the lives you were given, and that is your worst crime. For that offense I sentence you to start over, in hopes that you might get it right this time."

Before the eyes of dragon and wizard alike, Keldric and Dee became infants. The two babies looked around and began to cry. Barkin picked up baby Keldric and wrapped him in his wide scarf. Betto lifted the tiny hatchling and bounced her gently.

Talon was impressed, both with the punishment and with the power Neesha possessed to carry it out.

"May I suggest," Neesha said wisely, "that Keldric be renamed Kel, so that he is not associated with his past life. Let him be raised with a kind family."

Barkin nodded. He checked the baby over to make sure everything was in its proper place. A tiny hand reached out and gripped the white beard and drooled.

"Shall we change Dee's name to Zalfia?" Neesha asked Betto. "I have corrected a slight defect in her sorn gland. She should grow to proper height and have the use of magic. Please find a nice maternal dragon for her."

Betto nodded and kissed the cute brown hatchling on the forehead. The tiny red wings fluttered. "I'm hungry!" a shrill voice screeched.

"And *you*." Neesha pointed a menacing claw at Nymna. "Your life was saved today by a girl you have sentenced to death. How shall you repay her?"

The Head Wizard stood resolute. He was not going to let this beast give him ultimatums. "Nothing has changed. This girl is an abomination to wizardry. The decision of the Council is final."

Angry dragons on both sides crowded in. Neesha's look held them back.

"Then I make this pronouncement: your life is bound to Brinn's. On the day she meets the fate you have assigned her, your life will be forfeited. Dragons everywhere will hunt you down."

"Now, as for the rest of you," Neesha said in a voice loud enough to be heard all over the valley. "As the eldest dragon, I hereby decree that a proper site be chosen where an independent colony can be set up for any dragon who wishes to live outside matrilineal rule without prejudice. Those choosing to live in this colony will have to decide on your form of governance, still keeping the Laws of Dragon.

"Betto, please take your place at Pallan Cliffs. Do not take revenge on those who were swept up in Dee's charisma. I know you have put off the laying of the

Queen Egg for various reasons. Now is the time. The Pattern awaits her arrival.

"Py, you are a great leader, not only of your colony but all Dragonkind. But times are changing and they require younger leaders. With the laying of your Queen Egg, five years ago, the duties to your colony can be passed on to her. You might consider retiring and take time to relax.

"Larn, Fredik, Oret, Tellyanar, Barkin, and Poldrun, you are a credit to your profession. Whether you approve of us dragons or not, let it not be said that we do not deserve your respect. There is room enough on this world for both our races.

"Krrig Daa, Talon, much is expected of you, but you do not have to bear the burden alone. Even today, you have shared your task with another. Remember, prophesies have their own timeline."

"Lastly, Brinn. You have more courage than common sense should allow. Don't spend your life dreaming of heroic deeds. Heroes come and go; a life well lived is truly heroic.

"And as for my own transgression, it is long overdue that I make amends. Please forgive me." In a whirlwind of mist Neesha disappeared. On the ground where the mighty black dragon stood lay the figure of a woman.

Chapter 24

Brinn stood outside the large tent. She couldn't bring herself to go in. Fear glued her feet to the ground. She was afraid she would find the cot empty, or occupied by the black dragon. She was afraid of not being able to find the words she longed to say to her restored mother, and afraid the words would spill out in a torrent of emotions.

Barkin, having just put Kel down for a nap, brought a cup of hot cider to Brinn. "Come sit by the fire, your hands are freezing. She is sleeping soundly, there will be plenty of time to become reacquainted."

Brinn allowed herself to be led to a bench beside the crackling fire. She held the cup of cider but didn't drink it.

"She looks exhausted." Agnar looked at Barkin. He, himself, had only recently recovered from the young wizard's extraordinarily thorough examination of his body.

"She's been through a lot. Give her time," Barkin said in his healer's voice.

"I know what to give her." Telis launched a fireball at the girl's head. But rather than divert the flaming sphere into the fire or quench it with a ball of water, the fireball bounced harmlessly off Brinn's shoulder and onto the ground where it hissed and faded. "Those blasted Rings won't let me have any fun."

Brinn smiled at her friend's annoyance.

"Those *blasted* Rings are probably what kept her alive." Talon came out of his tent and joined the group around the fire.

"Yes," Larn said thoughtfully. "That had to be why she didn't fly to pieces with so much energy pouring into her. The Rings protected her." He seemed pleased to know that he didn't have to adjust his concept of wizardly limits. His wits had already been strained to the breaking point after seeing Keldric and that little dragon unaged, and that...Neesha transforming into a woman. He would have liked to put it down as a simple swapping trick every beginning wizard learns, but he had been assured over and over that it *really* happened. Knowing this new puzzle could be soundly explained with magic, Larn happily toasted a roll over the fire.

"Where's Graldiss?" Agnar asked Talon.

"He's gone back to Crinnelia. Py felt Ittra needed to be apprised of the situation in person. Betto left as well, she's anxious to put things back in order."

"And get to work on that egg, too, I bet." Telis said slyly.

"Do you think my books survived being buried in that pit?"

"Draega, can't you think of anything but your precious books?" Agnar swatted at his friend with his tail.

"Sure, I bet it will take a week for you to shake the dirt out of old Morisa's rugs," Draega stuck his tongue out.

Poldrun smiled at the young dragons. It was somehow reassuring to know that younglings of both species behaved the same way.

Talon looked around the fire at the odd mix of dragons and humans. Agnar, Draega and Telis refused to leave Brinn's side and had taken up residence next to her tent. Talon had to get on them more than once to keep their voices down while Brinn was getting some much needed rest. It came as no surprise that Nymna left immediately after Neesha transformed left without saying a word. Talon had hoped he would get a chance to speak to Nymna, to find out what his part in Keldric's plot was, and to try to convince him to rescind his edict against Brinn. The elderly wizard had not been at all comfortable with so many dragons around, but looked even greener after speaking to Tellyanar. That was another person Talon would like to have spoken to before they hastily vanished. Tellyanar, who had only recently encountered dragons for the first time, was so taken with them that he jumped at the invitation to stay at Tor Akkra for a few months. Before he left, Tellyanar shouted a cryptic message that he had taken the wind out of Nymna's sails.

All in all, the day turned out much better than it had a right to. Talon considered. The dragon mind can be amazingly elastic. After the mist cleared and Neesha was no more, the two armies became one gathering of dragons. All thought of defender and opponent vanished. Neesha's authority had been accepted and her decrees were as binding as law. Arrangements were made to place Zalfia with a mountain colony. Locations were being discussed for the new independent colony to be named Tonista for the town that almost fell because of treachery and deceit. When Py's egg was ready to hatch the mighty queen would step down and find a nice quite mountaintop to retire.

And here was Brinn. Her life had changed forever, again. Talon laughed. Well, their lives were never boring, that was for sure. "What will you do now?" he asked Brinn.

Brinn sighed, that was a good question and there seemed no end to the possible answers. "I will see to Mother's well-being first. Barkin said she is physically sound but thinks she has no memory of the last ten years. And there are quite a few dragons that would like to know if she retains any of Neesha's memory. She needs some time to adjust." She sipped her cold cider.

"So do you." Talon said quietly. "Both Py and Betto would let you stay with their colonies."

Brinn nodded. "I'll hire a coach from Tonista. Barkin volunteered to accompany Mother to Enoa. I promised to travel with Agnar and the others to Pallan Cliffs before I return home. I'm thinking of taking a set of clutchmates back to Enoa with me."

"You're going to let it be known that you're a wizard?"

"I think so. Either way, I can't wait to see the look on Madam Vorcha's face when I come down the street with a carriage full of dragons." She laughed at the thought.

"We wanted to go with her," Agnar said, joining the conversation, "but she said her butler wouldn't put up with a gang of rowdy dragons tearing up the place."

"I think we would be a good deterrent for those nasty wizards out to get her," Telis said with bravado.

Brinn smiled knowingly. "Oh, I don't think I will have to worry about them for long. Tellyanar had a long talk with Nymna before the little rat left."

Talon leaned anxiously across Agnar's shoulder. "I've been trying to figure out what that conversation was about. Tell me, tell me."

Brinn had to laugh at this mighty wizard acting like a little kid anxious to get in on a bit of gossip. "First, did you know that Tellyanar can see wizard auras like dragons can?"

Talon nodded, that had been a surprising bit of information when the old wizard had told him.

"Well, apparently female auras are a different shade from the male wizards."

Talon nodded again. Graldiss had told him this after Brinn arrived in Crinnelia.

"And from what Tellyanar said, there are more of us than just Shawni and myself. Close to twenty, all together."

It took a moment for this information to make its full effect. Talon laughed. "And Tellyanar told Nymna! Oh I bet the old goat busted a blood vessel!"

"A what?" Brinn didn't have a clue what a blood vessel was. "Anyway, Nymna was not pleased at all to find out there were enough of us around to cause a fuss if we wanted to."

Talon shared this news with the other wizards, who got as big a laugh out of the story as Talon had. Hot cider was passed around and a toast was drunk to Tellyanar, oldest and most cunning of wizards.

After the evening meal, Talon went to the edge of the cliff. The valley floor was now devoid of dragons. The town and surrounding farmlands were again bustling with life. He smiled. Sometimes ignorance was bliss. Those people would never know the monumental events they had slept through.

"It almost seems like a dream." Brinn joined Talon at the precipice.

Talon nodded. "But was it a good dream or bad? A lot of dragons were injured. A lot of lives changed forever."

"Oh, I'd say it was a good dream, a very good dream."

The End

*How in the world do you say that?
I tried to make the names I use easy to pronounce but
that's not as easy as it looks.
I hope this helps if you have trouble.

Syllable stress indicated with **bold**	Sounds like:
Agnar	Ag-nar
Ah'sha	Awe-sha
Barkin	Bar-kin
Betto	Bet-toe
Borda	Boar-daw
Brinn	Brin
Ce**li**sa	Sell-lisa
Cri**nnel**ia	Crin-Nell-Leah
Dissal	Dye-sill
Draega	Dray-gah
E**nikk**a and **Ori**ana	En-eeka and Ory-anna
E**no**a	In-Noah
Felgrig	Fell-grig
Fernley	Fern-lee
Fredik	Fred-ick
Gallia	Gal-leah
Graldiss	Grawl-diss
Grindle	Grin-dle
Grissa	Griss-ah
Gundrim	Gun-drim
Issic	Is-sick
Ittra	It-ra

Kaalla	Kay-la
Kartek	Car-tech
Keldric **Finn**elias	Kell-drick Fin-alias
Krrig Daa	Krig Daw
Krillik	Krill-ick
Krittlik	Krit-lick
Livia	Live-ee-a
Loris	Lore-us
Madam **Vor**cha	Mad-am Vorch-a
Magrid	Mag-rid
Manett	Man-et
Martek **Will**it	Mar-tech Will-et
Mellisiannarita	Mell-iss-ee-anna-rita
Morisa	Morris-ah
Neesha	Knee-shaw
Nessig	Ness-igg
Nethra	Neth-rah
Nymna	Nim-gnaw
Olwin	Ol-win
Oret	Or-Rhett
Pallan	Pal-in
Paygor	Pay-gore
Poldrun	Pole-drun
Pre**can**lin	Pre-can-lynn
Py	Pie
Riddliak	Rid-lee-ack
Riffa	Riff-a
Ruthic	Roo-thick
Selane	Sell-ay-n
Sencha	Sen-ch-a

Shawni	Shaw-knee
Silgaa	Sill-gah
Tagga	Tog-ah
Talon	Tal-in
Targis **Or**lag	Tar-giss Oar-log
Te**leb**iok	Tell-ebby-ock
Telis	Tell-is
Telly**anar**	Telly-ay-nar
Thal	Th-all
To**lag**o	Tuh-log-oh
Tollina	Toe-lee-nah
Tonista	Toe-niss-tah
Tor Akkra	Tore Ack-raw
Vanyett	Van-yet
Yorel	Your-ell
Zal**fia**	Zall-fee-ah

Diana spent her childhood in the lush green Willamette Valley of Oregon. She knew there had to be dragons hidden in the forests. Diana studied History and Mythology at Oregon State University. In 1992 the Metz family moved to Rock Springs, Wyoming, where there are very few trees and only small dragons. Diana started writing stories for her three children in 1997 and published her first novel, *Talon and the Dragons of Crinnelia* in 2002. She relies on her family for inspiration and editorial assistance.

Other books from M.O.T.H.E.R. Publishing

Talon and the Dragons of Crinnelia
by Diana Metz

Talon had no intention of becoming a wizard when he accepted an errand from a strange old man. Now an evil wizard is after him, he's living in a cave, and a dragon queen has mysterious plans for his future.

ISBN # 0-9718431-1-2   Fantasy

The Women of Eden
by A. K. Pyatt

Erde, high priestess of the great Mother Goddess, her daughter Eve and granddaughter Cain are caught up in murder, intrigue and adventure when a patriarchal warrior society invades their world.

ISBN# 0-9718431-0-4   Feminist Spirituality

Old Woman's Garbage
by Kayne Pyatt

Old Woman begins a magical adventure when she forgets to put her garbage out. Join her as she meets a talking bird and snowman, an icicle that laughs, and she receives a wonderful gift.

ISBN# 0-9718431-3-9   Children's Picture Book

Return of the Yin
A Tale of Peace and Hope for a Troubled World
by Diane Wolverton

A mythical story of a star-crossed princess and a Goddess of old who set out to break the spell of conflict and war that has gripped their world for thousands of years. Their adventures reveal a vision for planetary healing, balance and peace. A beautiful little book with big, big meaning.

ISBN# 0-9718431-4-7   Mythology

Renewable

ources

Andrew Solway

www.raintreepublishers.co.uk
Visit our website to find out
more information about
Raintree books.

To order:
☎ Phone 0845 6044371
🖷 Fax +44 (0) 1865 312263
✉ Email myorders@raintreepublishers.co.uk

Customers from outside the UK please telephone +44 1865 312262

Raintree is an imprint of Capstone Global Library
Limited, a company incorporated in England and
Wales having its registered office at 7 Pilgrim Street,
London, EC4V 6LB – Registered company number:
6695582

Text © Capstone Global Library Limited 2010
First published in paperback in 2011

The moral rights of the proprietor have been asserted.

Edited by Sabrina Crewe
Designed by Sabine Beaupré
Original illustrations © Discovery Books Limited 2009
Illustrated by Stefan Chabluk
Picture research by Sabrina Crewe
Originated by Discovery Books Limited
Printed and bound by CTPS (China Translation and
 Printing Services Ltd)

ISBN 978 1 406211 70 2 (hardback)
13 12 11 10 09
10 9 8 7 6 5 4 3 2 1

ISBN 978 1 406211 78 8 (paperback)
14 13 12
10 9 8 7 6 5 4 3 2

British Library Cataloguing in Publication Data
Solway, Andrew.
  Renewable energy sources. -- (Sci-Hi)
  1. Renewable energy sources--Juvenile literature.
  I. Title II. Series
  333.7'94-dc22

Acknowledgements
We would like to thank the following for permission to
reproduce photographs:
© Ballard Power Systems p. **36**; © Bergey Windpower
p. **21** top; © DONG Energy p. **7**; © Aubrey Fagon p. **16**;
© Getty Images pp. **4–5** (Raymond Patrick), **6** (Yuri
Cortez), **13** (Andrew Wong); © Lasse Hejdenberg p. **11**
left; © Hydrogen Association p. **35**; © iStockphoto pp.
8, **20–21**, **29**, **43**; © Library of Congress p. **18**; © Marcus
Lyon: p. **23**; © NASA pp. **22**, **34**; © Nuclear Energy
Institute pp. **39–40**, **41**; © Ocean Power Delivery
pp. **3** bottom, **32**; © PAC-Car II–ETH Zurich cover inset,
p. **7**; © Photodisc pp. **3** top, **28**; © Practical Action pp.
9, **17**; © Sky Wind Power Corporation p. **42** (Professor
Roberts); © Solar Cooking Archive p. **26**; © Solar Park
Gut Erlasee, Germany pp. **24–25**; © US Department of
Agriculture: pp. **10**, **11** right.

Cover photograph of the Bahrain World Trade Center
reproduced with permission of Shutterstock/Orhan.

We would like to thank content consultant Suzy
Gazlay and text consultant Nancy Harris for their
invaluable help in the preparation of this book.

Every effort has been made to contact copyright
holders of material reproduced in this book. Any
omissions will be rectified in subsequent printings if
notice is given to the publishers.

Contents

Where is this energy coming from and how is it used? Find out on page 28!

How does this giant sea snake create electricity? Find out on page 32!

Some words are shown in bold, **like this**. These words are explained in the glossary. You will find important information and definitions underlined, <u>like this</u>.

New sources of energy

Every day we use energy to help us in our lives. We use it for electricity, for heating, and to travel. Energy makes our lives easier.

The energy supply

<u>Most of our energy comes from **fossil fuels**—oil, coal, and gas.</u> We use billions of tonnes of them every year for fuel and to produce electricity. Today, there is just about enough energy to go round. Demand is growing, however. Eventually, supplies of usable fossil fuels will run out. So what about the future? We will have to conserve our **resources** and develop new ones. Scientists and energy experts are developing power from **renewable** sources.

Energy is used constantly in cities day and night.